D·E·A·D
AS A DINOSAUR

Books by Frances and Richard Lockridge

D · E · A · D

AS A DINOSAUR

FRANCES & RICHARD

LOCKRIDGE

HarperPerennial
A Division of HarperCollins*Publishers*

This book was originally published in hardcover in 1952 by J. B. Lippincott Company.

HarperCollins books may be purchased for educational, business, or sales promotional use. For information, please write: Special Markets Department, HarperCollins Publishers, Inc., 10 East 53rd Street, New York, NY 10022.

First HarperPerennial edition published 1994.

Designed by R. Caitlin Daniels

Library of Congress Cataloging-in-Publication Data
Lockridge, Frances Louise Davis.
Dead as a dinosaur / by Frances and Richard Lockridge.—1st HarperPerennial ed.
   p. cm.
  ISBN 0-06-092510-8
  1. North, Jerry (Fictitious character)—Fiction. 2. North, Pam (Fictitious character)—Fiction. 3. Private investigators—New York (N.Y.)—Fiction. 4. Women detectives—New York (N.Y.)—Fiction. I. Lockridge, Richard, 1898–   . II. Title.
PS3523.0243D42   1994
813'.54—dc20   93–46511

94 95 96 97 98 ❖/CW 10 9 8 7 6 5 4 3 2 1

• 1 •

Detective Vern Anstey of the Tenth Precinct listened with politeness, although almost from the first he had realized that what he was up against was one of those things. New York was full of those things, and always had been and always would be. You jammed too many people too closely together, so that they could not move without pushing and shoving one another, and you got those things. Detective Anstey was always running into them; to run into them was, he sometimes thought, the purpose for which he had been created. He took a dim view of this, which did not in any way affect his attitude, which at the moment was one of efficient attention.

He listened to a small, nimble man of, he guessed, about sixty-three. The man, who was restless in a cluttered room, had much gray hair on his head and more of it, in a border of tufts, on his chin. Detective Anstey shook his head appropriately, made a small, suitable, clucking sound with tongue and teeth and wondered whether Dr. Orpheus Preson did not now and then pull out small sections of his chin whiskers to further some purpose of his own. Detective Anstey found himself speculating as to what such a purpose might be, and returned his vagrant mind, under arrest, to the subject at hand. He said, "The trouble is, doctor—" and was interrupted, as he had expected to be. He said, "I understand, doctor," and was given more to understand.

It was a rather dusty room Anstey sat in and around which Dr. Orpheus Preson prowled as he talked. It was large enough, and had two good-sized windows on the street; it even had a fireplace, into which, it appeared, Dr. Orpheus Preson was in the habit of throwing almost any object for which he had, momentarily, no further use. There was much crumpled paper in the fireplace, which was to be expected. But there was also a starched collar and what appeared to be, from some feet distant, half a loaf of bread. "The trouble is, doctor—" Detective Anstey said again. "Yes, doctor, I appreciate that," he said. "Ummm," he said.

Dr. Preson was about five feet six and probably weighed not over a hundred and fifteen pounds. That part of his face visible above the tufts—"swatches" he took out of the beard; that was the word Detective Anstey had been trying to remember—so much of his face as was visible was ruddy with evidently healthy blood, at the moment in a state of agitation. Dr. Preson wore a gray sweater of notable cleanness and white duck trousers and tennis shoes. He picked up a bone and waved it at Detective Anstey for emphasis.

The bones did, certainly, add a note to the whole affair. They were on a long table toward the end of the room most distant from the windows, but there was a shaded light hanging over them. The bones seemed—but Detective Anstey was again at some distance from the display—to be of most conceivable shapes and of a variety of sizes. The one Dr. Preson now waved, with probably unintentional belligerency, was a sizeable bone. Detective Anstey thought it must once have been a leg of something. It appeared to be a very old bone, which was to be expected.

Dr. Preson became aware that Detective Anstey was regarding the waving bone and regarded it himself. "Hoplophoneus," Dr. Preson said. "Pleistocene." Detective Anstey said, "Oh." Dr. Preson put the bone back on the table. "Well?" Dr. Preson said.

"A crackpot, of course," Detective Anstey said. "New York's full of them, you know." He paused, and selected what he hoped would prove a suitable word. "Troublesome," he said.

"I," said Dr. Preson, "put it in your hands. What do you propose?"

That was the trouble. Detective Anstey had nothing to propose. There was nothing to propose. It was just one of those things. But tact was indicated.

"Of course," Detective Anstey said, "we'll do what we can."

"In short," Dr. Preson said, "you are without a suggestion. It would appear to me, Detective Anstey, that—"

"Doctor," Anstey said, and smiled, "doctor, I know how it appears to you. Believe me, I do. We all do. There are millions of people in New York and God knows how many crackpots."

"The purpose of the police," Dr. Preson began. Anstey shook his head. He still smiled; he made it clear that he wished things were otherwise.

"I know, doctor," he said. "We'll do what we can. But—I don't promise much. You see, whoever's doing this is using your name. He—or she—is paying cash across the counter. If we had a hundred men to spare we might—" he shrugged. "We might not, too," he said. "And we haven't a hundred men."

"The point is," Dr. Preson said, "that you regard it as trivial. I assure you—"

"Dr. Preson," Anstey said. "Listen a moment. Half the time I work nights. That's the way we're set up. I live out in Queens. I've been married a couple of years. Well, about six months ago, when I was on the night shift, the telephone at the house rang about—oh, a little after midnight. It kept on ringing until my wife got out of bed and answered it. She said, 'Hello?' and whoever had called hung up. You see, she's not much more than a kid and the first thing she thought was that something had happened to me. You see how she'd feel? Just a kid; not married very long. She called in and I was out on a job, of course. It was about three before I got in, and got her message and called back. She didn't go to sleep. And the next night—about one, that night—the same thing happened again. It kept on happening for about a month, whenever I was on night duty. Like I said, a crackpot. Maybe somebody whose toes I'd stepped on. It was just one of those things. Like this thing of yours. I didn't think it was so damned trivial, doctor. Neither did my wife."

"For about a month, you say?" Dr. Preson told Anstey. "Then, I take it, you stopped it?"

"Sure," Anstey said. "I had the telephone number changed. The new one isn't listed. Sure I stopped it."

"And whoever was playing this trick?" Dr. Preson said. "You mean he still—"

"Sure," Anstey said. "A crackpot. You never catch up with them." He paused. He stood up. "However," he said, "we'll try, as I said. There won't be much we can do, but we'll do what we can. It could be we'll get a break. You might try to make some arrangement with the papers themselves—arrange for identification in the future. Of course, there'd be a good many to cover, in town and in the area."

He did not intend to sound encouraging. He did not sound encouraging.

"I," said Dr. Preson, "am a taxpayer. As it happens, a very considerable taxpayer." He had sat in a chair; now he jumped out of it and clutched his beard. None of it came out; there was, apparently, another explanation of its condition. "I will not be subjected to this—this *persecution!* I expect that the police will—"

Anstey stood up, too. He was smiling still; his voice was gentle.

"I know how you feel, doctor," he said. He sought to look into Dr. Preson's eyes, hoping to convey sympathy and reassurance. He found this difficult, since he was distracted by Dr. Preson's glasses. They had, looked at closely, very curious lenses. They were, basically, bifocals. But above the semi-circular lower lens, there was a narrow band of what appeared to be another lens and above that, still another. Anstey blinked, partly in surprise and partly in sympathy. Although he had intended to continue, soothingly, to amplify his knowledge of the way Dr. Preson was feeling, the glasses distracted him from speech.

"Trifocals," Dr. Preson said. "If that's what's the matter, Mr. Anstey. Surely you've seen trifocals before?"

"No," Anstey said. "Well."

"When it is necessary to have three foci," Dr. Preson said. "With certain eyes, under special conditions. Your only suggestion, I gather, is that I have a change made in my telephone number?"

"I would," Detective Anstey said. "Meanwhile, we'll do what we can."

"I had hoped to find—" Dr. Preson began, and stopped and shook his head. The movement disparaged the police force of the city of New York. Detective Anstey once more promised that everything possible would be done—short, however, of a hundred men in full cry—and went down in the elevator of the elderly, not immaculate, apartment hotel in West Twenty-second Street. He made brief enquiries of the bright-eyed, white-teethed, brown-skinned young operator, who said sure he knew about it, that everybody in the place knew about it, and that they were doing what they could. They were trying to see that visitors to Dr. Preson's apartment were announced in advance.

"But what's to keep them from just walking up the stairs?" he asked Anstey. "See what I mean?"

Anstey saw what he meant. Anstey went toward Twenty-third Street to consider the next squeal on his list. It appeared that, in Twenty-third Street, there was an outbreak of dog poisoning. Another crackpot, of course; this time one to be regarded with special animus by Detective Anstey, who owned, and was extremely fond of, a toy poodle. Still, it was just one more of those things. Anstey wondered if his transfer ever was going to come through. When he got back to the precinct, he would see if Lieutenant Weigand had heard anything about it. On Homicide they gave you something to work on—something that really mattered a damn.

Mr. Gerald North of North Books, Inc., stopped in the middle of page two hundred and sixty-seven and looked out his office window to rest his eyes and to consider the cause of a feeling of uneasiness. Something, he realized, didn't jibe. He sighed, thought further, and went back to page seventy-four. He read through to page eighty and found it. He made a note: "Eyes, color of, 80–267. Blue on eighty." He made check marks on the manuscript and began on page two hundred and sixty-eight. He read one sentence three times, failed even on the third to discover a verb or any substitute therefore, and made another note: "268 L 22." He made another check on the manuscript. Frankel was casual about verbs.

It was Tuesday afternoon and there was a cold rain and Mr. North, feeling the need of a cocktail, of an apartment's warmth and of other warmths, looked reproachfully at the sheaf of manuscript pages still unread. Frankel liked them long. Mr. North sighed. So, however, did the public. Mr. North began on page two hundred and sixty-nine. The trouble is, Mr. Gerald North thought, I'm reading it all for the third time; that's the trouble. That's why it tastes of sawdust. Breasts on page two hundred and sixty-nine strained at thin fabric. Sawdust. The girl's clothes were too small for her; that was what it came to.

Mr. North put down the manuscript, took off his reading glasses and rubbed his eyes. He was doing nobody any good—not Frankel, nor the seventeenth century (with which Frankel was, as the blurb for his last book had remarked, "saturated"), nor Gerald North nor, when it came to that, "Inc." Sufficient unto the morrow would have to be the seventeenth century thereof, although that would make the morrow a tangle. Lunch at one with Miss Eaton; an appointment at two-thirty with Gallagher's agent about the new contract—neither of those could be postponed. The sensible thing to do would be to take Frankel's seventeenth century home with him, and see how it tasted after dinner. Mr. North sighed again. He had thought he and Pam might go to a movie. He—

The telephone on his desk rang. Gerald North said, "Yes?" to it, in no tone of encouragement, and listened. Each word he heard postponed further the warmth of an apartment, of three greeting cats at a door—most of all of a lady named Pamela.

"Has he," Mr. North asked the telephone, "got a manuscript with him?"

The telephone paused for a look; it reported no evidence of a manuscript. It reported that he was walking around and seemed to be talking to himself.

"Ask Dr. Preson to come in, then," Mr. North said. From the seventeenth century he would go now to the Pleistocene, conceivably to the Pliocene. This was retrogression on a major scale. Furthermore, Dr. Orpheus Preson would be, by and large, incomprehensible, since he mentioned the intricacies of fossil mammals to his publisher with a touching confidence that publishers understand all things. It was fortunate that Dr. Preson had no such illusions about the reading public, which he guided tenderly through prehistory. It was remarkable, Mr. North thought, how many people were nowadays fleeing to the past— the twenties, the seventeenth century, even the Pleistocene. Or, perhaps, it wasn't remarkable.

Dr. Preson came into the office like a released watch spring. He did not have a manuscript with him, which meant that he had come to report delay in the second of the three volumes of *The Days Before Man*. Gerald North hoped that this would not mean Dr. Preson had decided he must go to the Middle East and try to dig up something. In another year or two, non-extinct mammals might find it less painful to live in the present.

"Good afternoon, doctor," Gerald North said, standing.

Dr. Orpheus Preson darted at Mr. North, his whiskers vibrating. He shook hands sharply. He said, "Somebody is trying to drive me mad." Then he sat down vigorously on the edge of a chair and looked at Mr. North.

"Insane," Dr. Preson said. He momentarily considered. "Crazy," he said.

"Oh," Jerry North said. "That is—"

"Dogs to board," Dr. Preson said. "A butler. French lessons. A pony to rent. Somebody to lay brick. A *bushelman!*" He glared at Gerald North. "Three of *them*," he said. *"Three!"*

Gerald North sat down in his own chair. He grasped the arms of his chair and held on.

"For a week," Dr. Preson said. "A week ago yesterday. First it was a tree surgeon. A *tree* surgeon!" He paused for a response. Mr. North gasped slightly. "I have no trees," Dr. Preson said. "Everybody knows that. Then it was the first bushelman. Do you know—"

"Tailoring," Mr. North said, grasping at something fleetingly tangible. "It's one of the crafts in the garment trade, I think."

"Precisely," Dr. Preson said. "It appeared I desired to employ a bushelman. That was last Tuesday. But there were tree surgeons left over from Monday. You see?"

"I'm afraid—" Gerald North said. His fingers strayed toward a call-button on his desk.

"Wednesday afternoon," Dr. Preson said, "the pony and the dog to board. It seemed I had the dog but that I wanted the pony. There were still bushelmen from Tuesday, of course, and one tree surgeon. Fortunately, he telephoned."

"I am afraid," Gerald North said slowly, in a voice a little raised, "I am afraid, doctor, that I have no idea at all what you are talking about." Dr. Preson started to speak. "No idea at all," Mr. North repeated, spacing the words. "Are you feeling—that is, are you all right?"

"Would you be?" Dr. Preson demanded.

"I don't know," Gerald North said. He sounded dazed. He ran the fingers of his right hand through his hair. He sought to pull himself together. "Could you begin," he said, and paused. "That is, could you begin some place?"

"The *New York Herald Tribune,*" Dr. Preson said. "Some newspaper I never heard of out on Long Island. That was the dog boarding one and, apparently, the pony. Then one up in Westchester. The tree surgeon. And what do the police say?"

The question was clearly rhetorical, but Gerald North was tempted to answer it. He thought of the second volume of *The Days Before Man* and did not. Also, in a fashion, he liked the jumping little man. Also, Dr. Orpheus Preson was in some sense a great man. Or, Jerry North amended, had been.

"I don't know," Jerry said. "What did the police say?"

"Change my telephone number," Dr. Preson said. "I suppose the next step would be to move. That's what the police say."

"Oh," Jerry said. "You mean you think somebody is sending these—these people."

"I should," Dr. Orpheus Preson said, "think that obvious, Mr. North. Entirely obvious. For an obvious reason. What use would I have for a pony?"

The point was well, if obscurely, taken. Jerry North nodded to show he realized the validity of the point. He removed his hand from the vicinity of the push-button, put his elbows on his desk and cupped his chin in his hands, and explored. He was patient, and Dr. Preson grew calmer. It was not so complicated as Dr. Preson had made it seem, but it remained bizarre.

Among the want ads in a White Plains newspaper on the morning of Monday, November 26, there had appeared a statement that Dr. Orpheus Preson, of Apartment 3C, at the Greeley Arms, in West Twenty-second Street, Manhattan, desired to offer permanent employment to a qualified tree surgeon. Applications were to be made in person. Reimbursement would be made for railroad fare to New York from a distance of not over fifty miles.

Since it was a slack season in tree surgery, the response had been brisk. At a little before noon the first tree surgeon had knocked on the door of Dr. Preson's apartment. Dr. Preson was then engaged in writing a description of Daphaenus, the "bear dog," which in the end became a bear—was, in fact, in the middle of a discussion of the relative plasticity of mammals, using Daphaenus as an example—and was unprepared for a tree surgeon who, apparently anticipating an emergency, had brought a saw. The interview had been confusing to both mammalogist and arboriculturist, and had degenerated in the end into a somewhat sharp discussion of the railroad fare from Goldens Bridge to New York. Dr. Preson had paid. With amicability thus restored, the two had agreed that it was somebody's idea of a joke, and not a good one. The surgeon had summed it up by saying that there were a lot of nuts around.

There were also, as it turned out, a good many unemployed tree surgeons. Three more applied in person during Monday afternoon and several telephoned. Tuesday morning there were letters from half a dozen more—two of whom suggested that Dr. Preson advance the railway fare if he wanted them to appear—but by then Dr. Preson had begun to have bushelmen, in response to an advertisement in the *New York Herald Tribune*. The bushelmen were much more numerous than the tree surgeons had been, and several of them were indignant in various languages. One of them had said, flatly, that people like Dr. Preson were crazy and ought to be locked up and had insisted, at considerable length, that he "had a right." A right, Dr. Preson supposed, mentioning the matter to Gerald North, to see personally to the locking up. The discussion of the plasticity of the Canoidea progressed no further.

The subject was not, however, entirely changed. On Wednesday, there was active response to Dr. Preson's request—this time in a Long Island newspaper—for someone to board his Doberman bitch, who, according to the advertisement, needed homelike surroundings, not the institutionalism of a kennel. Long Island proved well-filled with men and women anxious to provide foster homes for Dobermans and, while many of them telephoned, four appeared in person. (One, who had read the advertisement only casually, brought with him a Doberman male, having misunderstood the nature of the need.) By midafternoon of Wednesday, the pony people had begun to mingle with the dog people and Dr. Preson, although in theory all out for mammals, was beginning to fly apart. (He had almost kicked the Doberman but, on looking more carefully, restrained himself.)

It had, he told Jerry North, become more and more difficult to adopt a sympathetic attitude toward the various applicants. It was one thing to realize that they, also, were victims of this—"this *depravity!*"—but it was another to resist a human temptation to hold them, individually as well as collectively, responsible.

"I," Dr. Preson told Jerry North, "am an even-tempered man. You know that."

"Well—" Jerry said, compromising.

"You're thinking of Steck," Dr. Preson said. He jumped up and then, in almost the same motion, jumped down again. There was, Jerry thought, no other way to describe his movements. "There are limits," Preson said, and grabbed his hair. "On the taxonomy of the felids, Steck—!" Words failed him; comprehension failed Jerry North.

"It is entirely untrue that I threatened to hit the last bushelman with part of Smilodon," Dr. Preson said. "For one thing, it's very brittle, of course. For another thing, it isn't mine and—" He paused, seemingly having lost his place.

"You're an even-tempered man," Jerry North told him.

"Certainly," Dr. Preson said. "I am a scientist, Mr. North."

"Look," Jerry said. "To get back. They wanted to sell you a pony? Was that it?"

"Well trained, broken to saddle and cart," said Dr. Preson. *"A pony!"* He almost screamed, and jumped up again, and clutched at his beard. "All day Thursday they kept coming—coming, telephoning, writing letters. Ponies, dog people, bushelmen. The tree surgeons stopped, but what good did that do?"

"Well—" Jerry said.

"The next day—*masons!*" Dr. Preson said. He gripped the edge of Gerald North's desk, and struggled obviously for control. "Masons," he repeated, more quietly, but with a kind of desperation. "I wanted a stone chimney built. I wanted to be sure it would draw." He laughed, a little hysterically. "I left, then."

He had, he said, done precisely that—he had fled his apartment. He had gone to the home of his brother, in the Riverdale section of the Bronx, and there had found sanctuary. He had also, it appeared, found sympathy; he had been urged to remain until, as his brother had said, "This crackpot gets tired of it." But on Monday, he had returned to his apartment.

"Got to get this book done," Dr. Preson told Gerald North. "Can't work out there. People all the time."

He had returned rather cautiously, but on Monday morning it did seem to have blown over. Until evening there had been nothing to interrupt Dr. Preson, and he had begun to get on with the plasticity of the Canoidea. It had been hard to settle down to it, of course; a sense of insecurity remained; Dr. Preson was conscious of listening always for a ring on the telephone, for a knock at the door. But all day nothing happened, and he was beginning to compose himself. Then, at nine-thirty in the evening, it started again.

It was butlers this time—butlers coming in response to an advertisement in the early edition of the *New York Herald Tribune*—butlers needed immediately, to apply in person, bringing references. They had done so until after midnight. The next morning—that morning— he had telephoned the police. He told Jerry of his interview with

Detective Anstey. "Who isn't going to do anything," Dr. Preson told
Jerry.

"Well," Jerry North said, "it is a crackpot, of course." Dr. Preson
glared at him. "I realize how upsetting it is," Jerry said. "How—"

"*Upsetting?*" Dr. Preson repeated, and jumped up again. "Upsetting, you call it?"

"More than that, I know," Jerry said. "But—"

"I tell you, somebody's trying to drive me crazy," Dr. Preson said.
"Don't you see that? Making it impossible for me to work, to think,
to—to—"

The spare, wiry little man was very excited again. Excitement
seemed to come and go, in waves. He leaned forward, now, on Jerry
North's desk, and banged the desk with small, hard fists.

"I'm not making it up!" he said. "You think I am? I'm—imagining it?"

"No," Jerry said. "Of course not."

"Putting these advertisements in myself?"

"No," Jerry said again. "Take it easy, doctor."

"Then," Dr. Preson said, "somebody is trying to do something to
me. I think to drive me mad—to—to—I don't know. Can't you see
what it is? There's—hatred there. Something you can't reach—something out of sight, out of touch—hating. Something—"

"Wait," Jerry said. "Listen to me, Dr. Preson. It's what the police
say, what your brother says. It's some crackpot. It's not directed
against you—not against you personally. It isn't hatred. Somebody
found your name somewhere. That's easy, you're well known. It's
just—just crazy malice. Surely you understand that?"

"Would you?" Dr. Preson said. "Would you—" He broke off.
"Maybe you think it's funny?" he asked.

"Well," Jerry North said, "in a way it is, isn't it?"

"I suppose," Dr. Preson said, with great but artificial calm, "it will
be very—very comical when this 'crackpot' kills me? Because don't
you see—"

Jerry leaned across the desk, put his hands on Dr. Preson's shoulders and gripped firmly. The little man was hysterical; it wasn't pleasant. Jerry managed to laugh.

"Kills you?" he said, and managed to laugh again. "It's a practical joke, Dr. Preson. Nothing but—some kind of crazy humor." He shook the older man, just perceptibly. "Get hold of yourself," Jerry said, spacing the words.

To Jerry's own surprise, it seemed to work. Dr. Preson looked at him for a few seconds and then, only then, began to see him.

"All right," Dr. Preson said. "I'm upset. I realize that, of course. I've—I've been working hard, lately. Trying to get the book done by the time I said. I suppose I'm—"

"Of course you are," Jerry said. "I'll tell you. We'll go out and have a drink and—"

But then the telephone rang, and when Jerry answered it was for Dr. Preson.

"Told them I'd be here," he said. "If the police actually found out—yes?"

He listened. Above the scraggling beard his face reddened; with his free hand he clutched his hair. Suddenly, he thrust the telephone at Gerald North. "You listen!" he commanded.

Jerry North listened. There were four men in the lobby of the apartment hotel in West Twenty-second Street. They were there to see Dr. Preson; they intended to remain there until he returned. They were large men, and stubborn, and the hotel management wanted to turn them over to Dr. Preson as soon as possible.

"Dr. Preson will not be back this evening," Gerald North said. "Tell them that. If they don't leave, call the police." He hung up; he looked at Dr. Preson, who was sitting again in the chair across the desk. He had his face in his hands.

Dr. Preson had masseurs, now. He had advertised for them.

• 2 •

TUESDAY, 10:15 P.M. TO WEDNESDAY, 12:15 A.M.

Mr. and Mrs. North looked at the chair in which Orpheus Preson, Ph.D., D.Sc., curator of Fossil Mammals of the Broadly Institute of Paleontology, author of *Tertiary Mammalian Dispersal* (1941); *Felid Myology* (1943); *Taxonomic Memoirs* (1948) and *The Days Before Man*, Vol. I (1950), had been sitting.

"My!" Pamela North said. She looked at Martini, who sat on the floor in front of her and blinked up. "Felid," Pam said to Martini. "There are irreconcilable differences of opinion regarding your phylogeny." She looked at Jerry North. "Why badger a mammalogist?" she asked. "I'd think they had enough to bear. And speaking of bears. Do you believe they used to be dogs?"

On that subject, and on subjects which were related, Jerry North was, he told his wife, willing to take Dr. Preson's word, assuming he could understand it. They were, he told her, away from the point. Pam agreed that they were, but pointed out that it was Dr. Preson who had taken them there.

"Because he was as excited about Dr.—what's his name?—Stick?"

"Steck," Jerry told her. "He—"

"As about the bushelmen," Pam said. "What does he want you to do?"

"Among other things, he's an author," Jerry told her. "He wants me to hold his hand. Or—" He broke off. "As a matter of fact, I'm not sure I know," he said. "I suppose he needed an audience. It is a damn funny thing. Damn irritating, too, of course."

"I keep thinking of the Doberman," Pam said. "It ought to be—funny. It all ought to be funny."

"In a way it is," Jerry said. "As I told Preson. But—"

"But you brought him home for a drink," Pam said. "Because it wasn't—well, only funny. It isn't, is it?"

Somebody, it had to be presumed, thought it was funny, Jerry told her. What other reason could there be for all of it, for any of it? It was a crackpot's idea of a rousing joke; on that the man from the precinct was right. There was nothing much to be done about it; on that the man from the precinct was right again.

"Why Dr. Preson?" Pam asked.

Presumably, Jerry said, and made them drinks—presumably there was no "why" to it, any more than there was a "why" to the direction lightning took, the victims it chose. Any object which stood above its immediate environment—even if it stood no higher than a small boy, playing with a puppy—was enough "why" for lightning. The small boy died; the puppy lived. Prominence was relative—a towering tree, a little boy on a level field. He brought the drinks back.

"Preson is prominent enough," he said. "People have heard his name, particularly since *The Days Before Man.* There've been stories about him. We saw to that, of course. He's made good copy—a scientist, a subject dry as—as fossil bones—and a best seller out of them. A target for a crackpot."

Pamela North patted her lap and Martini jumped to it. She stroked

Martini, who purred faintly. Pamela North said she supposed so, but her tone was without confidence. She sipped the drink.

"You know what the catch is," she said. "He does too, doesn't he? That's why he—he dragged in this Dr. Stick—Steck. It's going on too long. Wouldn't a crackpot get bored?"

It depended perhaps on the width of the crack, Jerry suggested. But his tone, too, lacked assurance. The alternative was deliberate persecution—meaningless persecution. Why should anyone persecute a curator of fossil mammals?

"Particularly," Pam agreed, "a nice one. He is nice, isn't he? In a jumpy, prickly way? In spite of the whiskers and those—those very strange glasses. I'd think you'd go crazy deciding what part to look through." She paused. "You don't think he has?" she asked.

Jerry didn't. He said Dr. Preson's book—the popular book—was entirely sane. He said that Dr. Preson had proved sane enough in contract negotiations. He pointed out that Dr. Preson was being victimized, was not making it up—as evidence the authenticated arrival at the apartment hotel of four masseurs. He paused.

"This Dr. Steck," Pam said. "Do you know him? The one he's feuding with. The one he calls a 'splitter.'"

"By correspondence," Jerry said. "He looked over the manuscript for us—Preson's manuscript. It was beyond us, so we called in Steck and a couple of others, just as a precaution. As specialists in a field we didn't—"

"All right," Pam said. "Did he like it?"

Jerry did not at first remember. *The Days Before Man* had been, at any rate, not technically disapproved by the consultant scientists, which was all that was wanted. (Lay opinion was unanimously favorable.) He had a vague feeling one of the consultants had indicated certain reservations. Then he remembered.

"It *was* Steck," he said. "Said the book probably was all right for the kind of people who would read it, since it didn't make any difference what they thought anyway. Said Preson was a 'lumper' and unsound on something or other. The genera of the Felidae, I think. Oh yes—said there was no point to Canoidea since everybody knew what Arctoidea meant. I remember looking that up." He stopped.

"All right," Pam said.

"Couple of names for the dog family, is all," Jerry told her. "You can call it Ursoidea, too, but authority will be against you."

Other things would be against her also, Pam pointed out. She asked what kind of a man Dr. Steck had sounded like.

"Was he feuding back?" Pam asked.

It had not appeared from his letter, so far as Jerry could remember. But it was a couple of years ago.

"Anyway," he said, "I gathered from what Preson said that what you call the feud was pretty special—pretty private. Not anything you'd invite outsiders to. Anyway, would people really feud about—about the classification of extinct mammals?"

"People will feud about anything," Pam told him. "Don't you know that, Jerry? Particularly about anything they're enough interested in. Dr. Preson cares a great deal about old bones, probably. Probably Dr. Steck does."

It was a long way from an interest in old bones, however mammalian, to bushelmen, masseurs and Shetland ponies, Jerry pointed out. It was a long way from paleozoology to what Jerry, with some reluctance, brought himself to call crackpotism. He could, in effect, imagine no one less likely to annoy a distinguished mammalogist than another mammalogist.

"The trouble is," Pam said, "that Dr. Preson doesn't seem to think so."

There had been that, certainly, during the hours Dr. Preson had spent with the Norths—hours which included a cocktail or two and a dinner stretched by Martha from two to three; which included, also, a subsequent period of conversation in which living dogs, variety Doberman; animals that, a million years ago, approached dogdom; the taxonomic errors of Dr. Albert James Steck and the unanticipated appearance of tree surgeons; the race history of cats and the lack of enterprise of the New York Police Department—in which these and other subjects were rather inextricably mixed. Toward the end, particularly, Dr. Preson had rather harped upon Dr. Steck. But it was not clear whether Dr. Steck had become topical because of things which had happened during the past week or of zoological changes which had, on the best evidence, taken place a few millions of years ago. To be a "genera splitter"—a vice only vaguely comprehensible to the Norths even when explained—was also, Dr. Preson indicated, to be a crackpot. Speaking of crackpots—there was a man who split the existing and prehistoric cats into twenty genera. Speaking of crackpots—there was a man who inserted newspaper advertisements to annoy Dr. Preson. Yet Dr. Preson, possibly because he spoke to laymen of a confrere, did not specifically accuse Dr. Steck.

"You can't deny that Dr. Preson wanders a good deal," Pam told Jerry, who had not thought to deny it; who did, however, now attribute it to a mental uneasiness natural in one who was being assailed by bushelmen. Usually, Jerry said, Dr. Preson kept pretty much to one subject—prehistoric mammals. Jerry had to admit, however, that he did not know a great deal about Dr. Preson.

He told Pam what he did know. Preson was a paleozoologist widely known in his field, which was a field into which laymen seldom ventured. He was important at the Broadly Institute of Paleontology as a scientist and also as a man who could, and did, finance expeditions, not only, although chiefly, in his own special field. A good many of these expeditions he had led; where interesting bones were found, there hastened Dr. Preson, with pick and spade. He had been doing this for years, and publishing what he discovered and speculating on the meaning of what he had discovered. He had remained unknown to the readers of the *Daily News,* whose interest in mammalogy was more immediate, and also to all but a handful of the readers of the *New York Times.*

And then a literary agent had telephoned Gerald North, of North Books, Inc., and had said he had something pretty special. Possibly, he had said, a little out of Jerry's line, but still—. Perhaps of interest to a special audience. ("But, by God, Jerry, it interests *me.*") A book which would have to be illustrated and which was, admittedly, a little long. Well—of which one volume, in itself pretty long, was presently at hand. A book now called "Some Aspects of Paleozoology" which, certainly, few readers could be expected to ask for at Macy's book counter. Still and all—

"Well—" Gerald North had said, in a tone of extreme doubt. He had nevertheless read the book; he had read it most of one night and part of the next day, and the next night strange monsters had stalked his dreams and the time of man had seemed trivial and wan—a moment during which evolution or nature, or whatever one chose to think of as the animating Force, had grown bored between marvels. "Some Aspects of Paleozoology" had, in short, turned out to be quite a book, and Jerry could not remember another like it. The public, when given the opportunity, appeared to agree.

Dr. Preson, alone among those concerned, was unsurprised that *The Days Before Man* appeared on lists of best sellers and remained there. He pointed out that paleozoology was a very interesting study and always had been. He said that the trouble was people usually got it in bits and pieces from popularizers who didn't, as a matter of fact, know Machairodontinae from Nimravinae, and never would. He excepted certain publications of the American Museum of Natural History, and lamented that they were not more widely read. He was, however, gratified and surprised at the size of the royalty checks. Ancient bones are most readily uncovered by modern dollars.

"Do you mean," Pam asked, "that he was running out of his own money?"

Jerry could only shrug to that. He had only an impression, not certain knowledge, that Dr. Orpheus Preson was well off by—well, call it by nature. Call it by inheritance, since, until *The Days Before Man,* mammalogy could hardly have paid highly. Now he knew that Dr. Preson had, so far, made a little under fifty thousand dollars in royalties—and that, for income tax purposes, he probably could spread the amount over three years, which would help. He had been told, however, that, over a period of years, Dr. Preson's financial contributions to research had been very considerable.

"Apparently," Pam said, "he hasn't any family."

The connection escaped Jerry North, who waved at it in passing.

"Few wives really care much about old bones," Pam said. "Of course, wives are just an example. I don't suppose cousins and nephews and aunts do either. I mean, I'd just as soon my aunts didn't go in for

Smilodons, and I don't think I'm mercenary." She paused. "Or am I?" she enquired, proving an open mind.

Jerry reassured her.

"So," Pam said, "has he?"

"I don't—" Jerry began, and remembered. "He's got a brother, apparently," he said. "Lives up in Riverdale, I think. Dr. Preson went up there last week when things got too tough. Stayed a couple of days and went back to his own place. I don't know whether there are any more."

"Sometimes," Pamela North said, "one relative is enough." She paused and considered. "I'll admit I can't see any connection, though," she added.

If she meant between relatives and uninvited masseurs, Jerry North couldn't either. Then he remembered Frankel's novel, ignored in his briefcase, and sighed. He mentioned the Frankel novel to his wife. He said that, interesting as Dr. Preson was, he would have to get on with it.

"From mammalogist to mammaries," said Pam, who had read novels by Mr. Frankel. "I'll wake you when I go to bed."

Jerry blinked momentarily, and inwardly. He decided to skip the point, if there was one. He took briefcase and—after only a momentary pause—a newly filled glass, into his study. Pamela began to read. The cat Martini wriggled around the book and lay over it. People whom cats have honored are not supposed to have other interests. Pamela moved Martini, who voiced an opinion better not translated from the original cat, and crawled back into a position to obstruct. Then the telephone rang.

Pam did not need to remove Martini, who jumped angrily. Gin, the junior seal point, dashed from a retreat with the impetuosity of any junior who has been expecting a telephone call, Sherry ran part way after her and stopped abruptly to wash her tail. Pam answered the telephone.

She said, "Yes," and "well he is, but—" and then listened briefly and said, "Oh!" She put the telephone back in the cradle and for a second or so looked at it in surprise. Then she went to the door of Jerry's study and opened it. Jerry looked up from the manuscript.

"It was Dr. Preson," Pam said. She spoke slowly and carefully, as if repeating something she had memorized. "He said, 'Tell your husband somebody has taken the labels off my bones.'" Pam paused and shook her head slightly. "That," Pamela North assured her husband, speaking in a voice somewhat strained, "is what he said."

The newest attack on the composure of Dr. Orpheus Preson was not quite so drastic as it had sounded. To the Norths, who went to West Twenty-second Street as much because of disturbing curiosity as concern, Dr. Preson admitted that his construction had perhaps been weak or, at any rate, not entirely precise. The bones involved were not his, in any real sense. They were bones, and other fossil remains, which currently belonged to the Broadly Institute, their original owners having no longer need for them. They were in Dr. Preson's apartment because he found it easier to work there than in his office at the Institute. But it was true that someone had got into the apartment and taken all the labels off the bones. The intruder had then, evidently with some care—since not even the most brittle was broken—jumbled the bones into a heap. Fragments of Cranioceras, a Tertiary browser with a horn growing out of the back of his head, were mingled, in most unscientific fashion, with particles of a very elderly Viverridae. Since there had been a great many bones on a long table, and most of the bone fragments had been small—although the piece of Smilodon was quite substantial, as was appropriate—the situation was discouraging. Dr. Preson's bone table looked like the inside of a gardener's garage.

There was only one word for it, and Pam used it. "My!" said Pam North.

Dr. Preson was very red of face and his whiskers were more than usually tufted. His profuse gray hair stood indignantly upright on his head and he peered rapidly, almost convulsively, through first one and then another lens of his trifocal glasses. For some little time after the arrival of the Norths, coherence failed him, although words did not. Bushelmen, tree surgeons, masseurs—now maniacs. It was too much. And, indeed, it seemed a good deal to Pam and Jerry North.

"Can you ever straighten them out again?" Pam asked, when, after a disorderly ten minutes or so, Dr. Preson appeared a little calmer. The result was unexpected.

"There is no reason to be insulting," Dr. Preson said. "Or do you think I'm out of my wits entirely?" He then advanced toward Pam North and waved his tufted chin at her.

"Please, Dr. Preson," Pam said. "I didn't mean anything. Of course you can."

Dr. Preson moderated at once. He said, "Didn't mean to shout at you, young woman. Seem to be a little upset."

"Of course," Pam said. "It's terribly upsetting. So *many* bones."

It was, Dr. Preson made it clear—although with a good many verbal spurts in a variety of directions—merely another annoyance. It was a meaningless annoyance, as was the effort to sell him a pony. The labels were on the bones merely as a convenience; in most cases they served no particular purpose; most of the bones Dr. Preson knew as if they were his own, or even more intimately. He could, obviously, tell Smilodon from Hemicyon at ten paces. It was true that to differentiate between some of the smaller remnants he would have to look twice, as would any paleozoologist. And certainly it was true that, to proceed at all, order would have to be re-established in this chaos, where now Carnivora rubbed bones with ruminants in a manner pleasing to neither. It was true that the bones would have to be relabeled and that, under the circumstances, Dr. Preson was the man who would have to do it. Involved were loss of time, and tedium. Until things were straightened out, work on the second volume of *The Days Before Man* must stand still.

"A damned nuisance," Jerry North said.

The description was, Dr. Preson agreed, precise. The de-labeling of the bones was merely another nuisance added to the nuisances already imposed. Nothing did permanent harm—as theft of the bones, or their destruction, would have done permanent harm; as the actual introduction of a pony into Dr. Preson's apartment would surely have done harm. Dr. Preson was merely being stuck with pins.

"What it comes to," Dr. Preson said, "is that somebody doesn't want me to finish this book. That's the least of it, of course. Somebody's trying to drive me insane."

He was relatively calm by then. He was at the table, picking up small fossil bones, looking at them, making words with his lips unconsciously, setting the bones aside—making a preliminary separation of sheep and goats. He stopped suddenly.

"You know," he said, "suppose Steck is writing a book? Wants to get in ahead of me? He hasn't been able to any other way."

Jerry North gave the point consideration, then shook his head. Unless Steck was authentically a crackpot, it was not a case of literary jealousy or of desire for literary precedence. The Preson book already had impetus; had already preëmpted its segment of the field. With the publication of the second volume announced, no publisher in his right mind would bring out a similar book against competition so well established. In fiction, perhaps; in this sort of general book, Gerald North greatly doubted.

"Anyway," Pam said, "if Dr. Steck were doing this, it would take as much of his time as it does of yours. More. He'd be cutting off his own nose."

Dr. Preson looked at Pam for a moment. He shook his head slightly.

"Exactly," Jerry said. Dr. Preson, after looking briefly at Jerry North, said, "Oh, of course." Then he said, "All right, you two tell *me*, then."

That was more difficult; at that stage, it was impossible.

It was Jerry who suggested that the police be called in again; Dr. Preson who saw no use in it; who seemed, suddenly, to grow fatalistic, perhaps thinking that it would all make no difference in another million years. The change was vaguely surprising; the refusal of police aid was unexpectedly definite. It was as if, being denied Steck, Dr. Preson wanted nobody; wanted only to get on with the reorientation of ancient bones.

"We'll all think about it," he told the Norths, and the implication was that they might as well think separately.

It was not until the Norths were in a cab bound again for home that Jerry said, "Look, those bones might have had fingerprints on them," and leaned forward as if to speak to the cab driver.

"I wondered about that," Pam North said.

"And now," Jerry told her, "Preson's handling them himself—ruining any prints."

"You know," Pam North said, "I wonder if he really is?"

Jerry leaned back again in the taxi seat. He looked at his wife.

"Why would he take the labels off?" Jerry asked.

"That's the hardest part," Pam said. "I haven't the least idea."

• 3 •

WEDNESDAY, 9:45 A.M. TO 6:45 P.M.

Twice weekly, on Wednesday and again on Friday, Dr. Orpheus Preson spent mornings at his office at the Broadly Institute of Paleontology, there briskly performing those tasks which fall to the lot of a curator of Fossil Mammals. He conferred, he read letters and sometimes dictated answers, now and then he associated himself in the evaluation of newly discovered antiquities. On this Wednesday of tribulation, he went to the Institute as usual, except that he went by cab. He was tired; he had been up until three o'clock sorting out old bones.

His office at the Institute, which is housed in a large building on upper Fifth Avenue, not far from the Museum of the City of New York, was a long room with two windows and a desk at one end and a table down the middle. The table was covered with fossil bones, but these were neatly ordered and properly labeled. Unconsciously, Dr. Preson sighed when he saw the familiar table, and the sigh was partly one of relief and partly one of weariness—the neat array of these bones reminded him unhappily of the confusion of those others. He straightened a small skull, stroking it absently and as absently wondering how, a million-odd years ago, the creature this had been would have responded to the caress. With something like a bark, or something like a purr? The former, probably, although one could not, of course, be certain. There are no fossil sounds to guide the paleozoologist; no sure way of guessing what yips and grunts, what screams of anger and caterwauling of love, may once have torn the prehistoric silence. One could assume, of course, that the ancient cats made cat sounds, and that the first true dog barked, after a fashion. There was no doubt at all in Dr. Preson's mind that the early monkeys had chattered. "We are noisy little beasts," Dr. Preson told himself, being out of sympathy with primates.

He went, then, briskly enough about his tasks and became engrossed in them. His whiskers waggled indignantly as he skimmed through a recent publication on Muroidea, not so much because he disagreed with the author's remarks as because the idea of mice was momentarily antipathetical. Already he felt as if he were being nibbled by them. He dictated several letters and attended a brief, preliminary conference on a proposed expedition, which he had tentatively agreed to finance, in part, if Auerbrecht handled it. Not otherwise, and he said so. Certainly not Steck. It was tentatively agreed that it should be Auerbrecht; there was an expression of regret that Dr. Preson was not in a position to take it over himself.

Preson did not discuss his personal difficulties with any of those he met at the Institute, and only one of his confreres noticed any particular change in him.

"Preson's jumpy today," this confrere—Brown of Fossil Invertebrates—remarked to Cornwall, associate in Quaternary Mammals. "Always jumpy," Cornwall said in reply. "Always wondered whether a beard is itchy."

"Good man, however," Brown said.

"Quite," said Cornwall, and went off to look at some Quaternary bones.

Dr. Preson had cleaned his desk by eleven-thirty. He had a quick lunch in the basement cafeteria and took a cab home again. He reached the door of his apartment at nine minutes after one, found ten seconds later that the door was unlocked, and went in at once. His sister Laura was sitting in a chair facing the door. Her head leaned back against the chair and her mouth was slightly open. Laura Preson was obviously asleep. She was breathing rather stertorously. Standing looking at her, Dr. Preson announced, aloud, that he'd be damned.

Laura Preson was thin and wiry, like her brother; she was about fifteen years younger than he, and there was not a little family resemblance. It was true, of course, that Laura had no beard; her glasses, which remained on her nose while she slept, had each a single lens; she was dressed in a dark suit and Orpheus wore tweeds. Also, of course, Orpheus was awake, which was a further difference. This difference he at once sought to erase.

"Laura!" he said. "Wake up, Laura!"

Laura Preson did not wake up; she showed no indication of intending to wake up. It was several minutes before her brother got around to shaking her; it was some seconds later that he discovered even this had no apparent effect.

"*Now* what on earth?" Dr. Preson then enquired. "Wake *up*, Laura!" He shook her more resolutely. "Wake *up!*" he ordered. Laura Preson's nose glasses fell off into her lap. She did not wake up.

Ordinarily, Laura rather annoyed Dr. Preson. She collected glass dogs, for one thing, which was ridiculous. The dogs were not even anatomically sound. There was no sense whatever in collecting glass dogs. There was nothing one could do with glass dogs, except dust them; there was nothing to be learned from glass dogs. And Laura had the absurd effrontery to contend, when challenged, that anybody who collected old bones was in a poor position to talk. "Dead *animals*," Laura was inclined to say, somehow making the matter seem unpleasant.

But at the moment Laura was saying nothing whatever, and she was, after all, a sister. Dr. Preson was by no means a slave to family affection; still and all, it was disturbing to find Laura so unshakeably asleep in a chair which did not, after all, belong to her. It was, as a matter of fact, the only really comfortable chair in the room. That, Dr.

Preson thought, was like Laura, and shook her again. Her head bobbed.

It was then that Dr. Preson realized, perhaps belatedly, that this was not a natural sleep—that something was the matter with Laura Preson; that, after annoying him with strangers for a week, the malignant influence which was impinging on his life had now got around to annoying him with relatives.

"Somebody's given her something," Dr. Preson thought, and felt concern—and acted. He telephoned for an ambulance. He got down on his knees in front of the chair and said, over and over, more and more loudly, "Wake *up*, Laura! Wake *up!*" He was thus engaged when someone knocked on his door. Thanking God that the ambulance people had come so promptly, Dr. Preson hurried to the door. He opened it and was startled to see, at first, no one there at all.

"You the man who wants midgets?" a voice enquired, and then Dr. Preson looked down. He looked down on a midget—a very small midget. And then he looked along the corridor, and coming toward the door was another midget.

"So," the second midget said, "you got here first. I might've known."

"Hold your horse, Charlie," the first midget said. "Says here he wants five, don't it? So there's only one of you, Charlie." The first midget laughed. "Maybe only half a one," he said, and laughed again.

"Aah-uh!" Dr. Orpheus Preson said, and tore at his hair.

Both midgets looked up at him.

"What's the matter with this square?" Charlie enquired.

"You got me, Charlie," the first midget said. "You sure got me."

Then the elevator door opened with more than its usual violence; then men in white came out, along with men in blue. The ambulance was there, and the police with it.

"In here," Dr. Preson said, loudly, gesturing above the midgets. "Somebody's—"

"Take it easy, mister," one of the policemen said. "Everything's going to be all right."

At that, Dr. Preson laughed more loudly than he had spoken; he laughed shrilly, almost hysterically.

"I tell you, Charlie," the first midget said. "This square is nuts. That's what it is. Nuts."

Detective Vern Anstey finished typing his report, looked it over, sighed deeply, and sent it along. He'd have a sandwich—although whether as a late lunch or an early dinner it would be hard to say—and get on with his part of it. He started out of the West Twentieth Street station house and encountered Acting Captain William Weigand, also on his way out. Anstey said, "Hi'ya, lieutenant" and then, "sorry, keep forgetting you're a captain now."

Bill Weigand told Anstey it didn't matter. Bill said, "By the way, about that transfer. I'm doing what I can, but the inspector—" Bill ended that with a shrug. Deputy Chief Inspector Artemus O'Malley was known to one and all.

"Thanks," Anstey said. "Thought for a while this afternoon I'd worked you up a case. Overdose." He paused outside the door. "Screwy one," he said. "One of those things but—well, it's not your worry."

"Right," Bill said. "However, if it's screwy enough." he hesitated. "Anybody named North mixed up in it?" he asked, as casually as the topic permitted.

Detective Vern Anstey said he hadn't heard of anyone named North People were named Preson. An old guy some crackpot was badgering; his sister, who had, apparently, run accidentally into something meant for brother. But now—

"Well," Anstey said, walking along toward the diner down the street, "it comes out attempted murder, I suppose. Which is a bit more than we bargained for."

"Preson?" Bill Weigand said. "Not Preston?"

"That's right," Anstey said, and stopped and asked, "Why?"

"A scientist?" Weigand asked him. "Let's see—mammalogist? Write a book about prehistoric animals, d'you know?"

"That's the guy," Anstey said. "Why?"

"Well," Bill Weigand said. "Well. Oh—a friend of mine published the book." Bill paused. "Friend of mine named North," Bill Weigand said. "I think I'll have a cup of coffee with you, Anstey."

Anstey talked while the counterman made hamburgers, interrupted himself to eat them with enthusiasm, and talked again. He began at the beginning, with tree surgeons and bushelmen. "So, it was just one of those things," he said, and Bill Weigand nodded. "Sometimes," Anstey said, "you get to feeling that half the city's nuts." "Right," Bill Weigand said.

But then came this last thing—these last two things. There was no reason to think that they were not part of the pattern, the work of the same crackpot. But when you came to phenobarbital, and a good deal of phenobarbital, it was no longer merely an irritating thing.

"The whole bottle was full of it," Anstey said, and then explained what bottle he was talking about. "Or," he said, "the bottle this dame is talking about. Preson's sister."

Miss Laura Preson probably was, by now, out of the hospital to which she had been taken. She had come out of it quickly. She had not, the doctors said, got much of the stuff—only a little more, apparently, than many people took every night at bedtime. Perhaps no more at all; since Miss Preson was not an habitual taker of barbiturates, a little might have gone far enough.

"So that was all right," Anstey said. "Of course, there were the midgets, but we got rid of them. Fast." He took a drink of coffee. "It would be a hell of a thing to be a midget," he said.

"Right," Bill said. "You talked to Miss Preson?"

Anstey had, as soon as the doctors permitted. Her story was a simple one. She had been downtown and, forgetting that Wednesday was her brother's day at the Institute, gone around to his hotel, thinking they might have lunch together. She had asked for him at the desk and, when Orpheus Preson—"Orpheus, for God's sake," Anstey said—proved to be out, had identified herself and been let into his apartment. Tne clerk had used his judgment, and Anstey was not inclined to question it. "For one thing," he said, "there's quite a bit of resemblance. For another—well, nobody would pick Miss Preson as somebody up to monkey business. Anyway, she's fifty or so."

Anstey, Bill Weigand guessed, was around thirty. Fifty still seemed a long ways off; by achieving fifty, one passed beyond the realm of monkey business. Of course, there were fifties and fifties, and Anstey had talked with Dr. Preson's sister.

"Right," Bill Weigand said.

Miss Preson had gone to the apartment at about twelve-thirty, perhaps a little earlier. She had waited for fifteen or twenty minutes, and begun to feel hungry.

"Had breakfast early, she said," Anstey told Bill Weigand. "They live up in Riverdale."

The connection was not instantly apparent. Then it was. Riverdale, although it is part of the Bronx, has rural aspects. In the country, people got up, and hence had breakfast, earlier than in the city. That was Anstey's connection; Anstey was very urban.

"Right," Bill said.

Miss Preson had gone to her brother's kitchenette and to her brother's icebox. She had found a bottle of milk there, poured herself a glass and, fifteen minutes or so later, had become very sleepy and gone to sleep. She had awakened, very surprised, in St. Vincent's Hospital.

"The bottle was still there," Anstey said. "We took it along, naturally. Full of phenobarbital. If anybody drank all of it, he wouldn't wake up."

"Quart bottle?" Bill asked.

It had been. Anstey seemed puzzled for a moment. Then he nodded.

"Hadn't thought of that," he said. "You wouldn't figure anybody's drinking a quart of milk at one time."

"Right," Bill said.

"That fits, of course," Anstey said. "It's still the same screwy business. Whoever put the stuff in the milk didn't plan to do Preson in. Just to knock him out for a while."

Bill merely nodded.

"For one thing," Anstey said, "it wasn't the old boy's milk. So he says, anyway. He does drink milk—drinks warm milk every night. Finished off what was in the only bottle he had early this morning sometime, after he got through working on the bones. I told you about those damned bones?"

"Yes," Bill said.

"So," Anstey said, and finished his coffee, and pushed the empty cup toward the counterman, "so—somebody brought him a nice fresh bottle of milk, filled with nice fresh phenobarbital. But not, probably, planning to kill him. Too much milk and, of course, there are better things than phenobarbital. That is—worse things."

It was, Bill Weigand pointed out, apparently very easy to get in and out of Preson's rooms at the hotel—to get in and out unnoticed.

"One elevator," Anstey said. "The desk's off at the other side of the lobby, and kind of around a corner. The stairs are handy." He drank from the new cup of coffee. "It's a pretty run-down place," he said. "Clerk, girl at a switchboard—she's clear out of sight of everything. One elevator operator, on in the daytime. The thing's automatic and there's nobody on it at night. They don't make much effort to keep people from going upstairs if they want to. But what hotel does, if you come to that? Anyway, I don't suppose many of the people who live there have a lot worth stealing."

Bill Weigand nodded again. He asked whether Dr. Preson didn't lock his door.

"Sure," Anstey said. "And half the keys that fit closet doors would unlock it. They do put Yales on if asked, but Preson didn't ask. I suppose he figured nobody would want a lot of old bones."

"Right," Bill said. "About the midgets?"

The arrival of the midgets, although rather dramatically inopportune, was merely another part of the pattern. There had been an advertisement that morning in the *New York Times*. It had carried Dr. Preson's name and address. It had—

"Here, read it," Anstey said, and produced a clipping from his billfold. "Under 'Help Wanted, Male.'" He handed it to Bill Weigand. It read:

"MIDGETS. Five midgets needed connection product exploitation. Temporary; unusual remuneration. Apply O. Preson, Greeley Apartment Hotel. West Twenty-second Street."

The first two midgets had applied while Dr. Preson had been attempting to awaken his sister. Six more had applied later. All eight, incidentally, had been incensed; one had threatened action for damages.

"Rather academic phrasing," Bill said, and handed the clipping back to Anstey. "Why not just 'high pay,' if that's what was meant?"

"Well," Anstey said, "he's a professor or—but no, he didn't put it in, did he? Could have been another professor. You think—"

"I don't know," Bill Weigand said. "You'll have to try to trace it down now, of course."

That Anstey knew. Had he not, as a good policeman, known it already, the captain in charge of the precinct detective detail would have informed him. The captain had anyway, if needlessly. As soon as Anstey finished his coffee—which he then did—he was going up to the *Times* to see what he could find out. He'd start with the main desk in Times Square, but he was not sanguine. The chances were a hundred to one that the advertisement had been telephoned in or, if not that, mailed in.

"Even crackpots have that much sense," Anstey said, and slid off the stool.

Acting Captain William Weigand of Homicide West walked with Detective Vern Anstey to the door. Anstey said, "Well, thanks for listening, lieu—captain."

Bill Weigand said, "O.K., Vern" and started to leave the other policeman, and then hesitated. He turned back.

"I'm going uptown anyway," he said. "I'll drop you off."

It was swell of him, and he was told so. He had been going north anyway, Bill repeated, and then realized why he had used that word to indicate direction—and, at the same time, why he had offered to drop Anstey. It was a funny thing about the Norths, Bill thought, walking with Anstey toward his parked Buick. They did get into the damnedest things. (As Sergeant Mullins said, the screwiest things.) It would be like them to be involved with a mammalogist and old bones—and midgets and bushelmen, if you came to that.

So, in the end, Bill Weigand did not actually drop Anstey. He went with him to the main want-ad desk of the *New York Times,* and listened while Anstey identified himself and produced the clipping; waited while the source was checked from filled-out blanks of the night before; was as astonished as Anstey when the blank was turned up, the appeal for midgets typed on it. It had been handed across the counter; the receiving clerk had initialed it. The receiving clerk could be identified, and was. Her name was Alice—Alice Farbmann. She was not on duty; her address, on the upper West Side, was available. Anstey took the blank and the address. Bill Weigand took Anstey, north again, in the Buick.

Their luck held. Alice Farbmann was at home; she was also an alert young woman; she also remembered the advertisement.

"Of course," she said. "I asked him, were they for kites?"

Bill Weigand blinked. Anstey, however, remembered. The summer before, some press agent had made an attempt to fly midgets from kites in Central Park, an attempt the police had rendered abortive. The press agent (whose purposes remained obscure throughout) had had no permit to fly midgets from kites in Central Park. He had tried Prospect Park in Brooklyn, where it was found that the flying of midgets would create a disturbance.

"He said, 'Of course not,'" Miss Farbmann told Anstey, while Bill Weigand listened. "He said, 'This is entirely legitimate, young woman.'"

"He?" Anstey repeated. "Do you happen to remember what he looked like?"

"Sure," Miss Farbmann said. "A little man. Red faced. Sort of jumpy. He wore glasses. Funny-looking glasses. He had a muffler up around his chin but I could see most of his face."

"Oh," Anstey said. He produced a photograph of Dr. Preson. "This man?" he asked.

She looked; then she nodded. "That's him," she said. "He had this muffler over his chin, but that's him, all right." She nodded. "Preson," she said. "That was his name. It's on the blank. It had to be. That's Mr. Preson."

"Yes," Anstey said, "I guess it is, all right. Well—thanks, Miss Farbmann. Probably nothing'll come of it."

"Look," Miss Farbmann said, "did something happen to the midgets?"

Anstey reassured her. Nothing had happened to the midgets.

"Just checking up on something," he told Miss Farbmann, and she was satisfied, since it was obviously the task of the police to check up on things. She went back to washing stockings, and Anstey and Bill Weigand went back to the Buick. On the way, Anstey reported that he would be damned. He said that, still, he didn't get it.

"He was putting these damn things in himself," Anstey said. "Wearing his 'funny-looking' glasses. *He* was the crackpot all along. What do you know?"

Bill Weigand didn't, except what was obvious. Nobody was trying to drive Dr. Orpheus Preson insane. Nobody needed to. Dr. Preson had made it on his own.

"The labels were off the bones," Anstey said. "Where'd that get him?"

Bill didn't know. He said he didn't know.

"And the stuff in the milk?"

Again, there was no ready answer. But the actions of the insane need no reason, are susceptible to no answer. Presumably, Preson had planned to drink the milk himself, himself succumb to the barbiturate, presumably be discovered in drugged sleep, and thus add new, and more dramatic, lines to the picture he was himself painting of a man persecuted.

"A crackpot," Anstey said. "God, what a crackpot. He ought to be locked up."

"Perhaps," Bill said. "I suppose he might get dangerous, although so far he seems merely to be giving himself a headache."

"His sister," Anstey pointed out.

Hadn't been seriously harmed, or put in much danger, Bill pointed out. However— He shrugged. It wasn't his problem. It was Anstey's problem, and the problem of the precinct and, more than of either, of Preson's relatives. Bill Weigand drove home, leaving Anstey with his share of the problem.

Bill told his wife, who had greenish eyes, and moved almost as lithely as a cat, and was named Dorian, about the odd case of Dr. Orpheus Preson, mammalogist and crackpot, over a cocktail.

But he did not need to tell her all of it. She had lunched with Pamela

North, and had heard a good deal already, although, of course, nothing of the sleeping sister or the animated midgets. Dorian was able to tell Bill that Dr. Preson was finishing, or ought to be finishing, the second volume of his book about ancient animals; to tell him that Jerry North was apparently counting on it.

"Of course," Dorian said, "Ezra Pound got a poetry prize even though they did have to lock him up. So I suppose Dr. Preson could still write about mammals?"

But she did not sound convinced, and Bill was not. Pound was, after all, a poet to begin with, Bill pointed out. Dr. Preson wrote in prose.

"I think," Dorian said, "you'd better tell Jerry what's happened, don't you?"

Bill Weigand agreed, and reached for the telephone. The result of that was cocktails in the Algonquin lounge and dinner afterward, Norths and Weigands again together.

• 4 •

WEDNESDAY, 5:15 P.M. TO 11:20 P.M.

Detective Vern Anstey, having flicked a hand at the departing acting captain of Homicide West, found a telephone and reported to the precinct. He was told he had better get on with it, and took a subway downtown again. He went to the apartment hotel in West Twenty-second Street and discovered that his luck had run out. Dr. Preson was not there. Anstey nevertheless went to the mammalogist's apartment, looked around it—noticing that the bones still were disordered—and found a typewriter under a black, oilcloth cover. Detective Anstey used the typewriter, copying on it Dr. Preson's application for the service of five midgets. He didn't suppose—

He examined the results. It was a matter for experts, but after scrutiny, Anstey found that he did suppose Preson had procured a want-ad blank, taken it home, typed his advertisement on it and then carried it back to Times Square. This involved procedure made no more sense than any of the rest of it. Anstey consoled himself with the thought that since Preson was a crackpot sense was not to be expected. He took his copy and its original to the station house, for passage on to experts, and was advised that, since he seemed to be doing fine, he might as well keep at it. He telephoned his wife and broke the news. She expressed wonderment that she had ever consented to marry a policeman and was told, with affection, that she had not been married for her judgment. Since he was in the privacy of a telephone booth, Vern Anstey mentioned one or two of the reasons she had been married, and was told to go on being a policeman. He went on.

He telephoned the apartment house in West Twenty-second Street and was told that Dr. Orpheus Preson still was out. He telephoned St. Vincent's Hospital, and was told that Miss Laura Preson had been released, as good as new except for a slight headache, half an hour earlier. Where she then had gone was her affair, or was so considered; the presumption was that she had gone home. Yes, her brother had been with her when she left the hospital. Anstey replaced the telephone receiver, thought briefly and shrugged his shoulders. He went to Seventh Avenue and took a subway north. He didn't much like what was coming up, but there were a good many things about being a cop he didn't greatly like. You often brought bad news, if you were a cop. Sometimes, of course, you were, yourself, the bad news, but that was different. Those to whom you were bad news had bad news coming. It was tougher to tell a mother her son was dead—or a family that they had better have a member of it checked by a psychiatrist, privately, unless they preferred the observation ward at Bellevue.

"Tell his sister, whoever's responsible, how it looks. Say we don't want to horn in—and haven't any grounds anyway—but that somebody ought to see to him. Make it tactful."

Those, in effect, were Vern Anstey's instructions: Tell somebody to lock brother Orpheus up before he does something else, and we have to. To be administered with tact. Damn it all, Anstey thought, I sort of liked the old crackpot. Funny thing, I didn't think he *was* a crackpot. It showed, Anstey decided, how you could be fooled even when, as a cop, you had been around—been way around, and all around. After a bit, Anstey shrugged, picked up a discarded copy of the *Journal-American* and began to read. He struggled a short way into a Pegler column and struggled out again. He sought refuge among the sports pages, which were merely soporific, as befitted early December, when major sports hibernate. It was a long distance to Riverdale. Even from the end of the subway line, the distance was considerable; even from the nearest bus stop, it was still three blocks.

The house was large, on a lot too small for it. But the Hudson was visible below through leafless trees, and the wind, blowing now across the Hudson and from the west, was as fresh as it was cold. Probably, Anstey thought, it was all very well in summer; probably there was that to be said for it. The house was of clapboard; it was square and tall—an ungainly house, painted grayly. Anstey verified the house number, walked onto the porch and rang the doorbell. The door opened almost instantly. A slender, dark young woman stood in the doorway and seemed to vibrate. The young woman said, "Yes? What is it?" and spoke as if she had been running.

"Is Miss Preson—" Anstey began, and the young woman interrupted him.

"Yes," she said. "I'm Miss Preson. Emily Preson. What is it?"

Again there was a kind of excited insistence in her speech; it was as if she were saying, "Hurry up, hurry up"; as if he were something heavy, unwieldy, which she must needs prod into motion, as if already it were too late for— For what? Anstey wondered.

"Miss Laura Preson," Anstey said. "She had a—a little difficulty today. I'm from the police."

She merely looked at him, now, but her eyes, her whole manner, said, "Hurry, hurry, do I have to drag it out of you?"

"My name's Anstey," he said. "A detective. From downtown. We wanted to find out how your—how Miss Preson—"

"My aunt," the young woman said, impatiently. "Laura Preson's my aunt. She's all right now." She continued to speak very rapidly.

"Good," Anstey said. "We wanted to make sure. We—"

"You want to see her, don't you?" Emily Preson said. She opened the door wider. "Come in," she said. And then, before he could move, "Come *in*."

Anstey went in. He found that, without intending to, he moved in rapidly.

"Sit down," Emily Preson said. "Sit down. I'll get her." She waved, urgent still, toward a door off the entrance hall. Anstey went into the room she indicated and sat down. He found he was sitting on the edge of a chair. He felt as if, at any moment, it might be necessary to jump. He looked around the room, and then looked around it again. It was filled with glass dogs, china dogs, of all sizes, all kinds. There was a glass-doored case of dogs; there were dogs on the mantelpiece and on the window ledges; there was an oblong table of glass dogs. The dogs were of various colors and sizes—there were bulldogs, and Dalmatians and dogs which must have come from China. There was, in glass, a dog of indeterminate breed giving suck to pups.

"My pets," Miss Laura Preson said from the doorway. "What do you think of them, Mr. Anstey?"

There was no sensible answer to that. Anstey thought there were a lot of them. "They're fine," Anstey said. "Very interesting."

"You probably don't think so," Miss Preson said. "Few people do. My niece said you wanted to see me? I have already told all there is to tell." Anstey had stood up when she came in. "However," Miss Preson said, "sit down, Mr. Anstey. There is something more?"

There was merely a desire on the part of the police to make sure that she was quite all right, Anstey told her. To be sure that there had been no ill effects from her experience.

"Nonsense," Laura Preson said. "It's quite evident I'm all right. Has something else come up?"

"Well," Anstey said. "Well—is your brother here, Miss Preson?"

"I have two brothers," Miss Preson said. "Which one are you talking about? Orpheus? Or Homer?"

"Dr. Preson," Anstey said. "The—er—" He realized he had almost said, "the crackpot." The younger Miss Preson had, he discovered, left him jumpy. The present Miss Preson was not, herself, soothing.

"Gone back downtown," Laura Preson said. "He brought me home, said, 'Look at those damn dogs!' and went back downtown. To play with bones."

"Umm," Anstey said. "Miss Preson, has your brother told you about—about these advertisements?"

"Certainly," Miss Preson said.

Anstey waited, but Miss Preson waited for him.

"What did you think of it?" he asked. "You and—your other brother? Your niece?"

"That it was very silly," Miss Preson said. "What would anybody think?"

It was that, Anstey admitted. It was silly. Also, it was malicious. Didn't Miss Preson agree?

"I have no idea what's in this person's mind," Laura Preson said. "Malice is in the mind, Mr. Anstey. This—whoever is doing these things to poor Orpheus may think merely that it is all very amusing. Funny. There are men like that, you know." She considered. "A great many, probably," she said. "Most men are quite—irresponsible."

Clearly she meant "men" when she used the word, not merely "people."

"Why are you so certain it is a man?" Anstey asked her. "Do you think you know who is doing it?"

"Certainly not," she said. "No woman would be so silly. But you wouldn't know that, I suppose."

"Being a man yourself," her tone said.

Anstey said, "Umm." Then he said, "Does your other brother live here, Miss Preson?"

"Since it is his house," Miss Preson said. "He lives here. I live here. My niece lives here. What has that to do with it, Mr. Anstey?"

"I'd like—" Anstey began. But then the young woman who had greeted him at the door stepped into the room and looked at both of them. Her eyes, her whole attitude, seemed to demand something from them, to demand it instantly. But all she said was, "Father's here, Aunt Laura." She managed, however, to make this statement an imperative. Apparently, Anstey thought, her father had been long away; had not been, at this moment, expected.

"I told him a detective was here," Emily added, still on the same note of intensity.

"You're worse than usual, Emily," her aunt said. "You make me nervous."

But there was no sign that Emily really made Miss Laura Preson nervous. The girl herself flushed painfully, embarrassingly.

"So emphatic about so little," Laura Preson added. "Is— ?" But what she might have planned to add she did not add. A trim, slight man of, Anstey guessed, about forty-five—a man with glasses, smooth graying hair, smooth gray clothes—came to the door behind Emily Preson and, as she stepped aside, her face still flushed, moved beyond her.

"Good evening, Homer," Laura Preson said. "This is a detective. I had a—an experience today. At Orpheus's."

Homer looked at his sister through shining glasses.

"An experience?" he said. "You mean—something else has happened to Orpheus?" He did not wait for an answer, but turned to Anstey, who spoke his own name. Homer Preson repeated it; it was as if he put the name in a file and closed the file drawer with a snap. "What has happened to my brother now, Mr. Anstey?" he asked.

Anstey looked at Miss Preson. Miss Preson told her brother, succinctly, what had happened. He listened; he shook his head, his eyes on his sister.

"It's what we—" he said, when she had finished, and then apparently thought better of the sentence. "It's an almost unbelievable thing," he said, and this time spoke to Anstey. "Series of things. You have no way of finding out who's responsible?"

"This sort of thing is very difficult," Anstey said. "I told Dr. Preson that."

"So he said," Homer Preson said. "He was very excited. He's an excitable man. Brilliant, but excitable. It's all very unsettling."

"There was another advertisement this morning," Anstey told him. "In addition to the barbiturate in the milk, there was another advertisement. For midgets, this time. In view of Miss Preson's experience, we made a special effort."

Homer Preson looked quickly at his sister, who regarded him steadily, who seemed, Anstey thought, to be waiting for something she expected. Preson turned back to Anstey.

"From the way you say that," Preson said, "I gather you—made progress?"

Anstey looked from one to the other of the older Presons. It occurred to him that he was not going to surprise them.

"I'm afraid," he said, "that your brother has been putting the advertisements in himself. At least, it looks like that." He produced the clipping of the midget advertisement. He showed it to them, and let them read it. Each read it, word by word.

"What is it?" Emily Preson said suddenly, sharply. She moved further into the room and held out her hand. "I want to see it," Emily said. Her tone was still urgent, demanding. Her aunt handed the clipping to her, and she read it.

"It's crazy," Emily said. "Completely crazy."

"I'm afraid," Homer Preson said, "that that is what Detective Anstey is saying, my dear. More politely." He looked at Anstey.

"You don't seem particularly surprised, Mr. Preson," Anstey said. He looked at Laura Preson, then at her niece. "None of you seems much surprised," he said.

Again, Homer Preson and his sister exchanged glances, quickly, as if they sought counsel. Then Preson slightly raised his shoulders.

"It's very disturbing," he said. "In a way we're—"

"What's the point of this, Homer?" Laura Preson demanded. "No, we're not surprised, as you put it."

"I wish we could be," Preson said. "For about a year now—frankly, Anstey, we've been concerned about him." He faintly shrugged. "Little things," he said. "Intangible things. Nothing like this, of course."

"All of you?" Anstey said. "I mean, you've talked it over, I gather? You and Miss Preson? Your niece too? You've all felt that Dr. Preson was—what did you think, precisely?"

Laura Preson left it to her brother. Emily Preson crossed the room as if she rejected all of them, were seeking escape. She looked out of a window, into the darkness. Yet Anstey could feel the intensity of her attention, and a kind of impatience in her listening.

Homer Preson spoke slowly, with care. He did not want Anstey to jump to conclusions, or to think that, before the advertisements started, they had jumped to conclusions. He said that they had realized that Dr. Orpheus Preson was not an ordinary man and that, realizing this, they did not apply ordinary standards. Dr. Preson was engrossed in his work and his work, of course, was not ordinary. That, Anstey must understand, they had realized.

Emily did not turn from the window, but she spoke suddenly.

"You did, father," she said. "Do you think Aunt Laura did?"

"Really, Emily," Laura Preson said. She turned to Anstey. "She means, I suppose, that I did not share brother Orpheus's belief in the importance of—of what he was doing," she said. "I never concealed that. But I am not an ignorant woman, Mr. Anstey. Even by my niece's—high standards."

It was not clear to Anstey what the Presons were getting at.

"Do you mean, Miss Preson," he said, to Emily Preson's back, "do you mean you didn't think your uncle was becoming eccentric? As your father and aunt, I gather, did?"

"Does it matter?" the girl asked, without turning. But then she did turn. "All right," she said, "maybe I did. It's just that—" She stopped. "Leave me out of it," she said.

"You are saying," Anstey said, "that recently your brother has been behaving—has not been behaving normally?"

He said it to either of the older Presons who wanted to answer. Homer Preson, after a moment, did answer.

"I'm afraid so," he said. "Nothing so—so overt as these advertisements, this tampering with food." He looked at his sister suddenly. "You're all right now?" he asked.

"Certainly," she said. "Don't be ridiculous, Homer."

"It might have been serious, nevertheless," Homer Preson said. "That's true, isn't it, Mr. Anstey?"

"Well," Anstey said, "in a way, certainly. However, the dosage was not concentrated at all. It isn't often that anyone drinks a quart of milk at one time. At least, I don't suppose so."

"But all of it—" Homer said, and waited.

"Would have been serious," Anstey agreed. "Depending, of course, on how soon the person was found."

Homer Preson shook his head.

"Did you tell Orpheus you were coming?" he asked his sister. She shook her head. He looked, then, at Anstey.

"It is meaningless, then," he said.

"Yes," Anstey said. "I'm afraid it is. From any sane point of view."

"But even if my brother isn't—isn't entirely sane," Homer said. "It is still difficult to understand."

Anstey shrugged to that.

"All you're saying," Emily Preson said from her window, "is that the irrational aren't rational. Aren't to be understood by the rational." Her tone was impatient.

"I suppose so," Homer Preson said. He spoke slowly. He nodded. "I suppose so," he repeated. "You don't know about the other advertisements, Mr. Anstey? Whether he inserted those, also?"

"No," Anstey said. "I don't know. It seems probable, don't you think? We could check."

"Poor Orpheus," Laura Preson said. But her tone seemed, to Anstey, to reveal detachment. "What are the police going to do?"

"This, for the moment," Anstey said. "Tell you. Dr. Preson's relatives."

"And leave it to us?" Homer Preson asked.

As it now stood, Anstey told him; the answer was "yes." On what they had now; on what his instructions were now.

"You see," he said, "there are a good many people around who are—well, eccentric. In New York, everywhere. Most of them aren't dangerous. It doesn't seem that Dr. Preson is, except maybe to himself. Probably a psychiatrist can fix him up. Maybe a good rest will do it. Privately. Without fuss. When relatives are in a position to take care of these things—well, it's better all around to do it that way than to have us move in. Particularly with a man of Dr. Preson's standing." He paused. "Of course," he said, "if you wanted to make a complaint, Miss Preson, we'd have to act. I suppose we would, anyway. I don't know what the complaint would be, precisely. Technically, you went to his apartment uninvited and took something out of his icebox. Perfectly natural, of course. But—"

He shrugged again. He smiled at Laura Preson. She did not smile in return, but she did nod, briefly.

"However," Anstey said, "I suppose you could get him before a magistrate. I suppose he'd be committed for observation. Probably you don't want it that way?"

Homer Preson appeared for a moment to think it over. Then he said, "Certainly not."

"Then," Anstey said, "I'd try to get him to see a doctor, if I were you. The right kind of doctor."

There was another moment of hesitancy. Emily turned from the window and looked at her father; Laura also looked at Homer Preson. Preson tapped his lips with an index finger.

"I suppose so," he said. "I suppose that's what we'd better do." He looked at Anstey. "You're certain about this? I mean, that he is doing it himself?"

"I think he is," Anstey said. "There's not much doubt about the identification. I'm pretty sure the want-ad blank was typed out on a machine in your brother's apartment. Of course, I didn't see him hand the blank in. I didn't see him type it out. However—I don't think there's much doubt."

"You're having the typing compared?" Homer asked. He hesitated. "You see," he said, "I—I suppose I keep hoping. We're all fond of Orpheus and—well, you understand. I'm afraid you're right, but still—"

Anstey knew how Preson felt, and told him so. There wasn't, he added, any great hurry. It would be an idea to wait, at least, until experts had compared the typing, gone over the blank for Orpheus Preson's fingerprints. In addition, Anstey would talk to Dr. Preson, and see what explanation the mammalogist had. "Maybe," Anstey said, "he had a double. Maybe I'm wrong about the typing."

"You don't think so," Homer Preson told him.

"No," Anstey said, "I don't."

He left a few minutes later. He left the Presons. Emily was still at the window, looking out into darkness. He walked to the bus and waited, the cold wind from the northwest biting him; he rode to the subway station and waited on a cold platform. But he said to himself, well, that's that. A stop at the precinct to see if a report had come through—then he'd get home, finally. It could have been worse, he supposed.

The report had come through: samples matched, both typed on an Underwood Noiseless manufactured 1946; probably rebuilt since. Identifiable fingerprints on the blank did not include those of Dr. Orpheus Preson. The last meant nothing, of course; the blank had been handled freely by a good many people; earlier prints would have been smudged and overlaid.

Anstey reported orally and his report was approved. He could write it up the next day. Anstey, at long last, went home. It was too bad about Dr. Orpheus Preson, who was a nice enough guy, but it was just one of those things. Anstey got home a little after eleven and his wife had waited up. At least, although she had gone to sleep, she had gone to sleep on the living room sofa.

· 5 ·

WEDNESDAY, 11:30 P.M. TO THURSDAY, 5:35 P.M.

The Norths and the Weigands had not hurried over dinner, and afterward had gone to the Weigands' apartment for a nightcap. They had talked of a variety of things, but at the end had reverted to the troubled times of Orpheus Preson, Ph.D.—and, as simplified by Pamela North, "extinct mammalogist." It was Pam, a little after eleven, who led them back to him. She said she kept thinking about Dr. Preson and his bones. She said she had the strangest feeling that there was something wrong with everything about it.

Bill Weigand was afraid that what was wrong was wrong in the brain of Dr. Orpheus Preson, and said that for such things there was no accounting.

"No," Pam said, "that's just it. What's *wrong's* wrong." She looked at the other three. "The wrong wrongness," she explained.

"Now," Jerry said, "wait a minute."

"Because," Pam said, "he has delusions of not being persecuted

48

enough. He must have. And that's a crazy kind of delusion. Don't you see?"

It was Dorian who saw, or admitted seeing. She said it was mixed up.

"Here," Pam said, deciding to make it very clear, "here is what you think's happened. You and this Mr. Anstey. By the way, where's Mullins?"

"At home, probably," Bill told her. "Anstey's not a Homicide man. This isn't a Homicide case. Nothing to do with Mullins or me."

"Where was I?" Pam enquired. She looked around for guidance.

"You were summing up," Jerry said. "At least, I think so. What Bill thinks happened."

"Of course," Pam said. "First, Dr. Preson persecutes himself by putting advertisements in newspapers asking for things and people. Then he puts sleeping stuff in a bottle of milk, presumably with the idea of drinking some of it and being found unconscious. Only his sister gets it first. But, he doesn't *imagine* these things are happening. He makes them happen himself. Is he supposed to have—" She paused to figure it out. "A delusion he has a delusion of persecution? It's a crazy kind of craziness, isn't it?"

She paused for reply. Again it was Dorian who, after a moment, nodded slowly.

"It is, Bill," she said. "It's more as if he—as if he had some sane reason for wanting to appear persecuted." She paused. "Publicity?" she asked.

Jerry North shook his head at that. Dr. Preson had always been opposed to publicity which involved him personally. He had protested each interview arranged on the publication of the first volume of his book; after two television appearances had refused to make others, declined to become a "chattering ape." He has also insisted that what he was, and how he behaved, was of no importance to anyone. If people wanted to read his book, that was fine. If they wanted to write about his book, that was fine. In so far as was possible, Dr. Preson, as a man with a beard, as a person, was to be left out of it.

"So far as I could tell, he meant it," Jerry told them. "Very funny-type author, of course."

"Anyway," Pam said, "if he wanted to get publicity out of all this, he'd have got it, wouldn't he? Called up people and told them? Had a press conference? Couldn't he have done that?"

Jerry thought he could have; he was well enough known for that. If people were sticking pins—or midgets or bushelmen—into Dr. Orpheus Preson, author of *The Days Before Man,* the newspapers would find it of interest. It had the news advantage of the bizarre.

"It's much simpler," Bill Weigand told them, "merely to settle for the good doctor as a crackpot. Much simpler. Probably, much truer, too. Let's let a psychiatrist work it out."

"Bill's tired," Dorian told them. "Hard day at the morgue."

"I—" Bill began, with summoned energy, the Norths stood up to go and the telephone rang. Bill reached for it. He said, "Right." He listened. The Norths started toward the foyer, Dorian with them. Bill cupped the transmitter and said, sharply, "Wait!" They stopped. Bill said, "Go ahead." He listened again.

Weigand said "yes" several times, and "right" twice, and then, "Hasn't Anstey put a report through?" He listened after that, for a minute or more, finally said, once again, "Right" and added, "since that's the way he wants it." He replaced the receiver. He looked at his wife and the Norths. He said, "Well, the little man's certainly persistent." They waited.

"Dr. Preson has taken an overdose of a barbiturate," Bill told them. "Apparently he had some left and thought he might as well go through with it after all." He shook his head. "Poor little guy," he said. "I guess he'll end up in Bellevue after all."

"Bad?" Jerry North asked, and Bill Weigand shrugged as he answered.

"He's in a coma," Bill said. "At the hospital. Probably they'll bring him out of it. Unless he got more than they think or is particularly sensitive. Live for the observation ward, probably. For a sanatorium."

"Why you?" Dorian asked, and again Bill shrugged.

"Crossed wires, as much as anything," he said. "That was a relay from the inspector. He's working on the first premise—that somebody's persecuting Dr. Preson. So this looks like attempted murder, maybe. Something we should look into. Anstey's later report—that the doctor was his own persecutor—is still somewhere in channels. So the inspector says, 'Get Weigand over there for a look around' and—end of an evening. I'll find another bottle of milk with phenobarbital in it, one glass gone out of it and into Dr. Preson. When Dr. Preson comes around tomorrow, the story will be that somebody got in while he was taking his sister home this afternoon and provided another bottle of drugged milk, from which he dutifully drank."

"He wouldn't," Pam pointed out. "After one bottle full of barbital, anybody would think twice."

"Right," Bill said. "Are you looking for rationality, Pam?"

Pam North hesitated for a moment. Then she said, "I guess not. I guess I'm licked. And he's such a nice little man, in spite of the whiskers and everything. Let's go home, Jerry."

Bill Weigand dropped them; drove on to the apartment hotel in West Twenty-second Street; went upstairs to have his look around. Deputy Chief Inspector Artemus O'Malley was in one of his thorough moods.

Bill Weigand was thorough himself; a conviction that thoroughness would lead nowhere did not lessen his application. In half an hour he had what he needed, which was, at least in outline, what he expected.

Dr. Preson had been found, in a coma, at a few minutes before eleven. A nephew, Wayne Preson, had found him. The nephew had called Laura and Homer Preson, sister and brother of the mammalogist, and then for an ambulance. There had then been an empty glass in front of Dr. Preson, who had been sitting at the table in the rear of the room relabeling bones. The glass had contained milk. It was apparent that, as he wrote on gummed labels, licked the labels and applied them to the bones, Dr. Preson had sipped from the glass.

"Took the taste out of his mouth, probably," a uniformed precinct man suggested, and Bill said, "Right," and then, more or less absently, "should have used a sponge."

"Makes 'em too wet," the precinct man said, and continued to report. He had arrived in a prowl car before the ambulance from St. Vincent's; when he arrived, Wayne Preson had got the little curator of mammals to a couch. He was restless, then, stirring uneasily in his sleep.

From what Wayne said, it was easy to get the picture. Dr. Preson, sitting in front of his pile of bones, had written and licked and sipped and stuck labels onto bones. Slowly the phenobarbital in the milk had had its effect. The handwriting on the labels, at first firmly clear, had deteriorated; toward the end it was hard to decipher what Dr. Preson had intended. "Particularly with words like that," the precinct man said. In the end, Dr. Preson's head had come to rest on the table, with the bones of extinct mammals. Apparently as he lost consciousness, he had been reaching for another label from a box of them near his hand. How long he had rested so was anybody's guess.

The ambulance had come and Dr. Preson had been taken to St. Vincent's Hospital, his nephew in attendance. Laura and Homer Preson had also gone directly to the hospital. Precinct detectives had continued the formalities.

"Found a bottle of milk, less one glass, in the refrigerator," Bill Weigand said. "Dr. Preson's fingerprints on it, probably. No—he'd have wiped them off, wouldn't he? Phenobarbital in the milk."

"About that, captain," the precinct man said. "Good guess."

"Repetition," Bill told him. "It happened earlier. Didn't anybody tell you?"

"Who'd tell me?" the uniformed man said. "Don't you know we just think with our feet?" He interrupted himself. "Sorry, captain," he said. "Didn't mean anything."

Bill told him enough. He said, "Oh, one of *those* things."

"Did they find out when Dr. Preson got here?" Bill asked.

They had. The information had been left with the man from the prowl car. Dr. Preson had got back to the hotel a little before five o'clock in the afternoon. He had not left again. When Wayne had arrived, representing the family, he had first telephoned Dr. Preson from the desk, and had gone up when there was no answer.

"Any food sent up to him?" Bill asked.

There had not been.

"Carrying anything when he came in?"

There information failed; that had been overlooked, or not imparted to the precinct man. Weigand telephoned down to the desk. Dr. Preson had, the desk clerk remembered, been carrying something—a paper bag, he thought. Yes, come to think of it, it could have contained a bottle of milk. Yes, Dr. Preson had certainly been alone. No, he had not communicated with the desk thereafter. The hotel did not serve meals, but could have sent out for sandwiches. It had not been asked to.

The pattern held, then. Laura Preson's blunder into the trap Dr. Preson had set for himself had not stopped him. He had brought home another quart of milk, filled it again with phenobarbital, taken the overdose which was to prove a new step in "persecution." The poor little guy! So much innocent cunning—not to hide the bottle coming in, yet to rub fingerprints from it! The cunning of madness. Such a nice little man, Pam North thought him. The things that happened to people—

Bill looked at the bones on the table; wondered if Dr. Preson would ever be able to complete the task of rearranging them. If he did he would have to redo much he had done that night. Not only were many of the labels beyond decipherment, but some of them had not adhered to the bones to which they had been affixed. As his mind grew dimmer, as sleep came, Dr. Preson must often have failed to moisten the gummed labels from—Bill looked at a package of labels, waiting in reserve—from Dennison's, naturally.

Bill returned to the telephone. He had been right, his office told him, on the contents of the bottle of milk. The first analysis showed there had been phenobarbital in it again. He had been right about the absence of fingerprints on the bottle. The glass, however, had had Dr. Preson's prints on it, as well as those of another man. The other man, undoubtedly, was the nephew Wayne, who said he had, on seeing the glass, automatically picked it up and smelled of its contents. It was difficult to persuade people to keep hands off things; the human instinct is to touch. But this time, Bill thought, it didn't make any particular difference.

"I'll stop by the hospital," Bill told the presiding sergeant at Homicide West. "If nothing new comes up there, I'll be at home. If the inspector calls, tell him it doesn't look much like attempted murder. Tell him I'll report in the morning. Right?"

"Yes sir," the sergeant said.

Acting Captain William Weigand went to St. Vincent's Hospital. In an anteroom on the third floor of the main building, he found a thin, sharp woman of about fifty, a neat small man with gray hair and gray clothes and glasses, and a dark, slender man of, perhaps, twenty-five. Among them there was, Bill decided, a family resemblance. He introduced himself to Laura and Homer and Wayne Preson.

"Will this make any difference?" Miss Laura Preson said. She spoke to him sharply. "It is, of course, essential that we know."

"Difference?" Bill Weigand said. "In what way, Miss Preson?"

"Your man," she began, but then turned to her brother. "Tell him, Homer," she instructed.

"My sister means, any difference in the dispo—I mean, the treatment of my poor brother," Homer Preson said. "The detective this evening—I think his name was Anstey?—indicated that we would be free to arrange for my brother's—treatment. My sister wonders whether this—this incident—will make a difference in that plan?"

He was, Bill decided, a precise man.

"Not necessarily, I shouldn't think," Bill said. "Of course, that's in other hands. However, it does make treatment more imperative. You see that."

"Your coming here—" Homer Preson began.

That, Bill told him, was another matter. A certain routine was established; he was part of it.

"Since," Bill Weigand said, "it might have been attempted murder."

Three Preson countenances expressed incredulity. The family resemblance was enhanced. Weigand was told, by Miss Laura Preson, that what he was suggesting was nonsense. He was asked, by Homer Preson, who would want to kill a harmless man like Orpheus. Wayne Preson contented himself with a nervous gesture of rejection, but then stood up, moved to a window and looked out of it. The implication was of departure from stupidity.

All three of these slight, wiry people were keyed up. That was, of course, understandable. Bill Weigand was soothing. All contingencies, even the most improbable, had to be taken under consideration. Death—or the threat of death—from other than natural causes had always to be looked into. There was every reason to suppose that Dr. Orpheus Preson had prepared his own sleeping draught, for reasons that—well, that he was afraid were evident. For a time, that had not been so evident. Investigation had been started; inevitably it continued for a time through momentum. Bill Weigand was, he told them, merely tidying up.

But that it was inconceivable that anyone should desire the death of a "harmless little man"—that, academically, did not follow. Harmless little men, as well as larger and more harmful men, did die violently from time to time. Most often, they died because they had something somebody else wanted, and wanted badly. Wayne Preson turned from the window, at that, and laughed. Bill offered him a faint, receptive smile, and waited.

"You think the Broadly Institute put something in Uncle Orph's milk?" Wayne Preson enquired. He had an unexpectedly deep voice; he clipped his words. "A committee of curators, perhaps?"

"Wayne," his aunt said, "don't talk nonsense. Don't try to be funny."

"Not I," Wayne said. "This gentleman." He indicated Bill Weigand. "This gentleman" shook his head. "Oh," Wayne said. "Then you didn't know?"

Bill was afraid he didn't get it. He continued to shake his head, the faint smile still receptive. He had missed the point of the joke, the smile said.

"My brother has left his money to the Broadly Institute," Homer Preson said. "My son refers to that. The Broadly Institute of Paleontology, with which my brother is associated." He paused to look with disapproval at Wayne Preson, who was bland, who said, "Sorry, dad," without any conviction in his voice. "A very poor joke," Homer Preson told his son.

"You wanted to know who would profit," Wayne Preson told Weigand. "In the event Uncle Orph—er—shuffled off. Isn't that what the police always want to know? Well, there you have it. The Broadly Institute. Not his loving family."

"Wayne!" Laura Preson said. "Must you be so—childish?" She turned to Weigand. "I hope," she said, "that I do not need to tell you that we have no interest in whatever money my brother may have."

"None," Homer Preson said. "In any case, my brother is not a wealthy man. A few thousands."

"Which we don't get," Wayne said. "In any case," he added, his inflection faintly mimicking his father's. He still seemed amused. But then he looked at his aunt, at his father, finally at Bill Weigand. "Of course," he said, "they're right. I'm afraid I was merely—" He broke off. "It struck me as amusing," he said. "The Institute putting stuff in uncle's milk. Don't pay any attention to me."

"Right," Bill said. "I won't arrest the Institute." His tone dismissed the subject. Wayne Preson was an intelligent young man, in contact with his elders. Flippancy resulted. But the disposition of Orpheus Preson's "few thousands" was without interest, academic or other. There was no case. There was only one of those things, destined to proceed to the observation ward of Bellevue Hospital, unless there was family intervention.

"How is he?" Bill asked anybody who had an answer.

"Doing as well as can be expected," Wayne Preson answered. "As they always are."

Weigand expected rebuke, waited for amplification. But the elder Presons offered neither. Homer Preson, in response to Weigand's slightly lifted eyebrows, merely nodded. It was Wayne who amplified. A nurse had visited them about an hour earlier and used the familiar words. She had also suggested that they might as well go home, since no change was to be expected immediately; she had promised they would be notified when Dr. Preson awakened. But they had decided to wait a little longer. He looked at Weigand. "Couldn't you—?" he asked.

Bill could. He went in search of information. It carried him past a nurse and her familiar assurances. It carried him to a resident physician.

"Oh, coming along all right," the resident said. "These things take time, you know."

"He'll be all right, then?" Bill said.

"Why—" the resident said. "Oh yes, I'd think so, captain."

Now Bill Weigand waited, letting the physician feel that more was expected.

"You understand," the physician said, "that tolerance varies. Recuperative powers vary. There are—elements. Body weight enters in, of course. Other things." He managed, Weigand thought, to assume the appearance of a man who has said something.

"Right," Bill Weigand said, "go on, doctor."

"That's all," the doctor said. "All I can tell you at the moment."

"No," Bill said. "I'm not a relative, doctor. I'm a policeman. I take it you're not satisfied?"

"These things vary," the doctor said again. "There's quite a skin rash, in this case. Characteristic of the stuff, you know. The blood pressure's down, of course. Quite noticeably down, as a matter of fact. Still, he ought to respond to treatment. I'd have been happier if we'd got him sooner but—" He stopped. He shrugged.

"I take it," Bill Weigand said, "that he hasn't started to respond yet?"

"Well—" the doctor said. "No, he hasn't, captain. Not that that proves anything."

"He's still in danger?"

"Well—" the physician said again. "As for that, I suppose you could say that. It's just a word, after all. I think we'll bring him around all right. We usually do." He nodded, seeming to reassure himself. "Takes a while," he said. "You might tell his people that. Get them to go home. No use their sitting in there all night."

Bill Weigand told the Presons there was no change, and wouldn't be for hours. He got them to go home, Wayne in a jaunty British sport car; the elder Presons by cab. Weigand watched them go and went home himself.

It was not until a few minutes before ten o'clock the next morning that Dr. Orpheus Preson died of respiratory paralysis.

Weigand was reporting, at that time, to Deputy Chief Inspector Artemus O'Malley. An hour earlier, he had checked the hospital and been told there was no change. (There had been, however, no further contention that Dr. Preson was doing as well as could be expected.)

Oral reports to Inspector O'Malley were likely to prove protracted, especially when the inspector was in a mood both thorough and retro-spective. That Thursday morning he was. He sought a complete reca-pitulation of all that was known about Dr. Preson, and what he heard reminded him of things which had happened in the older days, when cops didn't fiddle-faddle. On this, and somewhat allied, subjects he was loquacious with Acting Captain William Weigand and also with Detective (First Grade) Vern Anstey, briefly called in to amplify. The inspector was reminded (obscurely, as it seemed to Weigand) of a crackpot he had himself come across back in 1915—no, maybe it was 1913—who had his furnished room full of snakes. It had been quite a thing; they had been killing snakes for hours. Their harborer had wound up on Blackwell's Island. "No Welfare about it in those days."

"I suppose this Preson will wind up in Bellevue observation," O'Malley said. "Keep him there for weeks, trying to find out what makes him tick, won't they? Waste a lot of time and money. Anybody can see he's a crackpot."

"Right," Bill said. "I take it you agree, then, that he took this stuff himself? For some—crackpot reason?"

"What've I been telling you?" O'Malley asked. "Don't make me do your thinking for you, Bill."

"No sir," Bill Weigand said, with a little more emphasis than he intended. O'Malley looked at him.

"I agree with you, sir," Bill said.

"Think you would," O'Malley said. "Nothing in it for Homicide. Anyway, he's not—"

The telephone rang at that moment, O'Malley said, "Yeh," into it, and handed it to Weigand, who listened, said "Right, thanks," and hung up.

"Preson died at 9:52," he said.

O'Malley assumed, briefly, the expression of a man who would have removed his hat, had he happened to be wearing a hat. He said, "Well, we've all got to go" and then banished, with some little effort, the melancholy into which this thought threw him.

"O.K.," he said. "It's suicide, then. Like I said, he was just a crack-pot."

It occurred to Bill that, to O'Malley, Dr. Preson had, by dying, finally proved that point. The logic was, possibly, less than convincing. But it was also true that, by dying, Dr. Preson had not proved he was not a crackpot. Suicide, while of unsound mind—whether Preson had meant to go that far or not. Bill stood up.

"Well," he said, "that's that, then?"

"Sure," the inspector said. "That ties it up."

Bill agreed. It would run its routine course, through reports, autopsy, the filing of papers without significance. But it was tied up.

The death of Orpheus Preson, Ph.D., D.Sc., was adequately reported in the *New York World-Telegram and Sun* that afternoon; the account appeared on page one, although below the fold, for two editions before a more important story ("State Department Janitor Once Red, McCarthy Charges") relegated it to page seven. The account was factual—Dr. Preson had been found in a coma due to an overdose of a barbital derivative and efforts to revive him had proved futile. The police were satisfied that Dr. Preson, author of the recent best seller, had himself administered the drug, probably taking an overdose through inadvertence. Homer Preson, head of a printing company bearing his name and well known as a type designer, said that his brother had been nervous and run-down for several months, but not under a doctor's treatment.

The *New York Post* found room for several paragraphs among its columns of opinion, but, since the rewrite man involved had not happened to read *The Days Before Man*—as the *World-Telegram*'s man had—the account was briefer. The *Journal-American* contented itself with two paragraphs well inside, headlined "Mammalogist Dies of Over-Dose." The item was read with disappointment by many *Journal-American* readers who, misled by a multi-syllabled word, had expected more lively things.

Gerald North read the *World-Telegram* account on his way home from the office and thought, first, "the poor little guy" and, second, "there goes the book." With these two immediate reactions felt, and noted, he was left with an intangible feeling of dissatisfaction, amounting almost to uneasiness. Damn it all, Jerry North thought, I could have sworn he was sane as anybody.

· 6 ·

FRIDAY, 10:15 A.M. TO 11:20 A.M.

It had been Pam North who first suggested that they might be too pessimistic about volume two of *The Days Before Man*. Perhaps, she said, the book was really completed and poor Dr. Preson had merely been fussing over it, as writers sometimes did. Perhaps it was almost completed, and somebody could be found to finish it off. "Since you've already got twenty-five hundred dollars in it," she said, by that time arguing with nobody. "I feel guilty every time I think I called him an extinct mammalogist," she added. "Once we all went to school and merely sat there and I said, 'Maybe Old Man Stevenson is dead.' He was the principal and he was. I waked up nights for a week."

"Um-m," Jerry said. "You could be right."

"Oh, I am," Pam said. "Of course, I was only about ten or eleven."

"I mean about the book," Jerry said.

"The book?" Pam said. "Oh—I'm sorry. I was remembering again.

None of us liked Mr. Stevenson, which made it worse, of course. For a week I felt that somehow I'd killed him."

She was, she was told, a bigger girl now. She had not killed anyone, certainly not Dr. Preson.

"The death wish," Pam said. "But I didn't have it. Jerry, we ought to have done something. Made him want to live."

It had been then the last drink before dinner Thursday evening—the drink of nostalgia and of aspirations not achieved; at the same time, often, the moment when all knowledge seems just beyond fingertips.

"People ought to want to live," Pamela North said, and regarded her almost empty glass.

Jerry smiled at her. He said one couldn't make them. He said that, by and large, people did.

"As a matter of fact," he said, "I'd have thought Preson did. I still don't—"

"I tell you," Pam said, "that's just it. It looks one way but it isn't. I keep knowing there's something wrong with it."

But Jerry North shook his head to that. He knew how she felt. But the thought was subjective; in a sense it was a turning away of the mind. He advised her to read again the story in the *World-Telegram and Sun*. There was no doubt that Preson had bought the milk, little doubt he had been alone in the apartment. The milk in the bottle had contained phenobarbital. But it had not contained phenobarbital when Preson bought it from the corner grocery. That he had himself drugged the milk he drank was inescapable.

"Of course," Jerry added, "it's quite possible he didn't plan it to end as it did, didn't plan to kill himself. It was to have been another move in this—persecution. Only, he got more of the stuff than he could handle. The effects vary."

"You've looked it up, then," Pam told him.

Jerry admitted that.

"Then it doesn't seem right to you, either," Pam said. "Suppose we're all wrong. Suppose there was somebody. Putting midgets in the newspapers, I mean. And phenobarbital—" She stopped. She looked at Jerry over her cocktail glass.

But Jerry shook his head. The real trouble was, he told her, that they had both been wrong about Dr. Preson. He had seemed sane to them; he had written as if he were sane. They did not want to admit they had been wrong. But facts confronted them. And this, he said, brought them back to the question of volume two of *The Days Before Man.*

"Well—" Pam had said, at a quarter of eight on Thursday evening, "well—I suppose you're right. And the police are right. Let's try the Plaza. It's so dark and—and thoughtful. Particularly the bar."

They had tried the Plaza's dark and thoughtful bar, and afterward the Plaza's less dark Oak Room, and talked of other things. But now, at a little after ten on Friday morning, they were driving in the Riverdale section of the Bronx, above the Hudson River. It was raining, without hurry, as if there were ample time to drown the world and enough water in the northeast to do it. They went down a side street through semi-circular tunnels dug for them by windshield wipers, and then came back up the side street, which was the wrong side street. It was almost eleven when they found an ungainly grayish house on a lot too small for it, and parked and dripped to a narrow porch. They rang a bell and after a time the door opened.

The man who looked at them was tall, but very thin. His shoulders were narrow under a suit jacket too wide for them; his face was narrow and wrinkled deeply, horizontally. His face was almost colorless, and the blue eyes in it were pale. Long, thin hands dangled below jacket sleeves.

"*Good* morning," the emaciated man said to Pam and Jerry North, in a voice almost intolerably cheerful. "Mr. and—" he paused for a moment and looked down at Pam—"*Mrs.* North?" he said. Pam nodded up at him. "Been expecting you," the man said, still with great cheer. "Left me to let you in."

Somewhat bewildered, the Norths went in. Pam looked around instinctively for spider webs, probably with spiders in residence, but the entrance hall was neat. The man preceded them into a living room which opened off the foyer.

Inside the living room, he turned and awaited them. He was even more emaciated here in the living room, lighted against the darkness of the early December morning, than he had been in the damp daylight. He was also somewhat grayer, except for his hair, which was white, and needed cutting. Under the lights, short white stubble appeared on his sunken cheeks.

"Landcraft," he said, in a voice of vigor and of youth. "Jesse Landcraft. Uncle Jesse." He was, it was evident, referring to himself. "Friend of the family. Sad thing about poor Orpheus. Very sad. Very good man on canids, especially. Eh?"

He paused.

"I'm sure he was," Pam North said. "We—"

"Came about the book," Jesse Landcraft told her. "Homer's on his way. Laura's out, you know." He paused. "Arrangements," he said. "Always that, you know. Much to be said for tar pits."

"What?" Pam said.

"Fell in them," Landcraft said. "Thought everybody knew about tar pits. Giant sloths. Big cats. All sorts of things. No arrangements then, eh? Good fossils in a few thousand years. No fuss, no bother."

"Didn't the cats fuss?" Pam asked. "All the cats I know—"

"Oh, everything fusses," Jesse Landcraft said, and his tone was almost jovial. "Probably fuss ourselves, eh? But there you are." He looked down at her. "Or will be," he added, and chuckled. "Don't mind an old man, my dear. Eccentric old man. Lives in a furnished room somewhere. Made you think of that artist chap, eh? Signs himself 'Chas.' Means Charles. What's his name?"

"Addams," Pam said. Then she flushed, slightly.

"Everybody does," Landcraft told her. "Do myself, sometimes. Can't all be pretty women, Mrs. North. Eh?"

"Do you—" Jerry began.

"Garrulous old fool, too," Jesse Landcraft said, and patted himself on the chest. "Can't do anything until my brother-in-law gets here, you know. I'm just a Chas Addams character to let people in. Have to talk to Homer about the book." He paused to shake his head. "Well, can't have everything," he said. "Can sit down, though."

He sat down himself. He sat down slowly, carefully, grasping an arm of the chair with either hand.

"Sixty," he said. "Look eighty. Feel like eighty. Poor Orpheus was the other way round." He nodded. "Would have been, anyway," he said. "Now look at him, eh? Good mammalogist, too. Not bad on the felids; tops on the canids."

"Are you one, too?" Pam asked him. Rain lashed the living room windows; the wind found an aperture somewhere and moaned through it. "I mean—"

"Know what you mean," the young voice said through the ancient mouth. "Used to be. Retired. Got something at a dig. Invertebrate man, myself. Not mammals. Never cared particularly for mammals. Worked with Orpheus, though. My sister met Homer that way. Married him. What you wanted to know, eh?"

The blue eyes in the creased face were not really pale. There was, remotely, laughter in them.

"Just out of curiosity," Landcraft told her. "Realize that. Curiosity useful in your business, eh?"

"Business?" Jerry said. "Publishing?"

"That too, probably," Landcraft admitted. "Thinking of the other thing. Detecting. Police work, eh?"

"We're not detectives," Pam told him. "Not really."

"Tell that to the Pinnipedia," Jesse Landcraft suggested, and arranged his folded face into a smile. He chuckled. The faces of the Norths remained blank. "Marine carnivores," Landcraft explained. "Seals and the like."

Gerald North paid the remark the faint smile earned. He repeated that they were not detectives.

"All right with me," Landcraft assured them. "Either way. I don't interfere, you know. On the side lines, eh? That'll be Homer now."

The Norths had not heard anything which was not wind or rain. But now they heard a door closing, and footsteps. Homer Preson came in to express regret that they had had to wait. They would, however, realize that there were a good many things to attend to.

"As to the rights to the book," he said, going to it now that he was there. "I really don't know, Mr. North."

Jerry shook his head at that. There was, as far as that went, no debate.

The contract bound heirs and assigns. The right to publish volume two of *The Days Before Man* was, securely, that of North Books, Inc.

"Oh," Homer Preson said, quickly. "I realize that perfectly, Mr. North. That is not in question. It is merely that, if formalities are necessary—whatever formalities are necessary—I am not your man. Because, you see, we are not my brother's heirs. My brother left everything he had to the Broadly Institute. He had told us that—oh, some little time ago. His attorney confirmed it to me today."

"All of it, eh?" Jesse Landcraft said. "Good man."

"All of it," Homer Preson repeated. "I don't question his decision, Jesse."

"Be hard to, eh?" Landcraft said. "Not that I doubt you, Homer. What'll Laura think, eh? Hasn't got the scientific mind, has she?"

"Laura knew Orpheus's plans," Homer Preson said. His manner was stiff. "We all did. I supposed you did too, Jesse."

"None of my business," Jesse Landcraft said, with youthful vigor. "As a matter of fact, I did know. Orph told me. In case I'd been expecting. Hadn't. Told him it was a fine idea. Find a lot of fossils with—how much do you figure, Homer?"

"My brother did not confide in me," Homer said. He still was stiff. "I question whether this interests Mr. North." He nodded, rigidly, toward Pam. "Or Mrs. North," he added.

"No reason why it shouldn't," Jesse Landcraft said. "Interesting subject, money. And where it goes."

"About the manuscript," Gerald North said. "Is it here, Mr. Preson? It's not at the—at your brother's apartment." They had checked on that early. All personal effects had been collected from the apartment the afternoon before; the hotel thought by the family.

"I imagine so," Homer Preson said. "We had everything packed up and brought here. Except the bones, of course. The Institute has collected the bones."

Jerry was polite, but he was not interested in fossil bones.

"I'd like very much to see the manuscript," he said. "Look it over—see how far he'd got. We may be able to salvage something, you know. I'd appreciate seeing it, if it isn't too much trouble to turn it up."

"Well," Homer Preson said. "Emily's going over things. She's my daughter, you know. I'll find out if she's come across it."

He went. After he had gone, Jesse Landcraft laughed shortly. His laughter was not so well preserved as his voice. His laughter sounded its age.

"Bearing up," he said. "Stiff upper lip. Stiff neck, too." He chuckled, this time. "Think it might be," he said. "Where he gets it, eh? I'd guess Orph had a hundred thousand left. Maybe more."

"He doesn't seem disappointed," Pam said, and Jerry, just perceptibly, shook his head at her. It wasn't their concern, the gesture told her.

"Had time to get over it," Landcraft said. "Known for a couple of weeks. Orph went to the trouble of telling all of them. Keep things in order. Liked order, Orph did."

"Still," Pam said, "it must be disappointing, just the same. He might—oh, he might have thought better of it."

"Orph?" Jesse Landcraft said. "I suppose he might. If Laura badgered him. He hated to be badgered. Took his mind off mammals. They might have worn him down. Academic now, eh? Can't think better of it now, can he? Good thing for the Broadly." He considered. "Best thing could have happened, probably," he said. "They might have talked him out of it."

The implication was somewhat startling. Both the Norths looked at the emaciated man with the young voice. He looked up at them.

"Shocked, eh?" he said. "Told you I was detached. Like Orph. Hate to see him dead. Still, he was getting along. Might just have lived the money up, eh? This way, it gets used." He nodded. "Real use," he said. "Worth something." He paused again. "More important than one man," he said. "You agree, eh?"

"Abstractly," Pam said.

"You're a woman," Landcraft told her. "Abstract, this side. Something to talk about. Real, this side. Something to see. Touch."

"It isn't a matter of gender," Pam said. "It's the way people are. Didn't you know that, Mr. Landcraft?"

"Not me," Jesse Landcraft said. "First things first, real *or* abstract. Because there isn't any difference if you look at things, eh? Scientifically, no difference." He shrugged very gaunt shoulders under the too-large jacket. "No need for you to agree," he told Pam North. "The Institute gets it anyway. That's real enough, eh? Concrete?"

"People come first, all the same," Pam said.

He shrugged again.

"Old bones," he said. "Bones not so old. We've got plenty of people. We've only scratched a little of the past. With a trowel in an acre—in a hundred acres. We don't know much, and that's a fact. Take the bovoids, for example. Tremendous gaps there."

"Cows?" Pam said.

"Among other things," Landcraft said. "A wide field, full of gaps. Just an example, of course. Gaps in the primates, if you come to that."

"But, after all," Pam said, "even if you had it all, what would you have? I mean—"

"Know what you mean," Landcraft said. "Knowledge, woman. Knowledge. What do you want?"

"Life," Pam North said.

"Oh," Landcraft told her, "there's plenty of that." His voice was, suddenly, not so young as it had been. Jesse Landcraft's voice seemed to have tired.

Pamela North was shaking her head, but Homer Preson came back before she had organized any answer to this last; to this, at best, elevation of the past above the present. This—

"Quite a good deal of it, Mr. North," Homer Preson said. He carried two boxes, tied with string. The boxes had contained typewriter paper; now, it was to be assumed, they held typewriter paper still, but now the paper was manuscript. Jerry opened the boxes and examined and was relieved. The typescript had been considerably corrected, in pencil. But it was still readable, and at least preliminary revisions had been made. He leafed through the two hundred odd pages in the first box and the more than a hundred in the second. The last page was numbered 315. He calculated. A hundred thousand words, perhaps. Volume I had run longer. Still— He came on four pages clipped together, numbered consecutively. At the start of the first was typed: "Chapts. 22, 23, 24—summary." The rest was terse; all too evidently a listing of topics still to be covered. It meant very little to Gerald North, who sighed. He re-turned and read the last two pages of the completed, or semi-completed, manuscript. It was concerned with the "bear dog" of prehistory; it was clear, interesting, now and then witty. When he wrote those pages, at any rate, Orpheus Preson had still had his wits about him, and the grace of mind—the unexpectedness—which had given life to his saga of old bones. He had ended with a half-finished sentence.

"I'll take it along," Jerry said. "We may be able to publish as it is. Perhaps somebody can finish it along his lines."

"I," Homer Preson said, "don't know. I'll have to ask that you con-sult the Institute."

"Of course," Jerry told him. "That's obvious, Mr. Preson."

"I am not familiar with the situation, technically," Preson insisted. "I should like to be certain that the Institute, whose property this is, or will be, approves your plans."

A very precise little man, Jerry thought. A pettifogging little man; a man who moved with short steps and cautious ones.

"My firm is entirely responsible," Gerald North said, and knew that he echoed Homer Preson's primness. "All contingencies will be con-sidered." He felt that the last would appeal to Homer Preson.

"Well—" Preson said. "I rather wish my sister—"

"I'll tell you," Pam North said, "we'll go up to the Institute right now, won't we, Jerry. Take the manuscript up to them, explain Mr. Pre-son's position, get their approval. Won't we, Jerry?"

It was Jerry North's turn to say, "Well—" and to say it doubtfully. He looked quickly at his wife; she nodded with emphasis. "Why yes," Jerry said, "we'll do that."

"Good," Homer Preson said. "I'm sure that is the correct procedure, Mr. North."

They were through the rain again, in the car again, in a few minutes. Preson had taken them to the door. Jesse Landcraft apparently had gone to sleep in his chair but, as Jerry started the car, Pam said, "He was wide awake, all the same. I looked back and he was just closing them."

"His eyes?" Jerry said, preparing to drive around a block, turning right at the first corner.

"Of course," Pam said. "Did he make you shiver?"

"Landcraft?" Jerry said. "He's a little Chas Addams, certainly."

"I don't mean that," Pam said. "Oh, that too. I mean what he said. The—the way he thinks. Feeding us to—to what? Prehistoric bovoids?"

"I imagine they ate grass," Jerry said, and made another right turn. He ought, now, to be headed back toward the parkway. He was going east, at any rate; the industrious windshield wipers shuddered in the wind; water slithered on the glass.

"A mad scientist," Pam said, and was told to come, now. She was told, also, that she should begin to avoid television.

"Not that kind," Pam said. "Mad about science. Don't you see? He'd—he'd grind people up. For knowledge."

"Nonsense," Jerry said. "You're being sensitive, baby."

Pamela North denied this. She said it was plain to anyone who listened.

"He *said* it," she told Jerry. "I think you have to turn down this one first and then get on."

Gerald North said he knew, and turned right on the feeder road to the parkway.

"About poor Dr. Preson," Pam said. "That it was a good thing he died, so his money would go to—to more old bones. To plug gaps in the bovoids. He really meant it."

"Academically," Jerry said and stopped where a sign commanded. He peered back into the rain and started again, bound downtown on the Henry Hudson Parkway. "By the way, why did you say we'd go to the Institute? Now, I mean? I'll have to go over the book and—"

"Oh," Pam said, "I'd think somebody there would know about Mr. Landcraft, wouldn't you? Whether it is, really, academic. Or whether, if he thought—oh, science—was in danger of losing something, he would really—"

"Losing something?" Jerry said, taking the easiest first.

"Like money," Pam said.

"Would really what?" Jerry asked her, but by then he could guess.

"Do something," Pam said. "Even—kill something."

It should, Gerald North told himself, sound grotesque. It went against all they knew; against the obvious fact that nobody had been, in the sense Pam meant, killed. It was because of the rain drumming on the car roof, because of the wind crying through an aperture somewhere in an old house, because of a too-thin man with dangling arms, that the suggestion was not immediately absurd. If the sun had been shining, if Jesse Landcraft had not been of so curious an appearance, Jerry would have laughed easily at Pam's imaginative flight into— well, into something close to the macabre. As it was he laughed. The laughter did not sound as he had hoped.

"You see?" Pam said. "Somebody at the Institute will know him, probably. Maybe he is famous." She paused. "In one way or another," Pamela North said, darkly in the dim car, only just audibly above the beating rain.

· 7 ·

FRIDAY, 11:45 A.M. TO 2:55 P.M.

The Broadly Institute of Paleontology, which has exhibit rooms open to the public between the hours of ten and five, Monday through Friday, ten to ten, Saturday and Sunday, occupies a large, square building on upper Fifth Avenue, but it is by no means as large as the American Museum of Natural History, on the other side of the park. Hurrying up its broad steps, in a futile effort to run between raindrops, Pamela North was a little surprised that the Broadly Institute was not larger, since it had begun to loom so large in her thoughts. But inside the door, in the Great Hall—which is two stories from floor to ceiling, and occupies most of the width and almost all the length of the building—she was sufficiently impressed. The Great Hall, shadowy in spite of numerous ceiling lights, was to a considerable extent occupied by a rearticulated Tyrannosaurus, which showed teeth at her and, impartially, at Gerald North also. Pamela North said, "My!"

As Tyrannosauria went, this one was not prodigious. Some millions of

71

years ago it had become personally extinct before reaching full growth, so that the skeleton stood not more than twice the size of a tall man and was barely thirty feet in length. No doubt its fellow Dinosauria had considered it something of a runt. It still showed big teeth to Pamela, who looked up at it.

"My," Pam repeated. "Whatever he says, people are better. And what difference does it make if they *did* live?"

"People like to read about them," Gerald North said, speaking as a publisher and removing the boxed manuscript from beneath his coat, where it had been sheltered from the rain. "Fortunately," he added. "I'll find somebody to talk to."

He consulted a guard. Pamela walked thoughtfully around the medium-size Tyrannosaurus, shaking her head. Nature had once been unrestrained. Tyrannosaurus, when clothed and on its hind legs, had been a very showy animal, even an excessive one.

Jerry North intercepted his wife; asked whether she wanted to stay among the exhibits or go with him to see Dr. Agee. "Paul Agee," he amplified. "The director."

Pam chose the human and, on reaching the third floor by elevator, the director's office down a long corridor by foot, was glad she had. Introduced, Dr. Agee showed his teeth also, but in a smile. He was a slight man, hardly larger than Preson had been, but a good deal more self-contained. He sat behind a modern desk in a modern office. He was, it proved, also efficient. He said that Dr. Orpheus Preson was, indeed, a great loss, not only to the Institute but to science. He said this as if he meant it, but he did not brood over it. As for the book—

"I'm told he left everything to the Institute," Dr. Agee said. "I'm not surprised. His life was here, I felt. He had signed a contract for this, I assume?" He indicated the manuscript.

"Yes," Jerry told him.

"Binding on his heirs, of course?" Dr. Agee said.

"Oh yes," Jerry said.

"Excellent," Dr. Agee said. "We were all pleased with the success of the first volume—all of us here. You people did an admirable job.

Wouldn't have thought there were so many people interested in paleo-zoology."

"It was an excellent book," Jerry told him.

Dr. Agee knew. He had read it. He had been surprised, as well as pleased. He had not known that Dr. Preson, whom he knew as a good—a very good—mammal man, had this—"knack," should he call it?

"Scientists often have, as a matter of fact," Jerry told him. "Do you want a copy of the contract?"

As a form, only as a form, Dr. Agee supposed it would be more businesslike. It was, however, early days, and he pointed this out to Jerry. The will had not yet been filed; until it was, the whole matter remained in, should he say, *incertae sedis?* He agreed, without prompting, that this was entirely a formality. At any rate, he assumed so?

So did Gerald North, and said so. Meanwhile, there were practical matters. Jerry explained the most pressing—the manuscript was not completed.

It might, presumably, be published as it stood. Jerry would know more when he had finished reading it. Possibly—and here he looked involuntarily at Pam—they were premature. But, if they were to try to complete volume two of *The Days Before Man,* they would need scientific help. Provisionally, could Dr. Agee suggest someone?

"Steck," Dr. Agee suggested without hesitation. "Far and away the best—" He stopped, and looked from one to another of the Norths. "The name seems to mean something," he said.

"Dr. Preson mentioned Dr. Steck once or twice," Jerry said. "There seemed to be an area of disagreement."

"Oh, that," Dr. Agee said, and waved a hand. "Nothing to that. One calls the other a 'splitter'; the other calls the first a 'lumper.' A technical disagreement about taxonomy. Actually, neither's primarily a taxonomist. Both very good zoologists. Both primarily mammal men although Preson did some very good work on invertebrates and Steck's excellent on reptiles. Set up Teddy downstairs."

"Teddy?" Pam North said.

"Oh," Dr. Agee said, and for a moment looked a little embarrassed.

"Force of habit. The Tyrannosaurus in the Great Hall. It—er—reminded somebody of—"

"Paleopolitics," Pam North said.

Dr. Agee was surprised and showed it. But then he laughed. "Exactly," he said. "The teeth, of course."

"To get back," he said, then. "I do suggest Steck, if you find you need somebody. He's a very good general man in zoology—paleozoology, neozoology. He writes very agreeably, it seems to me, although that isn't my line, of course. We'd feel great confidence in him for a job like this. And, of course, it's in the family."

"You mean he works here, too?" Pam North said. She was surprised, this time.

"Why—yes," the director of Broadly said. "He works here." His voice put the faintest possible emphasis on the word "works." "He's associated with us," he added. "As a matter of fact, he'll probably take over mammals. Been an associate, you know."

"With Dr. Preson?" Jerry North said.

"Yes," Agee said. "For the past year or so. Before that, he was with the Museum." He smiled. "Quite a compliment to us, his coming here," he said. "Usually the other way about, if they can make it."

There had been, of course, no particular reason why Dr. Preson, in his discussion of Dr. Steck as a possible persecutor, should have mentioned that Steck, too, was a Broadly Institute man. Probably, Jerry realized, Dr. Preson had assumed it was a fact generally known, as Jerry himself might assume the connection of a Mr. Cerf with Random House to be a phenomenon universally recognized. Then he realized, simultaneously, why he was surprised and the element he had overlooked: When he had written Steck for his opinion of *The Days Before Man,* Steck had been with the American Museum of Natural History. That had been two years ago. All that had happened was that, subsequently, Steck had changed jobs. Or, as Dr. Agee obviously would prefer, "associations."

"Didn't they fight?" Pam North said. "Over—splits and lumps?"

"Certainly not," Dr. Agee said. "I explained that. A minor scientific disagreement." He smiled. "I realize Dr. Preson could be—emphatic," he said. "That his emphasis might be misleading to people in another field."

Probably that was it, Jerry thought; probably it did not come to more than that.

"I don't want to seem insistent," Dr. Agee said. "But if you're thinking of what Dr. Preson's wishes would have been, I'm quite sure he would have approved Steck. After all, this isn't a Classification. We're not competing with Dr. Simpson. A difference in taxonomic approach hardly arises. Why not talk to Steck, when you're ready? Or now, if you like?"

"After I've—" Jerry began to say, but Pam said, more clearly, "Why *don't* you see him now, Jerry?"

"Well," Jerry said.

"Since we're here," Pam pointed out.

Dr. Agee communicated by telephone with Dr. Steck, found him available, advised him of the approach of Mr. and Mrs. North. The Norths stood up to go. Then Pam said, "Do you happen to know a Mr. Landcraft, Dr. Agee? A Mr. Jesse—"

Agee had stood up behind his desk, smiling them out. He ceased to smile. He shook his head.

"Poor old Landcraft," he said. "Preson's brother-in-law. Yes, I know him. Why?"

Pam had, she said, merely wondered.

"Used to be an invertebrate man," Dr. Agee said. "Quite sound, once. But he doesn't do much now, I'm afraid. Er—bad health. That is, not the man he was, I'm afraid. Why did you ask?"

Pamela North amplified, this time. She said they had just met him. She said she had just happened to ask. She said—"oh, he talked a little strangely."

"I'm afraid so," Dr. Agee said. "He does, I've heard. His interests have become channeled. Is that what you mean?"

Pam thought for a moment. It was one way of putting it, certainly. So she said, "Yes."

"Nothing that's happened in thousands of years means anything, really," she added. "I mean since thousands of years ago. That's what he made me feel."

"Millions of years, probably," Dr. Agee said. "Of course, we all get a certain frame of reference. Our interests get special. Perhaps our values do. It may be that Landcraft carries it to extremes. But—why? He isn't involved in the book?"

"Oh no," Pam said. "I'm just—curious. He is very happy that the Institute is going to get Dr. Preson's money. Even if Dr. Preson did have to die first."

Dr. Agee merely regarded her, his eyebrows slightly raised, his attention polite.

"The acquisition of knowledge," Pam North said, "seems to him more important than life. At least, he spoke that way."

"Academically, it is, of course," Dr. Agee said.

"I only wondered if he recognizes any difference," Pam said. "He said he didn't, actually. But people say things." She waited, but the director of Broadly, after a moment, did no more than shake his head. "Why would Dr. Preson kill himself, Dr. Agee?"

"We've all wondered," Agee said. "I suppose he'd been overworking. Although when he was in last—" He broke off. "Is there any doubt he did?"

"Oh, apparently not," Pam said. "But we're keeping Dr. Steck waiting, aren't we?"

Dr. Agee, who looked as if he were moving through a fog, did not deny this. He repeated directions for reaching the office of the new curator of Fossil Mammals. They went along a corridor from Dr. Agee's corner office, overlooking Fifth Avenue, down a long central corridor and found a door with a printed sign, "Albert James Steck, Associate Curator, Fossil Mammals." The door stood a little open and, after knocking and receiving no response, the Norths opened it wider and looked in.

They looked into a large room, lined with books. At the end were two tall windows, in need of washing. Under the windows was a long table, covered with objects. Halfway down the room, on the right, was a desk, its back to the book-lined wall, and at it there was a large man, crouched over the desk, his head resting on his hands. From the distance of the doorway, his attitude appeared to be one the utmost depression. Jerry North knocked again on the now largely opened door. Nothing happened. "Er-ah!" Jerry North said. The man looked up.

"Come in," he said. His voice was very deep. "Come in." He considered them. "Everybody does," he added.

The Norths went in. Dr. Albert James Steck stood up. He was a very large man indeed, being both tall and wide. He had a round, tanned face; his gray hair, cut short and bristling upward, grew vigorously, and low on his forehead. He spoke again, and his voice rumbled.

"You the people Agee called about?" he asked. "People about Preson's book?"

Jerry agreed. The Norths walked toward the large man at a desk which, as he bulked over it, seemed inadequate.

"Trying to get some work done," Dr. Steck said. "Always trying to get some work done. Too bad about Preson."

The Norths continued their advance.

"Mr. and Mrs. North. That's who you are," Dr. Steck rumbled. "Thought you were detectives."

Jerry explained that, as well as it could be explained. He also explained, more fully than Dr. Agee had on the telephone, his present mission. Before he finished, Dr. Steck was shaking his head. As he finished, Dr. Steck said, "Not your man. Sit down, anyway." He looked at two chairs by the desk. Both were already occupied, one with half a dozen books, piled precariously; the other with a box containing small bones. Dr. Steck came around his desk, removed the books from the chair, looked around the room, appeared to despair, and put the books on the floor. The box of bones he put on his desk. The Norths thanked him and sat down.

"I'm not a writer," Dr. Steck said. "Preson was. That's what it comes to."

"Dr. Agee doesn't agree," Jerry told him.

"Good of him," Steck said. "Perhaps he's not a judge, though. Actually he's an ethnology man, you know. Although I don't really know that that proves anything, does it?" Then, for the first time, he smiled. The smile faded quickly. "Too damn bad about Preson, isn't it? Everybody loses."

"Except the Institute," Pam North said.

"Everybody," Dr. Steck repeated, his deep voice rumbling. "The Institute gets a few thousands—and loses one of the best men in the field. When it comes to that, Preson financed a good deal of work here anyway. Just before—just the other day—he agreed to put up the money for an expedition in the southwest. We hear there are some interesting things down there. Leave out his taxonomy—he was an outrageous lumper, you know—and there wasn't a sounder man anywhere. Good general zoologist; good paleontologist to boot. Best man we had here, if you ask me. And he used to spend a good deal of time jumping down my throat, too."

"You didn't mind?" Pam North asked him.

"Mind?" Steck repeated. "Certainly not. I jumped down his. It didn't mean anything."

"Precisely," Pam North said, "what is a lumper?"

"Um-m," Dr. Steck said. "Well, you know what taxonomy is? The—call it the science of arranging. Classifying. Putting all the chairs in one room, even if they differ a good deal, and saying, 'these are chairs.' All the tables in another room. 'Tables.' It gets more complicated with animal life, principally because most animals are extinct. We establish and define relationships, or try to. Postulate orders, superorders, families and down to genera and species and put animals, living animals and extinct ones, where they belong, or where we think they do. Well—lumpers make fewer and larger units; big, simple groups. They come across a carnivore, say, and it isn't a dog or a bear. So, it's a cat. They call us splitters. Say if we can tell two animals apart, we place them in different genera; if we cannot tell them apart, we place them in different species. That's what Simpson said, anyway. Very clever man, Dr. Simpson."

"Oh," Pam North said. "Did you know Dr. Preson thought he was being—well, persecuted?"

"Preson?" Dr. Steck rumbled. "Nonsense." He looked with scrutiny at Pamela North, then at Jerry North. "Then he was being," Dr. Steck said. "He didn't imagine it. Does somebody think he had delusions?"

They told him enough to explain what had happened.

"He didn't imagine it," Dr. Steck told them.

That was obvious. What else was obvious, they also explained. "Doing it all himself?" Dr. Steck said. "I don't believe it. Why should he?"

"I'm afraid," Pam North said, "because he wasn't as sane as you think he was. You see, he did, in the end, take the sleeping medicine. The police are sure of that. So there isn't much choice about what to believe, is there? Whether he meant actually to kill himself or not, he fixed the milk and drank it and put stickers on those bones—" She broke off. "What happened to the bones?" she asked.

"They're here," Dr. Steck told her. He waved toward the long table under the window. He shook his head. "It's all to be done again, incidentally," he said. "The labeling, I mean. Almost all the labels came off." He paused, obviously in thought. "I guess you're right," he said, after a moment. "He wasn't himself. He never did anything halfway. Not even sticking a label on. It's still hard to believe." He shook his head again.

"About the book," Jerry said. "I'd like you to think it over, Dr. Steck. I'll have a look at it, get a general idea what we need, and then perhaps—"

"No," Steck said. "I'm afraid not. For one thing, as it looks now I probably won't be around for—oh, quite a few months, probably. This expedition I spoke about. It's not certain, but probably I'll head it up, now that Preson's—" A shrug of very broad, very heavy shoulders, finished the sentence. "The money he's left us will make the thing possible and—well, his death changes other things. He was anxious to have a young chap—good man, named Auerbrecht—in charge. Agee wasn't too enthusiastic. Felt that Auerbrecht ought to go as second, not first. I don't deny I think Agee's right. Auerbrecht's very young. So—"

"You'll take over," Jerry said.

Steck thought so; was pretty sure of it. There would first be the business of taking over as curator, getting the department running under his direction. Then the preparations for the expedition; then the expedition itself. Even if he felt himself qualified, as he did not, to finish the Preson book, where was the time to come from? He assumed that they didn't want to wait indefinitely for the book.

Jerry agreed to that, supposed he would have to seek further. Perhaps Dr. Steck had suggestions?

He had suggestions; he had several suggestions. As he made them, Pam North left her chair and walked around the room, looking at the books on the shelves, as she always looked at books on shelves. Few of these offered light, or even comprehensible, reading. She wandered to the end of the room—passing a door set into the book shelves of the right wall—and looked at the bones on the table. They seemed to be roughly grouped. The labels had, certainly, come off most of them. Either Dr. Preson, in his last few hours, had grown very careless or he had used very poor labels. He should have used Dennison's. Like those in the box on the table that Dr. Steck obviously had handy for a second relabeling. I must have Martha put on new shelf paper, Pamela North thought, and worked her way up the other side of the room, passing more books, another door. Obviously, a paleozoologist needed to do a great deal of reading. When she was back at the desk again, Jerry was standing up, thanking Dr. Steck. Pam smiled at the large mammalogist and made appropriate sounds. She and Jerry went back up the corridor, past Dr. Agee's office, and down by elevator to the Great Hall and Tyrannosaurus.

It was after noon, by then, and time to think of lunch. Before that, Jerry thought, he ought to stop by his office, or, at the least, call his secretary. He was told to call, and went in search of a telephone booth. Pamela, meanwhile, viewed the distant past, as re-created in the Great Hall of the Broadly Institute.

It was re-created in glass-fronted alcoves, so that antiquity lived, in effect, in show windows. Strange creatures posed in most of them, artfully reconstructed. There was something which looked like a rhinoceros, and probably had thought itself one; there were camels with necks like giraffes; there were animals with three horns, and one with a long horn on his nose and another who wore his third horn in the back of his head; there was an animal as much like an elephant as like anything living, but with tusks merged into a shovel at his lower lip. There were also very small horses, some of them with toes. All these creatures, the explanatory placard told Pamela North—who was suitably astonished—were native Nebraskans some seven or eight million years gone by.

Carnivores lived in another show window, with a background of prehistoric vegetation. There was a creature called—the placard insisted—"Hemicyon" which was as large as a black bear, and was indeed a little like a bear, but which was also a good deal like a dog. There were several cats, all with improbable names, and one of them was a saber-tooth. And in another alcove, a giant sloth went ugly on hooklike claws. He had lived in Florida when ice pushed life to the south. Pam gazed at him, shaking her head. Nature had, from time to time, made itself ridiculous. She moved on and found apes behind glass and, beyond them, a creature which was trying to be man and making what appeared to be minimal progress. He, with his mate, were at the entrance of a simulated cave. Something like a dog was with them, and a cat looked down, skeptically, from a tree. The cat, it was clear, had already made great progress in felinity when man began a—why, not more than a million years ago! A johnny-come-lately to the giant sloth; a freshman to the already feline cat. Pamela passed along, and found Jerry looking for her. She regarded Jerry.

"My, but you've improved," she told him. "You used to be shaggy."

"Got a haircut yester—" Jerry began and then, looking beyond Pam and getting a glimpse of early humanity, said, "Oh." He walked back a few steps. "Improved yourself," he told Pam. He rejoined her.

"It will have to be a fairly quick lunch," he told her, leading her toward the exit. "I've got an appointment at two." They went down the stairs and found the rain had stopped. "An appointment with one of the Presons," Jerry told Pam, when they were in the car. "With the nephew—what's his name? Wayne. Wayne Preson. He says he thinks there is something I ought to know about."

There was, they both agreed, no use in speculating as to Wayne Preson's message, since they would hear it shortly. So they speculated on it only so far as the Algonquin and, once at a table in the Oak Room, reconsidered the Broadly Institute and its occupants, antique and recent. Pam supposed, doubtfully, that it was useful to know that

Tyrannosaurus had once lived, and what he had looked like. It made one, at any rate, glad that he was not alive today. The prehistoric man indicated, she presumed, progress, at least toward diminished shagginess.

"On the other hand," Pam pointed out, "he only had a club, didn't he? Like the one he was leaning on in the showcase. And now look at him." They drank, perhaps to antiquity and simpler weapons.

"I suppose," Pam said then, "that they like to go on expeditions."

"They?" Jerry said. "Oh—paleontologists. Why yes, I suppose so. Be inconvenient if they didn't."

"And being curators," Pam added. "So it isn't quite true that everybody lost, is it? Dr. Steck didn't."

"Listen, Pam," Jerry said, slowly and carefully, "Dr. Preson died of a self-administered overdose of phenobarbital, presumably while of unsound mind. Why not admit it?"

She did, Pam said. Of course she did. She would have eggs benedict.

"I know there isn't any way around it," Pam said, then. "All I say is that, if there were, it would be interesting about Dr. Steck. Or about Mr. Landcraft. He's the one it ought to be, really. Since Dr. Preson did it himself, Mr. Landcraft is sort of wasted, isn't he? I mean, he would be so available."

There wasn't, Jerry told her again, any vacancy. There was no value in suspects when there was no crime.

"The trouble with you," he told her, "is that you've been spoiled. Another drink?"

Pam shook her head and then looked faintly surprised. She did, however, adhere to her decision. "After all," she explained, "we've got Wayne Preson coming up."

It occurred to Gerald North some time later that he might well have been surprised that Wayne Preson was a situation coming up not, simply, for Gerald North, as a publisher, but for the Norths as—well, as a unit. That he had not been surprised indicated (he realized, walking from the Algonquin toward his office, with Pam beside him) that he had, himself, some residual uncertainty about the whole matter. There was, he told himself resolutely, no reason why he should have, or why anyone should have. Wayne Preson had, or thought he had, some point to discuss about his uncle's book. It would be a point of seeming importance to him, of little to his uncle's publisher. It would be—

"Mr. Preson here?" Jerry asked his secretary, passing her desk.

He was; he had just arrived.

"There's a Miss Preson with him," the secretary said.

They were to be asked in. They came in. They were strikingly alike in appearance—both dark, neither tall, both slender. At a guess, they were both in their middle twenties. If he had first seen them out of context they would, Jerry realized, still have looked like people he had seen before. In context, it was simple—both of them resembled the late Dr. Orpheus Preson. About the girl, particularly, there was, in addition to a familiarity of feature, of bodily structure, an intensity of approach which was very like that of her uncle. She regarded both the Norths with anxiety, as if she were, somehow, thinking of them as problems which must instantly be solved.

"I'm Wayne Preson," the dark young man said. He spoke quickly, almost hurriedly, in a deep voice. "This is my sister, Emily. As my uncle's publisher, in view of the book, we—"

"We're going to contest the will," Emily Preson said. She said this very rapidly, as if it could not, because it was so urgently of importance, be said soon enough. "He wasn't competent. He—he hadn't been for months. He wasn't *sane*."

She stopped speaking, but it was as if she had not stopped. It was as if she were still, but not inaudibly, demanding of the Norths some response adequate to the urgency of her statement. *Don't just stand there,* she seemed to insist. *Don't you hear what I have just said? Don't you know that you must share this urgency with me?* She was screaming in silence.

"That's it," Wayne Preson said. "Our lawyer will communicate with the Institute, of course. But we—"

"Sit down," Jerry North said to both of them. "This is my wife. She knew your uncle."

"Well—" Wayne Preson said, doubtfully. "Well—" But he motioned his sister to a chair. She looked at him, and again there was a kind of trembling in the air. But she did sit down. "We talked it over," Wayne Preson said. "My father was opposed, at first. Aunt Laura said she didn't care one way or another. But Emily and I—"

"It isn't fair," Emily Preson said. "Don't you see that? Don't you both see it? He didn't know what he was doing."

I suppose, Pam thought, that decisions must be terribly important to her—the making of decisions, even about things not really vital in themselves. I suppose that is it. But at the same time Pam, unable to respond as Emily Preson demanded, was conscious of resenting the girl, resenting this unjustified demand on her and her own resultant sense of inadequacy—almost of dullness. Diminished in their own estimation are the dull of spirit, Pam thought. What does she want of us?

"Well," Jerry said. "It's up to you, of course. That is, I suppose it is really up to your father and aunt, isn't it? Since they're the next of kin?" He paused. "Up to all of you," he said. He was, he thought, saying nothing. What was he supposed to say?

"We realized you were concerned," Wayne Preson said. "Because of the book."

Jerry North considered. He shook his head slowly.

"Interested," he said. "Naturally. But not actually concerned, Mr. Preson. If you mean involved, as I suppose you do. As far as the book goes, it doesn't make any difference. We'll merely pay the royalties to—well, to whomever the court finally directs. That's the legal situation."

"Father said he would say that," Emily said to her brother. She stood up quickly. "What are we doing here?"

"Wait a minute, Miss Preson," Jerry said. "What is it, precisely, that you and your brother want?"

The girl looked at Wayne Preson and he, for a moment, seemed uncertain.

"Well," he said, "we're going, of course, to claim that my uncle was mentally irresponsible. You know he was, don't you? Didn't everything show it?"

"A good many things showed it," Jerry said. "I suppose—yes, a good many things recently. Did he make this will during that period? When these odd things were happening?"

"Yes," the girl said. "Of course. But it started long before that. Tell them, Wayne!"

"She's right," Wayne Preson said. "Doesn't this new book show it?" He looked at Gerald North, and now he was insistent, almost as his sister was.

"I haven't read it," Jerry said. "I've dipped in here and there. It seems all right; seems very good, very clear. You're afraid that may upset your case?"

"I told you how it would be," the girl said. She had gone to a window and was looking out over the city. "Doesn't anybody ever learn?" She seemed to demand an answer from all the buildings below the window, and all the people in them.

"You don't understand," Wayne said. "That isn't what we're thinking about. We're going into court to prove my uncle was—well, insane at the time he made the will. Not competent to make it. The police will back us up, because it's all true. What will that do to the book? It's your company we're thinking of, for God's sake. We didn't want it sprung on you. The court will decide Uncle Orph wasn't in his right mind. Then who's going to buy his book?"

Their attitude was considerate; their concern for North Books, Inc., very generous. Their attitude was also surprising. Jerry North tried to keep surprise from being too evident in his voice; as he told them both they were very thoughtful—and that there might, of course, be something in what they said. That, however, he would have to chance. In any case, one could never tell about people who bought books, at best a peculiar and diminishing group. Often, so far as he could tell, they formed judgments on the basis of the books themselves, without too much regard for the idiosyncrasies of authors. He could hope that would be the case this time. So could the Presons.

"After all," he said, "if the second volume goes as well as the first, you'll profit. If the courts do upset the will."

Wayne Preson said he supposed so. He put hands on the arms of his chair and leaned forward, preparatory to rising. He repeated that he and his sister had thought North ought to know what they planned. He was glad that Mr. North didn't think the success of the book would necessarily be jeopardized. Then Emily Preson turned from the window, and her attitude was insistent.

"Mr. North," she said, "whose side are you on? What will you say?"

"Side?" Jerry repeated.

"Uncle Orpheus wasn't sane," the girl said. "Don't you know that?" She turned suddenly to Pam North. "Don't you?" she said.

You had to be in it, Pam thought. You had to respond.

"The things he did don't seem sane," Pam said. "The things he seems to have done."

"There isn't any doubt what he did," Wayne Preson said, still leaning forward in his chair. "The police can prove that. It's a matter of record. And—we'd known it for a long time before."

"He *couldn't* have been sane," Emily Preson said. "Don't you know that?" This was to Pam North. It seemed to be vital to her that Pam North should know that, should say she knew it. It was as if her brother had not spoken.

Pam North shook her head.

"How can I know?" she said. "What do you care, anyway, whether I know or not?"

The girl looked at Pam for a moment, as if it were impossible Pam should not add to what she had said. But then Emily Preson turned away abruptly, dismissingly.

"You, Mr. North?" Wayne Preson said.

"You want me to testify that your uncle acted irrationally?" Jerry asked him. He shook his head. "He talked rationally to me," he said. "He wrote rationally. It's obvious, now, that he wasn't, I suppose. But these irrational actions are only things I've heard about—that my wife and I've heard about. We couldn't help you."

"You're against us then?" the girl said. There was surprised violence in her voice, her whole manner.

"For heaven's sake," Pam North said. "Do we have to be one or the other? What makes you think we have to be in it at all?"

The girl looked at her, and now there was a puzzled expression in

Emily Preson's eyes, as if what Pam North was saying were incomprehensible.

"Miss Preson," Pam said, "we don't have to care. Don't you see that? We don't have to care one way or the other. Nobody does." But then she looked into the girl's eyes. "I'm sorry," Pam said. "You can't—can't tear things out of people, you know. Particularly not when the things aren't in them."

Then Pam felt as if she had slapped this dark, demanding girl—slapped her needlessly, in callous rejection. She wondered if Emily Preson were not often so slapped, and so rejected, because her demands on people were insatiable. She must be lonely, Pam thought, and I'm sorry.

"I'm sorry," she said to the girl, but Emily merely looked at her, puzzled.

"Come on, Emily," Wayne Preson said, and now he did stand up. "Can't you see she's right?"

Emily Preson did not say anything. She went with her brother, who said the conventional things, and who was again thanked by Jerry North for the spirit which had prompted him to give a warning.

"All right," Jerry said, after they had left the office. "What was all that about? Merely what he said—to give us, I gathered, a chance to get out of publishing the book? Or—" He shrugged. There were too many possibilities.

"She came," Pam North said, "because she wants to be reassured."

"Reassured?" Jerry said.

"That the world is real," Pam said. "That she can get through to it. Because, you see, she can't really." Pam paused. "Also that she is right about her uncle, probably," Pam added. "You see, she isn't sure, either." She paused. "I don't really know why *he* came," she said.

· 8 ·

FRIDAY, 3:55 P.M., TO SATURDAY, 10:18 A.M.

"You'll think it's important enough," Jesse Landcraft said into the telephone. He listened. "Better make it this afternoon," he said. "Might change my mind, eh?" He listened again. "After that, then," he said. "Let your dinner wait for once, eh? Might even have it with you." Once more he listened. "I know," he said. His surprisingly young voice was a little impatient. "I know. Not senile yet, eh? *Nor* lost my memory." He chuckled. "How's Teddy?" he enquired. He listened. "You'll be glad you did," he said. "About six, eh?" He listened once more and replaced the telephone receiver on its hook in the dark hall of the old house where he had a room. He went back upstairs to the room and looked at himself in a mirror. He rubbed a hand over his face, decided he had better, and went to the bathroom down the corridor to shave.

He left the house at a few minutes after four, and walked toward the bus stop in gathering darkness, made deeper by low clouds. The rain had stopped. The wind would back around in a few hours, Jesse Landcraft thought; it would be cold by the time he got home. He wrapped a long coat around his long body. It was cold enough as it was. You needed heat and a good deal of it as you got older; you needed now, would like now, the kind of heat you had endured in Nevada on the dig with Orpheus ten years ago. Was it only ten years ago?

His route to the bus stop took him past the Preson house. There was a sports car in front of the door—one of the little English jobs Wayne was selling. So Wayne was there; they were having a conference, probably. Jesse Landcraft hesitated for a moment in his not rapid progress—he seemed disjointed when he walked, badly hinged. He chuckled. Then he went on toward the bus. It would be like the Presons to confer on their next steps, although all they now had to do was obvious—get their lawyer to work. But Homer would want things worked out in precise detail; Laura would want to pick at them; the girl would want—Jesse Landcraft shook his head. It was hard always to understand what his niece wanted. More than she was likely to get, he thought. The trouble with Emily was that she scared people—scared them off.

A bus was waiting. He got on it, slowly. Because she wanted too much to be in things—deeply in them, wholly in them—she was often left out of them. Had been this time, so far as he could gather. He shrugged. He rubbed fog from the bus window with his hand and looked out, seeing nothing of what he had thus made visible. The window fogged again, but he continued to look into it, hardly realizing he could now no longer see through it, until the bus stopped with finality. He got out with the others and took the subway downtown.

It would have been quicker to leave the subway at Ninety-sixth Street and go cross-town by bus, but he had ample time. He rode down to Columbus Circle and walked east along Central Park South, past hotels and restaurants, finally past the Plaza. It still was early; he moved so seldom nowadays out of a small area in Riverdale, living there as he might have lived in a village, that he had forgotten city distances and the time it takes to cover them. Now it was only a few minutes after five. He hesitated at the curb of Fifth Avenue and then walked back to the side entrance of the Plaza. He had not been there—he had not been anywhere—for a long time; a long, long time. He went into the Plaza and down the corridor to the bar in the rear. He had not been there for—was it five years? Or almost ten? It had not changed; now, early for cocktail time, it was uncrowded. He went halfway down the bar, away from a group of young men—very young men—at the corner nearest the door. He hesitated a moment while the bartender waited; then he ordered scotch and soda. He drank it slowly, letting the room and the drink warm him. He spent too much time in Riverdale, he told himself—too much time in his room, too much time at the Presons', part of the family yet not part of it; not a confidant in its councils, yet too close, and sometimes too taken for granted to remain wholly an outsider. He had been, too long, only an observer; too long detached and passive. He was not old enough for that; perhaps no one is ever old enough for that. He finished, almost abruptly, what remained in his glass, paid and walked out of the Plaza bar, a long man in a long coat, moving a little stiffly.

He walked to Fifth Avenue and across it and caught a bus uptown. As the bus ground north, the course he was taking became increasingly familiar. How many times—but how long ago!—he had ridden up Fifth toward the Institute, toward work he knew and men he knew. Old Smith had been director, then; Agee hadn't even been there. No—Agee had just come. It was a long time ago.

Although it was dark in the streets Dr. Jesse Landcraft knew, without conscious referral to landmarks, when it was time to signal for the bus to stop. Leaving the bus, he went without looking around him, without need for further orientation, down the side street beside the Institute building to the staff entrance. He no longer had a key to that door, as all staff members had, but it had been arranged he would need none. His hand remembered the doorknob, his body the slight effort of pushing inward the rather heavy door. He stepped inside, leaving the door to close behind him, slowly on its pneumatic check. He was at the bottom of a short flight of stairs leading to a small foyer, in which was the staff elevator. He reached out toward the push-button which would bring the elevator down and heard the door at his right, the door which gave access to the Great Hall, open. That would be old Marms, the watchman. "All right," Landcraft said, "I'm—" Then he stopped. Marms wasn't opening the door.

The one opening the door—who now had opened the door—said nothing and Landcraft, although he drew his breath in quickly as if about to speak, said nothing. He heard the elevator coming down in the shaft, but he could not wait. Now he didn't have time to wait for anything. He turned to find a way out and as he turned—and only then—realized all that he had blundered into. Before he had only known part, thinking he knew the whole. That was the blunder.

He dismissed, without consciously dismissing, the door to the street. There would be no safety in the street. There was one other door, and, as the one who was not old Marms moved toward him, still not speaking, Landcraft lurched across the foyer toward it. He had only three steps to take; he took them convulsively, and reached the door and pushed it open. Then he was trying to run, shuffling a little, awkward on stiffening old legs, down a narrow corridor. The corridor ran toward the front of the building. The wall on the right was blank, windowless. On Landcraft's left as he tried to run there were regularly spaced doors. Midway of the corridor, which was narrow and straight for two hundred feet and ended in a door, there was a single dim light, dangling from the ceiling.

The other had been surprised by Landcraft's sudden flight; had not, perhaps, noticed the door into the corridor until Landcraft had got through it. But now the pursuer was coming down the corridor behind Jesse Landcraft, not even bothering to run. I'll be caught before the end, Landcraft thought and felt hatred of his feebleness, the stiffness of his legs; hatred of the other's insolent assurance. It was intolerable that the other did not need to run, and still would be quick enough. There was no hope in this flight down the straight and narrow hall.

What Jesse Landcraft did then he did almost without plan, his body thinking with its own fear; seeking, as if of its own volition, to put some barrier up against oncoming danger. Landcraft turned suddenly to one of the doors at his left, fumbling for the knob. His hand had remembered so easily, so surely, when nothing mattered; now it could only grope. But then the knob was in his palm. He pushed at the door and it did not open. That was wrong, then. He pulled the door toward him. It opened and he was through it. He pulled it hard behind him, and it cracked against the jamb. The sound was like the report of a pistol.

92 FRANCES & RICHARD LOCKRIDGE

The space inside was very narrow. Landcraft held the inner knob with both hands and leaned back to put his weight against the pressure which was to come. He had a few seconds of standing so before it came. Then the knob tried to turn in his two hands, and he fought to keep it from turning.

He tried to cry out, then, but then he had no breath to cry with. His hands grew wet with sweat; his body ached with the effort. And slowly the knob turned. It turned enough and the latch was free, and then the one outside was pulling the door open. Landcraft gasped with effort. There was pain in his arms and hands. It was no use.

Then, because it was no use, he let the door go and the other, with the resistance suddenly abandoned, staggered slightly as the door jumped outward. Landcraft had not counted on this. He had merely, suddenly, reached the end of hope, and so of strength. But he took advantage of the other's momentary loss of balance.

Landcraft moved to his left in narrow space, his back rubbing what seemed to be a rough wall, and then the wall behind him ended. But the other was inside, by then, edging toward him. Jesse Landcraft stepped backward into a clearer area and here, dimly, there was light. It came from the Great Hall, through a thick pane of glass.

The place was cluttered and the light was very faint. Landcraft reached the glass and stood against it, his two hands against it. He could see out into the Great Hall, shadowy, half lighted. He tried to beat on the glass, but his hands seemed soundless against it.

There was no one in the Great Hall; no one to help. Seeing that, Jesse Landcraft stood for a second as if he were pinned to the glass. Then he turned to face the other.

"You should have stayed out of it," the other said. It was said with little emphasis, stating a fact. And then Jesse Landcraft saw what it was the other held.

He raised his hands against the blow, but they did no good. Stone is harder than bone and flesh, and men have known it for half a million years. Stone is harder than the bones in hands, and harder than the bone which compasses the brain.

*   *   *

Dr. Paul Agee opened the door of his office at a little after seven o'clock Friday evening. He opened it with impatience and looked along the corridor, which was empty. He hesitated; then reached back into the office and flicked a tumbler switch. Lights in the office went out; Dr. Agee closed the door of the office behind him and heard a click, but he nevertheless tested the door. It was locked. He walked along the hall to the central corridor and looked down it. Near the far end, there was a lighted office. Dr. Agee walked down to it, further opened a partly open door and said, "Oh, still here?"

"I am," Albert James Steck, D.Sc., said from his desk. He spoke without looking up from a pamphlet he was reading.

"Yes, so you are," Dr. Agee agreed. "Anybody else around?"

"I'm sure I don't know," Dr. Steck said. Then he did look up. "I'm going to need help with those bones of Preson's. All his labels came off."

Dr. Agee made a sound indicating, absent-mindedly, regret at this news.

"Haven't seen old Landcraft around, then?" Dr. Agee asked.

"Landcraft?" Dr. Steck repeated. "Oh, Landcraft. Haven't seen him for years. Why?"

"He was supposed to come around," Dr. Agee said. "I've been waiting for him."

"I thought he retired years ago," Dr. Steck said. "Didn't something happen to him? Health?"

"Yes," Dr. Agee said. "He retired. All the same, he wanted to see me."

"Hm-m," Dr. Steck said. "Wasn't he some relation to Preson?"

"In-law," Agee said. "His sister married Preson's brother."

Dr. Steck regarded the director of the Broadly Institute.

"I don't know what he wanted," Agee said. "He said it was important." He waited a moment, but Steck said nothing. "Well, I guess he changed his mind," Agee said. "You want to run the expedition?"

"Yes," Steck said.

Agee merely nodded. He said then that he would be getting along. He went down the central corridor, turned left in a corridor at the rear of the building and then left again. He came to the staff elevator and pushed the button. The elevator sighed beneath, rattled itself together and came up. It took Paul Agee down and Paul Agee took himself out.

Left behind, Dr. Steck returned to his pamphlet. But he read only briefly and then looked up, and looked for a time at nothing in particular. After a few moments he shrugged and stood up. He got hat and topcoat from a rack and went out, locking his office behind him. He crossed the corridor to an office which was identified as that of Orpheus Preson, Ph.D., D.Sc., Curator of Mammals, opened the door and went in. He turned on the lights and looked around the large, unoccupied room. He looked around it speculatively for a minute or more and then walked to the desk and looked down at it. He went around the desk then, opened the central drawer, and looked into it. Nobody had got around to cleaning it out yet. He closed the drawer, looked around the room again and then left it, turning off the lights.

"Yes, dear, I know," Mrs. Robert Franklyn said at a few minutes after ten o'clock on Saturday morning to her niece, who was nine years old, named Rose, and Mrs. Franklyn's to protect until five o'clock Saturday evening. "I know there's a man in there. It's—that is, he's a prehistoric man. Some people think that a long time ago men looked—"

"I don't mean that man," Rose said. "I mean a real man. Only he looks funny."

"Just a model of a man, dear," Mrs. Franklyn said. "When he was just beginning to be man. You see—" She paused, a little doubtful of her ability to explain evolution at ten o'clock on Saturday morning— or, indeed, at any time—to a child of nine.

"A *real* man, Aunt Jane," Rose insisted. "Only his head's funny." She pulled at Mrs. Franklyn's hand. "You look," Rose directed.

It was simpler, obviously, to look. Mrs. Franklyn allowed herself to be led to a glass-fronted alcove which bore the instructive sign: "Neanderthal Man, Middle Pleistocene." Mrs. Franklyn looked into the lighted space, saw Neanderthal Man and—Mrs. Robert Franklyn began to scream. She pulled the little girl away from the glass, got between her and the glass, and kept on screaming.

It did not appear that any actual effort had been made to conceal the body of Dr. Jesse Landcraft. It had, however, fallen forward so that it was partly inside the cave which artificers had contrived, out of papier-mâché, to simulate the entrance to one of mankind's earlier dwellings. Most of Dr. Landcraft remained visible, however, and most of what remained of his head. He was sprawled only a little; his long black coat covered most of him.

Although the exhibit of Neanderthal man had been simulated—the appearance of Neanderthal himself is only a scientific postulation—one item in the tableau was authentic. Men had once chipped a stone into the rude shape of an axe head and other men, searching for fossils, had subsequently found it. It may be, although no one is certain, that half a million years elapsed between these events. In preparing the exhibit at Broadly, other men had lashed this ancient stone to a club, as they thought prehistoric man had done.

The rude stone axe head had not been stained as it now was in years too many to be counted.

· 9 ·

SATURDAY, 11:15 A.M. TO 4:15 P.M.

It was "the cave-man murder" from the start; it might have been "the Neanderthal murder" but "Neanderthal," in addition to being unfamiliar, is unadaptable to headlines. It was the *New York Post* which first, publicly, put one and one together, came up with a total and made it "the cave-man murders." The police had done it some hours earlier. Deputy Chief Inspector Artemus O'Malley had done so with reluctance. He had even been testy about it.

"This guy Preson kills himself," he told Weigand. "That's what you say."

"Said," Bill corrected.

"Kills himself," O'Malley repeated. "This other guy gets killed. Methods entirely different. It could just've happened."

Bill Weigand did not say anything. O'Malley looked at him and waited. O'Malley said, "Well?" Bill shook his head. "Why?" O'Malley insisted. "Not complicated enough for you that way? You young cops—" He sighed, deeply.

"Too complicated," Bill said. "You know that, inspector. Coincidence isn't simple. It isn't likely. We were wrong the first time."

"One time somebody goes through a long rigmarole to knock a guy off," O'Malley pointed out. "The next time he hits a guy with a chunk of stone. Chunk of stone somebody thinks is a million years old, maybe." He paused, considering this. "How the hell they know?" he enquired.

Bill, deciding against an attempt at explanation, chose to regard the question as rhetorical. He chose, indeed, to regard the whole conversation as essentially rhetorical. It had turned screwy on Inspector O'Malley. He was fighting it.

"You know they don't change methods," O'Malley said. "Not one time poison, the next time this hunk of rock. It's one of the first things a cop's got to learn." He looked almost anxiously at Bill Weigand. "You know that, Bill," he said. "Sure you know that."

"Well," Bill said, "I guess this one's different, inspector."

Then he waited. Inspector O'Malley swore. He pointed out that they had, already, told the press that Dr. Preson's death was self-caused. He said they would look like a bunch of fools.

"Right," Bill said. "Apparently we were." He corrected hastily. "I was," he said. "We can always tell them we are reopening the case. We've got to, you know."

O'Malley swore again, but more weakly. He said it looked to him like those Norths were mixed up in it somewhere. He said it was the sort of thing the Norths would be mixed up in. Bill Weigand kept his counsel. Inspector O'Malley sighed deeply and said, "All right, what're you waiting for, captain?" Bill went, by car, to the Broadly Institute of Paleontology, which was by then closed and fairly full of policemen. Police photographers were busy outside, and inside, the glassed alcove in which the body of Dr. Jesse Landcraft still lay, a shaggy approximation of mankind's past towering over him. Neanderthal's mate crouched a few feet from Landcraft's shattered head. She seemed to be staring at it.

"That guy look like anybody you know, Loot?" Sergeant Mullins enquired, looking at Neanderthal. "Seems to me like—" He paused, a little hurriedly. "I mean it would if he had clothes on," he said. "You see what I mean?"

"Now Mullins," Bill Weigand said. "Remember you're a sergeant."

"Who said anything about the inspector?" Mullins enquired, and they went on through the Great Hall to the staff elevator.

Dr. Paul Agee was playing host to several—to a lieutenant from the precinct, another lieutenant from Homicide East, to a man from the district attorney's Homicide Bureau. Bill Weigand and Mullins added themselves to the audience. Bill was told by the man from Homicide East to go back across the street, where he came from. Bill Weigand grinned. He said, just audibly to the other, "Here about a guy named Preson?" The man from Homicide East nodded slowly. He raised eyebrows slowly. Then Bill Weigand nodded.

"Let's go over it again, doctor," the man from the Homicide Bureau suggested. "You say he called you up about four? Wanted to see you about something important? He didn't say what it was?"

"No, he didn't," Dr. Agee said. "Of course, as I told you, I can guess now. At least, I suppose I can. I suppose he wanted to tell me about this plan to contest the will."

"Why should he?" the man from the district attorney's office asked. "That's what I don't get. Why make a trip all the way down here to tell you that? Your lawyer called you up this morning and told you that."

"The Institute's lawyer," Agee said. "Called one of the trustees, who asked him to notify me. As for the rest, I share your puzzlement. But I am unable to think of anything else. I hadn't seen Dr. Landcraft for years. He was no longer connected with Broadly. He'd retired, as a matter of fact. The Preson connection is the only one I can think of."

"The Presons contesting?" Bill asked the Homicide East man, speaking behind the fingers of his left hand. "So he says," the Homicide East man said, and nodded at Dr. Agee.

"All right," the Bureau man said. "You arranged to meet him here about six. Arranged to have the staff door left unlocked so he could get in. And he didn't show up."

"That's correct," Dr. Agee said. "I waited an hour or so and went home, as I said. Dr. Steck was still here. He hadn't seen Dr. Landcraft either."

"Well," the Bureau man said, "Landcraft got here, all right."

No answer was expected to this, and none was offered. Dr. Agee looked unhappy, Bill Weigand thought. That was reasonable. The Bureau man looked around at the others; nodded at Bill in greeting; said, "The Preson angle?" Bill Weigand said, "Right."

"By the way, doctor," Bill said, "you just heard this morning that the Presons plan to contest the will? I suppose on the contention that Dr. Preson was mentally incompetent?"

"That's as I understand it," Dr. Agee said.

"You think he was?" Bill asked.

"I certainly saw no indication of it," Dr. Agee said. "But I understand there had been some—some rather confusing developments in recent weeks."

Bushelmen, Bill Weigand thought. Midgets. Shetland ponies.

"There were," he said. "Some of them were quite confusing."

"I hate to keep going over the same ground, doctor," the lieutenant from Homicide East said, "but, so far as you know, there was no one else in the building after, say, six or so? Except you and Dr. Steck. Both of you in your offices on this floor?"

"So far as I know," Dr. Agee said. "But the building has four floors, you realize. There are offices and laboratories—work rooms—on two of them. There's a basement. There are store rooms. Obviously, several people—staff people—could have been here. In addition, the staff door was unlocked, as I said."

"And the watchman, this Marms, wasn't due on until eight?"

"That's right," Dr. Agee said. There was a pause. "When can we reopen the Institute?" Agee asked. "I mean, to the public."

"This afternoon, far as we're concerned," the man from Homicide East said. "You'll have a crowd, you know. Particularly at the prehistoric man exhibit."

They would curtain that off, Dr. Agee said.

"I still don't see," the Bureau man said, "why Dr. Landcraft should make such a point of coming down here to tell you what wasn't any secret. About this will contest. I wish you could clear that up for me, Dr. Agee."

Dr. Agee shook his head. He said he wished he could.

The telephone on Dr. Agee's desk rang. Agee answered it, said, "Just a minute, please," and, "Is one of you Acting Captain Weigand?" Weigand nodded and took the telephone.

"The commissioner wants us to handle it," Deputy Chief Inspector Artemus O'Malley said. "Says we started it. Says we dropped it. Says he'd like to see us pick it up pronto. Says the newspapers—"

"Yes, inspector," Bill Weigand said.

"So don't drop it again," Inspector O'Malley said. "Got to rely on you."

"Yes, inspector," Bill Weigand said.

"And for God's sake, keep those Norths out of it," Inspector O'Malley told him.

"Yes, inspector," Bill said. He hung up.

"The commissioner wants Homicide West—" Bill began, and the man from the other side of Manhattan grinned at him.

"Hell," he said, "I heard him. One thing about O'Malley, you can hear him. I must say you're welcome to it." He shook his head. "A stone axe, for God's sake," he said.

He was told he sounded like Inspector O'Malley. Bill took Mullins with him and went to find Dr. Albert James Steck. He found Steck working at a table full of ancient bones. Steck rumbled at him. He rumbled that he had already told somebody all he knew, which was nothing.

Bill Weigand was sorry. He realized they were repetitious. He wouldn't be long.

He was not long. Dr. Steck had worked late the night before. He had been visited, about seven or a little after, by the director, who was looking for Landcraft. Steck had not seen Landcraft.

"Saw him a while ago," Steck said. "Damned nasty thing."

It was, Bill Weigand agreed. Dr. Steck had no idea what Landcraft had wanted to see the director about.

"Something to tell him, Agee said," Steck said. "That's all I know. I don't know what about. Agee did say something about an expedition we've got coming up, but it couldn't be that. Nothing to do with Landcraft, who hasn't been around in years. You've asked Agee?"

They had. Steck said he would bet they had.

"You stayed around a bit after Dr. Agee left?" Weigand asked him.

"Ten minutes," Dr. Steck said. "Perhaps a quarter of an hour."

"You went straight from here? I mean from your office? You didn't go anywhere else in the building?"

"I went across the hall to Preson's old office," Steck said. "They may want to move me in there. It's always been the curator's. I wanted to see whether they had cleared poor old Preson's personal stuff out of it. They hadn't."

"You're taking over as curator?" Bill asked him.

Dr. Steck was.

"By the way," Bill Weigand said, "did you feel Dr. Preson had been acting strangely lately?"

"Not around here," Dr. Steck said. He was emphatic, in a heavy, rumbling voice. "Whatever anybody says. I told this publisher fellow that."

Jerry North went to his office briefly and returned to the apartment to pick up Pam for lunch. Pam North was in the kitchen. She had a saucer with a little water in it, and into the water she was crushing aspirin tablets. Three cats sat on the table and looked at her with round blue eyes. Jerry North joined them, his eyes almost as round, if not so blue.

"New recipe?" he enquired, gently. "I'd rather thought we would lunch out."

Pamela North said hello. She said, "I got to wondering why they weren't and remembered they were." She had reduced several aspirin tablets to a watery paste. "The trouble is," she said, "they keep on crinkling up."

"Well," Jerry said, "they often do, you know."

She stopped. She turned.

"The labels," Pam North said. "I thought it was the stickem. I wondered, why not Dennison's. Then I remembered Bill said they were Dennison's. So I wondered, suppose it wasn't really in the milk."

She waited. Jerry looked at her, which was pleasant; at the saucer of aspirin paste and then at a box of gummed labels on the table. He said he'd be damned. Pamela, back at her task, nodded abstractedly. She pushed away a cat which, mistakenly believing a special cat delicacy to be in preparation, moved forward to sample. Pam took a label from the box and sloshed it, mucilage side down, in the aspirin broth. She put it aside.

"The trouble is, they crinkle," she said. "I suppose this isn't the right way to do it."

Jerry thought of another objection. "The taste," Jerry North said. "Or doesn't phenobarbital taste?"

"A little bitter," Pam said. "I looked it up. I wish we *had* some phenobarbital. But the stickem—here, taste." She gave Jerry a label out of the little box. He licked. What Pam preferred to call the stickem was highly flavored. It was a flavor which would absorb considerable bitterness.

"I can get all of a tablet on five labels," Pam said. "It says they're five grains each, so that's a grain to a label."

"Some of it's starch or something," Jerry said. "Whatever the aspirin people use. Inert material. Phenobarbital's—" He paused.

"White crystalline powder," Pam told him. "Odorless and stable in the air, it says. I think you can get it in tablets. I suppose mixed with something, the way you say. I wonder if—Jerry, suppose we used a small paint brush? Maybe they wouldn't crinkle up afterward. This way, they get wet all over, and that wastes some of it, too."

They had no small paint brush. Jerry went out and bought one. He mixed them a round of martinis, for sustenance until lunch, and they tried it with the small paint brush—a brush such as a child might use to paint in water color a picture of a cow. It worked much better with a brush. They painted the mucilage sides of a dozen labels, and drank martinis while the labels dried.

They were still not quite as they had been; still a little crinkled. The stickem showed a granular white deposit. But, dried and stacked together neatly, they did not look much changed. Picked up, one at a time, stickem side down, and written on, the labels showed no change to a person not expecting change, or so Pam and Jerry North decided. When a label was taken up and licked, with the gummed side held down in preparation for the tongue, as was not only natural but almost inevitable, the white deposit on the mucilage was invisible. On the tongue, the acidity of aspirin was lost in the flavor of the stickem.

"Stick some on something," Pam said. "We haven't got any bones, I'm afraid. On anything. Except a cat, of course."

It was evident that she had already tried that part, but Jerry North was obedient. He stuck a label on the handle of a knife and another on the linoleum of a kitchen counter and another on the outside of a cocktail glass. The last did not even momentarily adhere, since the glass was damp. The other two seemed to stick; in applying them, one could feel adhesion. There was nothing abnormal, either to sight or sense of touch. But as it dried, the label on the knife handle fell off and that on the linoleum curled up at the edges.

"They'd do better on bones, probably," Pam said. "Bones are sort of porous. But you see, something happens to the stickem. It gets diluted, I suppose. Part of it washes off."

Jerry nodded, abstractedly. A grain to a label; say the licking tongue got three-quarters of a grain. Then from a dozen labels they had done, nine grains of aspirin might have been absorbed. Or—nine grains of phenobarbital. They went to a toxicology they had bought soon after they had, a number of years ago, met one Lieutenant William Weigand of Homicide.

It is true of all but a few poisons that toxic doses are variable and lethal ones even more so. Poisoners have been plagued by this fact for generations; carefully laid plans have gone astray because one person will die of a gram of this or that while another—and perhaps the very person most in need of killing—will take the same quantity and feel little the worse. A variety of circumstances enter into this, and a few of them are predictable—tolerance can be established to a variety of noxious substances, for example, and sometimes a hearty meal taken beforehand will reprieve the condemned man. But inherent susceptibility, which cannot be predicted, also enters in. Phenobarbital is, in its effects, variable. Less than a gram has caused death; people have recovered from ten times as much.

It appeared from the course of events that Dr. Orpheus Preson had taken a good deal of phenobarbital. It appeared to Pam and Jerry North, from the experiments they had just concluded, that he might have got a good deal. Jerry got paper and pencil and figured. Say three-quarters of a grain to a label; say—this he had to look up—15.4 plus grains to the gram. Say, then, twenty labels to the gram. (Pam, working simultaneously on the long division, came up first, gratifyingly, with two labels. Jerry, briefly, explained a matter of decimal points.) Say, to make it easy, he had had time to write a word on, lick, attach, sixty labels. It could easily have been enough; it began to look as if it had been enough.

And it began to look, inescapably, like murder. If Dr. Preson had wished to poison himself, fatally or otherwise, he would hardly have spent several hours applying a barbiturate to the mucilage side of labels so that he might subsequently lick it off. As Pam pointed out, there are limits even to insanity. He had had milk to put phenobarbital into and—

"But," Jerry said, "so would a murderer have had."

They were at lunch by then, the debris of experimentation left behind. Pam shook her head decisively and then had to say, "Oh, not you," to a waiter who, approaching, had shied away. The waiter came closer, a little doubtfully, and was instructed.

"No," Pam said, then. "We've been over that. Dr. Preson brought the milk in himself. He could hardly be expected, anyway, to drink milk which had been standing around in his refrigerator, because he had discovered what happened to that. That was the first time the murderer tried, I suppose." She paused at this, and looked doubtful. "They say there wasn't enough in the milk, though," she said. She brightened. "Probably went home and looked it up," she said. "Anyway, milk was out the second time."

Nevertheless, Jerry said, there was phenobarbital in the milk the second time.

"Of course," Pam said, "to make it look like suicide. Put in afterward—I mean, after Dr. Preson had licked the labels." She stopped again, and this time seemed to look through Jerry. "About the first time," she began, "I wonder if—" She stopped again. "I don't really know what I wonder," she said. "It's on the tip of my mind, but it keeps sliding off. It—" She gave up with a shrug and finished her drink in time for *canneloni*. The *canneloni* tasted somewhat of mucilage.

The *New York Post,* which is of tabloid size, can devote the whole of its front page to a headline and this day it did. "Cave-Man Axe Used in Slaying!" the *Post* announced. The Norths, having left the restaurant and walked to Madison Avenue, bought a copy of the *Post* and, as instructed, saw Page 3. They saw that "Dr. Jesse Landcraft, retired scientist, was found brutally murdered today in an exhibit enclosure at Broadly Institute, his head crushed by repeated blows from a stone-age axe which had formed part of the exhibit. The blood-stained axe, said by Institute authorities to be many thousands of years old, had been wrenched from the central figure of the exhibit, the model of a cave man. Dr. Landcraft's body lay at the cave man's feet."

It was, as Pam said automatically, dreadful. It also, the Norths decided—as O'Malley and Bill Weigand had decided some hours earlier; as the *Post* was to decide in its next edition—was, had to be, a violent sequel to the quieter death of Dr. Orpheus Preson. ("The police link," the *Post* was to say, when the *Post* thought of it.) The Norths found a telephone booth and called Homicide West. They did not find either Weigand or Mullins there. They left word. They went home by subway, since it was quicker—and in spite of Pam North's conviction that it is unnatural to travel below ground—and tried again to get Bill Weigand at Homicide West. As they hung up the telephone, they got Bill at the front door of their own apartment.

"Landcraft's been killed," he said. He looked at them. They were nodding. They showed him the *Post*.

"It means somebody killed Preson," Bill said. "But of course you see that."

"We think we know how," Pam said. "We were trying to get you."

"Right," Bill said. "They told me. You think what?"

"We've worked out how Dr. Preson was killed," Pam said. "It wasn't the milk. The milk was a red herring."

"The—" Bill said. "Oh. You're talking about the barbital?"

"You dissolve it," Pam said. "Suspend it, maybe. Anyway, in water. Then you—"

She told him of her experiment. Once or twice at the start Bill seemed about to interrupt her. As she went on, he listened more intently. At the end he moved his head slowly, in tentative agreement.

"It's going the long way around," he said. "But—"

"So are midgets," Pam North said. "Bushelmen, for that matter. The whole thing's going the long way around. Dr. Preson persecuting himself, if he was. Or somebody trying to drive him crazy. Shetland ponies. Repeated blows with a cave-man axe. Who was going the long way around to where? That's what it comes to."

Bill Weigand knew it did. His face showed it; he said it. Without too much urging, Bill sat down. He refused a drink, but admitted that coffee was a good idea. "I'm supposed to keep you two out of it," he said. "O'Malley tells me I am."

"As usual," Pam said, and Bill said, "Right."

"So," Bill said, "here's the setup."

He had, he said, just come from the Broadly Institute. The *Post* account was generally right, although Landcraft had been hit only twice, which had been plenty. Landcraft apparently had been intercepted by his murderer while on his way to tell something to Dr. Agee—presumably to tell him that the Presons now planned to contest Dr. Preson's will.

"We knew that," Pam said, and told how.

"Why do you suppose they made such a point of telling us?" Jerry asked. "All altruism?"

Bill Weigand shook his head wearily. He wasn't sure of anything; had too many theories about everything.

"Now this business of the labels—" he said and, so reminded, reached for a telephone. He made two calls: One to the medical examiner's office. Query: How much phenobarbital in Preson's body? One to Mullins at the Institute. Instructions: Find the labels which had fallen off Preson's bones and hold on to them. He gave the Norths' number each time. He sipped coffee and talked, to the Norths and to himself.

Jesse Landcraft must have had more on his mind than the knowledge that the Preson family planned to contest the will. That was information dangerous to nobody. What he had known was dangerous; he had been intercepted because it was dangerous, and killed because of that. There the pattern was classic. But the point was, "Why go to Agee?" Because Agee was the murderer? That, also, fitted the common pattern. That was simple.

"The trouble is," Pam said, "the rest isn't. Did you ever try to wrap up a toy?"

Then they both looked at her.

"Oh," Pam said. "Anything with things sticking out. Points and things. A—oh, a contraption. That's what we're trying to do. But we don't even know the shape. So how can we wrap it up in Dr. Agee?" She paused. "Anyway," she said, "I keep thinking of Dr. Steck, really. You say he was there. And—doesn't he—"

"I just talked to Steck," Bill said. "Yes, Pam, apparently he does profit. He gets to be curator. He gets to head an expedition which he appears to consider very important. With Preson alive he wouldn't have—" And then Bill Weigand interrupted himself.

"With Preson alive *and* competent," Jerry North said. "Not just with him alive."

"That's it!" Pam North said. She thought. "That could be it," she said. She looked at her husband, at Bill Weigand. "Why," she said, "we've converged. I can't remember that we ever did before, anyway so soon."

But Bill Weigand shook his head. It only started out all right, he said. It didn't finish all right. Suppose they started out with the theory that Albert James Steck, D.Sc., was the villain of the piece—that he, to a degree hard to believe in, wanted to become curator of Fossil Mammals of the Broadly Institute of Paleontology and to lead an expedition for the Institute. Suppose he felt, perhaps rightly, that Dr. Preson was in his way. Suppose then he tried to drive Preson mad by bizarre persecutions. Suppose—

"Wait," Jerry said. "Put it this way. Suppose he tried to make it appear that Preson was out of his head. That Preson had turned into a crackpot and was putting these advertisements in newspapers because he got some crazy amusement out of it. That would have served Steck's purpose. Anyway, I imagine the Institute would have eased Preson out if the directors thought that."

"Then," Pam said, "why go on and kill him? No—wait. Because Preson found out? Threatened to tell everybody what Steck was trying to do, and so discredit Steck? So that, in the end, Dr. Steck had to go further than he'd planned?"

But Bill Weigand was shaking his head through all of this. They had, he said, forgotten one simple thing: Preson *had* put the advertisements in himself. They knew that. But then, again, he paused and seemed uncertain.

"Actually," Bill said, "we only know, on the clerk's identification, that he put in the last advertisement. I suppose it's possible that someone else put in the others. It's far-fetched, of course." He shook his head over his empty coffee cup.

"The identification—?" Pam began, but Bill shook his head before she had finished. They would, now, check up on it again, of course. But the girl had seemed certain. He had been there when she made the identification. Almost always you could tell. The girl had been certain. She was intelligent, and the oddity of the advertisement had, of course, focused her attention. She had, also, described Dr. Preson before being shown his photograph. And, she had, unprompted, remembered his trifocal glasses, called them "funny-looking."

"Suppose somehow he put the last one in to trap Dr. Steck on the others?" Pam said. They waited. "Somehow," she said, with diminished confidence.

"Tell us how, Pam," Jerry suggested. She couldn't. Then the telephone rang.

It was the report from the medical examiner's office. Dr. Orpheus Preson's body had contained upward of three grams of phenobarbital. It was a dosage he might have survived. He had not survived it. Bill Weigand put in another call, this time for the police laboratory. He held on for the answer. According to a quantitative analysis, the milk remaining in the quart bottle in Dr. Preson's refrigerator had contained 1.12 grams of phenobarbital. The milk remaining had been twenty-two fluid ounces. A little less than a third of it had, therefore, been poured out and—although now this was merely presumption—been drunk by Dr. Preson. Assuming uniformity of the solution, Dr. Preson would have drunk about half a gram of phenobarbital.

It looked, Bill told Pam North, as if she were right. It also looked as if, by taking too much for granted, he had himself slipped badly. It had all been there for anyone with paper and pencil, and a rudimentary ability to add and divide. Bill Weigand swore softly to himself. The telephone rang. Bill Weigand listened to Sergeant Mullins at the Institute. Bill replaced the telephone and swore again, not so softly.

Dr. Steck had thrown the useless labels into a wastepaper basket, which had been emptied into a bag and, with other combustibles, into an incinerator.

Bill Weigand thought for a moment and reached again for the telephone. He got Mullins again.

"Get those bones and hold on to them," he told Mullins.

· 10 ·

SATURDAY, 5:45 P.M. TO 7:50 P.M.

Just before she left the room, she picked up the copy of the *New York Post*. As she left, she carried the newspaper with her, rolled in her hand. There was no logical reason for this action; all that mattered in the *Post* was indelibly in her mind. She did not need to read again the tense, rather excited, account of Jesse Landcraft's murder. It was only that the newspaper, as a physical object, as something she could hold in her hand, was an aspect of reality. Holding it would be enough, but if she needed to reassure herself that this was not a nightmare, dreamed by herself only, she could again read the quick sentences and be sure that it was a nightmare shared.

Leaving her room on the third floor of the tall house in Riverdale, Emily Preson took nothing else except her purse. She had about a hundred dollars in her purse and she wished it were more. Perhaps, from the savings bank, she could get more tomorrow; perhaps, if she went to the bank very early, just after it opened, it would be safe. She would have to wait and see. But now, here in the house, she could not wait.

Aunt Laura was in the house. Emily had heard her moving in her bedroom a little after Emily herself had first come home—before Emily realized she could not remain in the house. Then, standing by a window, looking out on the dimly lighted street, Emily had heard her aunt going slowly down from the second floor to the first and then, because sound carried so far in the old house, walking back along the corridor toward the kitchen. Emily should have gone then, she thought now. But then she had not yet quite decided.

Now she might encounter her aunt, who almost certainly—Emily had not heard her, but it was almost certain—would have finished whatever she had to do in the kitchen (saying something to the cook about dinner, probably) and gone back to the living room. It was a chance which had to be taken. If she waited any longer, the risk of being seen would be at least doubled, perhaps trebled. It was almost time for her father to come home and Wayne might come at any time. Her chance would not get any better.

She held the newspaper and the strap of her purse in her left hand and went out of her room as quietly as she could. She remembered to close the door quietly behind her. She went down the first flight of stairs cautiously, holding with her free hand to the rail. At the second floor landing she stood, for a moment, listening. She could hear sounds from the kitchen—a pan being got out from among other pans in the cabinet. She could not hear anything else. But, looking down, she could see light flowing out from the open living room door to make a wall of light across the downstairs corridor. She would have to break through that wall to reach the outer door.

She went on down the stairs, now more carefully than ever, and along the corridor to the edge of the light. She stopped, then, just in the area of semi-darkness, and could look diagonally into the living room. As she waited, her aunt stepped into Emily's line of vision. Aunt Laura had a cloth in her hand. As Emily watched, Aunt Laura picked up a china dog and wiped it very carefully, turning it in her hand, holding it up to the light to be sure that she got all the dust from it. She put the china dog down, finally, and reached out for another dog. She picked up a glass dog, this time.

Each Saturday, and again each Tuesday, Aunt Laura cleaned the glass and china dogs, carefully, one by one. The woman who came each day to clean the house was not permitted to touch the dogs; none of the cleaning women who had, through years, come daily to the old house had been allowed to touch the slowly growing collection of glass and china dogs. There were seventy-one of the dogs, now; once Emily had counted them. But, although she was scrupulous, Aunt Laura was also quick. In a little over an hour she could dust all of the dogs.

If she had started only after she had returned from the kitchen, Aunt Laura would be engaged with the dogs for another forty-five minutes. Emily could not wait that long; she would have to chance her aunt's turning as she passed, seeing her in the light from the open door. Emily waited until the glass dog was finished and put down and her aunt, her back partly to the door, was reaching for a china pug. It was as good a time as any; Emily went, visible but quiet, unprotected but very quick, through the light. She reached the outer door and pulled it toward her, knowing it would creak a little, as it always did.

"Homer?" her aunt said from the living room. "Is that you, Homer?"

Emily did not hesitate; she pulled the door to behind her and stood on the porch, a harsh wind snatching at her. She waited for a second then, but the door did not open behind her. Perhaps her aunt was still waiting for her father to speak; perhaps Laura Preson had decided that only the wind had made the sound she had heard. Emily went on, and now, since silence was no longer of importance, she went more rapidly. She did not quite run. She went toward the bus stop, although her father would come from there, along this unfrequented street. That, too, was a risk which had to be taken, if she were to get away, if she were to keep them from finding her.

She was a slender girl in a dark cloth coat, the coat held close to her body with her free hand. She seemed to be blown along the dimly lighted street by the west wind. She strained her eyes so that she would be first to detect, and to identify, anyone coming toward her, but the street ahead was empty. It was not until she was within a block of the bus stop—the last stop, the place where the bus turned around and went back—that she saw someone coming toward her. But, instantly, she realized that the man coming was not her father, and so she went on, although now walking more slowly so as not to attract attention by her haste. She passed the man, who was no one she had ever seen before, who did not appear to notice her, and then she was in the lighted block, with the drug store on the corner and the A & P next to it and, beyond, a bus just pulling up to the stop. She could see several people inside the bus, getting to their feet to leave it. One of them was her father.

She stopped, hesitated for a moment. Then she turned into the dark street which ran beside the drug store and, in the darkness beyond the window, stepped close to the wall. She waited there, looking toward the lighted sidewalk down which her father would walk on his way home. After what seemed a long time, but was not more than a minute, she saw him pass. She waited for what seemed, again, a long time and walked to the corner. She looked down the way she had come, and saw her father, walking quickly, pass under a street lamp. She hurried toward the bus. It was standing with the door open, and the lights on, but the driver was not in his seat. He would, she realized, be getting coffee in the room which was at once a minor office of the bus line and a kind of canteen for the drivers. She saw that there were no coins in the box, and dropped her own in. She went back into the bus, and found a seat. She willed the driver to come back and drive the bus away; she wanted to scream for him to hurry. She sat on the side of the bus farthest from the sidewalk, because many people in the neighborhood might know her by sight—although she herself knew almost no one, she had discovered that many people saw and remembered; the difference was part of that difference between herself and other people which she could not ever fully understand, and always fought and could never alter.

She was still conscious that she was as visible in the lighted bus, standing here on a familiar corner, as she would have been on a lighted stage. He must come! she thought. It must be time for him to come out of the place they go and drive away! A woman walked toward the bus and Emily, instinctively, turned, so that her face was away from the

entrance to the bus, and looked out of the window. The woman got into
the bus, making a small sound of effort, and Emily could feel herself
being looked at. She did not look at the woman. She heard coins drop-
ping into the box, and turned her head further to the left, so that only
the back of her head was visible to anyone walking down the aisle. But
the woman took a seat well forward in the bus. After a moment, Emily
ventured a glance at her. She was sure she had never seen the woman
before. Nevertheless, she turned her head away again, and looked out
into the empty street.

Then, quickly (but quickly enough?) she raised a hand to shield her
face. Wayne's sports car passed the bus, moving down the street toward
the house. Wayne, almost as unmistakable as the car, could have seen
her if, idly, he had taken his eyes from the road. She waited for any
change in the car's course which would indicate he had seen her, was
turning to come back. But the little car went on down the street.

Then the bus driver came, with evident reluctance, out of the office
and toward the bus. He heaved himself into it, looked at Emily and the
other passenger, but only as if he were counting them, and then into the
coin box. Passengers and payments came out even; he touched something and the box whirred and the coins vanished. He looked at his
watch, then, threw out the door the cigarette he had been smoking, and
closed the door. The bus lumbered off. Hurry! Emily thought. Hurry!
But the bus driver was broad shouldered, heavy shouldered, impenetra-
ble. The bus lumbered toward the subway station.

Only on the subway train, headed downtown, did Emily's sense of
urgency a little lessen. With its lessening, there came to take its place a
feeling of uncertainty. Emily began to realize that beyond the immediate steps of escaping from the house, she had hardly planned at all. She
had had to get away. That was, for the moment, accomplished. She had
to keep from being found and that was still to be achieved. She could
not plan far into the future, because she felt—a little vaguely, with
uneasiness—that the future would depend on things which she could
not control, which she might not even understand. But she still had,
certainly, to plan at what station she would leave the subway train and
where, having left it, she would go to spend the night.

She thought first of the area around Columbia University, since it was in that area she most nearly felt at home. She went there four times a week, sat in classes there; from Columbia, at the end of the following term, she expected to get her master's degree. But, again, she had been in the streets around the university, and in the university's buildings, many times over half a dozen years. There might be there, as at the bus stop in Riverdale, people who would know her by sight and might remember having seen her.

In the end, she stayed on the train until it reached Forty-second Street and got off there and went up into that glaring block of Forty-second where second-run motion picture theaters are wedged solidly together, seem to scream together. It was not quite seven o'clock, but the sidewalks were crowded. She walked slowly, was pushed and jostled by the people of Saturday night. She at once hated this, and envied the people she saw—they seemed young, for the most part; younger than she. They laughed loudly, and screamed at one another, and held on to one another. They all seemed alike to Emily Preson, and it was that very likeness of one to another she envied. Each could reach out so easily, through so little strangeness, and touch another. They did this, quite literally, but to Emily their touchings, which were sometimes overtly caressings, seemed symbolic of more subtle contact.

She was touched herself, jostled by the many people of Saturday night, but that was different. She was touched, jostled, merely because she was there, because there was not room enough for everyone to walk untouched on the sidewalk, not because she was Emily Preson; not even because she was a slim young woman; not because she was a person at all. A couple jostled her and the man said "sorry" and then he and the girl with him laughed, not at her, not with her—laughed at something she did not understand. Somebody touched her arm and she moved it a little, getting once more, in so far as she could, out of the way of what she could not share. The pressure remained on her arm, and she moved away from it, to the side. She did not look around.

"You're quite a way from home," a voice said, among other voices. She did not suppose anyone was speaking to her. Then she realized the pressure on her arm was not the accidental contact of someone passing, or trying to pass, in a crowd. "Aren't you, Miss Preson?" Dr. Albert James Steck asked her. He spoke down to her from superior height. He smiled down at her and released her arm, but continued to walk beside her in the crowd.

"I," Emily said. "I'm—going to a movie."

"Well," Dr. Steck said. "A movie."

"I'm meeting someone," Emily said. "I'm meeting a friend." In spite of herself, she spoke violently. It was always in spite of herself.

"All right," Dr. Steck said. He looked down at her, and smiled again. "An exciting friend," he said.

"What makes you say that?" she demanded. "Why do you say, 'an exciting friend'?"

"No reason," Dr. Steck said. "Except that you seem excited. Very keyed up."

"What difference does it make?" she said. "You don't care, do you? Unless—" She stopped suddenly. Someone bumped into her from behind. She was only half conscious of the contact, but Dr. Steck took her arm again and, in response to the message of his hand, she walked on. Now she was conscious that she was shaking.

"My dear Miss Preson," Dr. Steck said. "You're cold, aren't you? Why don't you let me buy you a drink somewhere? Before you—meet your friend. It's natural you'd be keyed up." He indicated the newspaper she held. "You've read about Landcraft."

"How do you—" she began. She looked at the newspaper she held. "It's horrible," she said. "How can you be so calm about it?"

"I?" Steck said. "I'm not indifferent. It is very unpleasant, Miss Preson. Very shocking."

"Did you follow me?" she demanded, and heard her voice rising; heard in it that insistence, that note almost of violence, which she never planned upon, which did not—until it was there, in her voice, inescapable—represent anything she knew to be in herself. "What are you following me for?" Again she stopped to look up at the large man beside her. Again his hand on her arm urged her forward.

"Following you?" he repeated. "Why would I be following you?" But, before she could answer, he turned her toward the curb, opened the door of a taxicab standing there. She held back. "You need a drink," he told her. His hand urged her into the cab. "Algonquin," he told the driver, and got in after her. "Algonquin all right?" he asked her. She did not answer. "What makes you think I've been following you?" he asked. "Why should I?"

"You found me," she said. "I—nobody saw me leave. How did you know where I was?"

"Know where you were?" he repeated. "I'd just come up out of the subway and saw you in front of me. Don't you ever just happen to run into people, Miss Preson?"

"No," she said. "What do you want?"

"It happens all the time," he said. "Probably you just don't see people. I don't want anything. Except to buy you a drink. Get you some place it's warm."

"Why should you?" she demanded.

"God," Dr. Steck said, "I don't know. Do you always act like this? What're you afraid of? You meet an acquaintance, get offered a drink. Anyone would think I'd come after you with a club. I—" He stopped, seeming to have heard his words.

"Like Uncle Jesse," she said. "Like somebody went after him."

"Oh," said Dr. Albert James Steck, "for God's sake, Miss Preson. Do you want a drink or do you want to get out?"

"It doesn't—" she began, still in the intense voice. But then she caught herself. Perhaps he was telling the truth; perhaps he had not been following her, did not want to force anything out of her, had really met her by accident. "I am keyed up," she said and, although it was very difficult, managed to lessen the violence in her voice. "Perhaps I need a drink."

"You do," he told her. "The Algonquin," he confirmed to the taxi driver. "O.K.," the driver said. "But you could walk to it quicker. You know that?"

"All right," Steck said.

"Some people think I'm trying to run up the fare on them," the driver said. "You know how it is? Can't make a left offa Forty-second, so some of these people—"

"It's all right," Steck said.

"S'long as you know how it is," the driver said, and went the way he had to go.

"Beginning to feel warmer?" Steck said.

"Oh yes," Emily said. "Much warmer."

The Algonquin lounge was crowded, but there was a table in a corner. After a time there was a waiter. Steck looked at Emily, who said, "Anything."

"Bring the lady a stinger," Steck said, "and me a scotch. On the rocks."

"When do you have to meet your friend?" Steck said. He held out a package of cigarettes as he spoke. Emily took a cigarette.

"I'm not meeting anyone," she said. "That was—I'm not really meeting anyone. Dr. Steck, did you think my uncle was—was insane? You did, didn't you?"

He held a lighter toward her cigarette; lighted a cigarette of his own. He was very large at the small table, the cigarette was very small between his big fingers. He shook his head.

"No," he said, "I'm afraid I didn't, Miss Preson."

"But he must have been," she said. "He did those strange things. He drugged the milk and then drank it. He must have been. He killed himself."

"Why—" he began, and stopped as the waiter came with drinks. "Drink some of that," he told her, after the waiter had left. She drank.

"Isn't it clear to you," he said then, "that he didn't kill himself? That must be clear to you. Now that Landcraft's been killed, too."

"I don't believe it," she said. "Whatever else happened, he killed himself." She looked at him anxiously. She seemed to seek reassurance. But Steck shook his head.

"You'd better face it," he said. "It went further than you thought. Perhaps than anybody planned." He leaned forward, massive over the small table. His voice was heavy, rumbling. He seemed to have forgotten the drink in front of him. She merely looked at him. "Drink your drink," he told her. He drank from his own.

"You know," he said, "Agee's got quite a setup at the Institute. I don't know whether you realized that, Miss Preson. It's a one man show, for practical purposes. The trustees don't bother with it, so far as I can tell." He paused and drank again. "Finish your drink," he told her. "I'll get you another." She shook her head. "Nonsense," Dr. Steck said. "You need it. You were pretty close to shock, back there, whether you know it or not." She shook her head again. "Oh yes," he said. "I'm a doctor, too, you know. What people keep calling a 'real doctor.' Know shock when I see it."

He beckoned to the waiter, made a gesture at the two empty glasses. The waiter said, "Yes sir," and went away.

"Sometimes," Steck said, "I wonder whether the trustees even bother to get an auditor in. That's a fact, Miss Preson. I wonder whether they do."

Acting Captain William Weigand and Detective Sergeant Aloysius Mullins were distracted by glass dogs, and by china dogs. Whichever way they looked, china and glass dogs looked back at them; dogs stood at attention, with chins up and tails extended; dogs sat with mouths open and tongues hanging; dogs sat up and begged. One dog, forepaws apart and forelegs bent, had chin to ground and appeared to be barking.

"My sister's collection," Homer Preson said. "She collects dogs."

"I see she does," Bill Weigand said, not adequately. "Jeeze," Mullins said, but he said it under his breath.

"I presume," Homer Preson said, "that you have come about poor Jesse. A shocking thing."

Bill Weigand was recalled from dogs of glass and china.

"Not primarily," he said. "About your brother, I'm afraid, Mr. Preson. Is your sister here? Your children?"

"Laura is here," Preson said. "You have something to tell her?"

"Right," Bill said. "But all of you. You see—your brother was murdered, Mr. Preson. We—"

"What did you say?" Laura Preson demanded, from the door of the living room. "What did you say?"

"That your brother was murdered," Bill repeated. "It was made to appear suicide—"

"Nonsense!" Miss Preson said, and came into the room. "Complete nonsense. Orpheus was insane. He killed himself." She looked at her living brother. "You just stand there," she told him.

He did. He stood there, and the expression on his face seemed to Weigand unreadable. But he shook his head to indicate dissent from what Weigand said.

"Please, Laura," he said. "Why do you say that, captain?"

"I'd like to talk with all of you," Bill said. "Tell all of you at once. Your daughter, Mr. Preson? Your son? Aren't they here?"

"No," Preson said. "Wayne—we expected Wayne for dinner, but he telephoned. Emily's"—he hesitated—"Emily has a class this evening," he said. "Why do you say my brother was murdered? Are you trying—" He apparently decided against finishing the sentence. Bill gave him time, which he did not use.

"It was meant to appear like suicide," Bill said. "Or, perhaps, an accident, if your brother took more than he intended. It wasn't that. I suppose Dr. Landcraft found out it wasn't."

"Nonsense," Laura Preson said. "Poor Orpheus didn't know what he was doing. Jesse—I don't know anything about Jesse. None of us knows anything."

"Please, Laura," Homer Preson said again. "Let the captain talk. I suppose you mean somebody else—not my brother—put the barbiturate in the milk?"

Bill shook his head.

"On the labels," he said. "The ones he was writing. To take the place of those someone had taken off, knowing he would prepare new ones and stick them on. So that he would write new ones and stick them on. Someone who knew him quite well, of course."

"What's he talking about?" Laura asked her brother. Preson said he didn't know. Bill told them both. Laura Preson said she did not believe it; that she did not believe it for a moment. "Don't drop that," she said to Mullins, who had picked up a glass pug dog and was turning it over thoughtfully. Mullins put the pug dog down, with care. "It wouldn't work. The stuff would taste."

"It did work," Bill told her. "It was done that way."

"You tested the labels?" Homer Preson asked. He still stood. His eyes were a little narrowed behind his glasses. "I suppose you must have."

"The used labels were thrown out," Bill said. "Dr. Steck got rid of them. The unused ones, which the Institute apparently picked up with the bones, hadn't been tampered with."

"But, you don't really know, then?" Homer Preson said. "It is merely a theory—an ingenious theory. For one thing, Laura's right. He would have tasted the phenobarbital."

"He apparently didn't," Bill said. "It isn't merely theory. We tested the bones, you see—enough of them. Where the mucilage had been there were traces. Very faint, of course. But—enough. You can take it as proved, Mr. Preson."

"I don't—" Laura Preson began, her voice sharp.

Her brother turned toward her and shook his head sharply. She looked at him for a moment. She did not finish her sentence.

"So you come to us again," Preson said. "Well?"

"You're his family," Bill told the neat, trim man; the wiry little woman. "You'll want to help. It is a new problem, of course."

"Certainly we will help," Preson said. "But I'm afraid I don't know how. I suppose you have a theory? One that will explain everything? The advertisements, Laura's experience? The fact that poor Orpheus put the advertisements in the papers himself? Or—do you think you can ignore all that?"

It had the effect of challenge. But it might be no more than precision, of speech and of thought. It did, certainly, sum things up.

"You're quite right, Homer," Laura said, with approval. "What is your theory about all that, captain? Since you do know—have said you know—that Orpheus inserted the advertisements. Invented this—persecution."

"I think now that your brother was impersonated," Bill said. "I think the girl at the counter was wrong when she identified Dr. Preson."

"She admits that?" Preson asked.

She had not admitted it when they had talked to her an hour or so before. She had barely admitted doubt. Say an impersonator had been the right size; say he had worn the funny-looking glasses. Could she be wrong then? She had not thought so. Of course, anybody could make a mistake. Of course, she had seen him only once. Yes, she had particularly noticed the trifocal glasses.

"She isn't as sure as she was," Bill Weigand told the Presons. He hesitated for a second. "As a matter of fact, she's most sure about the glasses. Whoever put the advertisement in was wearing trifocals. I think we can be sure of that. Was about your brother's size, wore the kind of glasses he did."

"Orpheus had a beard," Laura pointed out. "Do you contend that somebody—one of us, I suppose?—put on a false beard? Really, captain!"

"Your brother had chin whiskers," Bill told her. "Whoever put the advertisement in had a muffler up around his chin. It was a cold enough night to make that plausible. As for who it was—have I made any charges, Miss Preson?"

He was told that he might as well have made charges.

"No, Laura," Preson said. "The captain is being very fair. But—I think he is wrong in his assumption. I think it was really Orpheus. Have you ever tried to see anything through trifocals, Captain Weigand?"

Bill shook his head.

"You can't see through them," Homer Preson said. "A kind of distorted blur. Your impersonator would have been blind, captain. Completely blind."

"Right," Bill said. "And—that's what makes me pretty sure, Mr. Preson. I think he was. I think he knew before he went that he would be. I think that's why he had the advertisement typed out in advance." Bill shook his head. "I should have thought of it sooner," he said. "We should have thought of several things sooner."

"Typed in advance?" Preson repeated.

"Somebody," Bill said, "we assumed, at first, your brother himself, went to the *Times,* got a want-ad blank, took it to Dr. Preson's apartment downtown, typed out the advertisement, and took it back to the *Times.* It seemed like going the long way around. The normal thing would be to fill the blank out at the counter. But—the assumption was that your brother was eccentric, that it was a waste of time to look for logic. However, if it was someone impersonating your brother, wearing your brother's trifocals, it was quite logical. He didn't fill the blank out at the counter because he couldn't see to. He would have had to take the glasses off to write. But the whole purpose of trifocals is to provide a variety of foci, so that the eyes are adjusted to any need. The girl would have remembered—she was supposed to remember the whole incident, I think. If she didn't appreciate the discrepancy, still she would have remembered it. Eventually, somebody would have said, 'Hey! What did he do that for?'"

"He couldn't have seen to do anything," Homer Preson said. "Not enough to get around."

"He didn't have far to go," Bill said. "He didn't need to see much. He could have walked in a straight line from the door to the counter; he would have seen enough to avoid running into anybody. The girl would have been a blur, but that was all right. He didn't need to recognize her; he needed to be recognized. He could have had a large enough bill ready in his pocket; put the change in his pocket without counting. As soon as he got back to the door, he could have taken the glasses off."

Homer Preson hesitated. Then he said he supposed it would have been possible.

"Right," Bill said. "Now—do you know whether your brother had more than one pair of glasses? Of glasses with trifocal lenses?"

"I'm afraid we don't—" Homer Preson said and his sister's sharper voice cut through his sentence. "Oh yes," she said. "At his office. In his—" Then she stopped. The two looked at each other and neither, Bill Weigand thought, was pleased with the other.

"At least—" Laura began, and again a sentence was broken in two. "Oh yes," Preson said. "I believe he did have, come to think of it." Then he said, "Sorry. I'd forgotten for the moment. Laura's right, of course."

"Anyone there could have used them," Laura Preson said, and she spoke quickly. "Dr. Steck. Dr. Agee. Anyone. If it is really true that someone was pretending to be Orpheus."

"Right," Bill Weigand said. "However—" He paused, giving either of them a chance.

"It could hardly have been Dr. Steck," Homer Preson said, after a moment. "He is physically very unlike Orpheus."

"Agee isn't," Laura Preson said. She paused. "However," she said, "I do not believe in this impersonation. Not for a moment. For one thing, what would have been the purpose?"

Bill gave either of them another chance, but neither took it.

"To make it appear that your brother was insane," he told them. "To make us think he was insanely persecuting himself."

"Still—why?" Preson asked.

There could, Bill told them, be a good many possible reasons. He gave them one—to make it appear that Dr. Orpheus Preson was no longer competent to act as curator of Fossil Mammals at the Broadly Institute. He gave them another—to invalidate in advance something that Dr. Preson might have planned to say, or someone might have feared he was planning to say. He gave them a third—to invalidate something Dr. Preson had already said or done.

"By the last," Homer Preson said, "I take it you mean his will, captain? The will we have, admittedly, decided to contest on the grounds you mention?"

"Right," Bill Weigand said. "I do mean that." He waited a moment. "Well?" he said.

"Nonsense!" Laura Preson said, with emphasis.

But her brother shook his head. He said they must be fair. He said he could see a certain logic in the theory. He had the appearance of a man impartially weighing an abstraction. But then he shook his head.

"I am sure you see the flaw, captain," he said. "A flaw much more fatal to the theory than any denials we could make. Of course, we do deny any such—stratagem. But—" He paused, and now it occurred to Bill Weigand that it was he who was being given a chance.

"Go on," Bill said.

"Orpheus was killed," Homer Preson said. "That is the flaw. You assume we want Orpheus's money. As things are, we will have to go to court to get it, and the outcome is, of course, uncertain. Assume we are unscrupulous, if you like. But do not assume we are fools, captain. I assure you, we are not. You follow me?"

He was an instructor propounding a syllogism.

"Go on," Bill suggested.

"We wish to get hold of Orpheus's money," Homer said. "We wish, naturally, to do this with a minimum of risk. We decide to make it appear that he is insane. We are successful in this, to a point. Now, as I see it, we have two courses. We can threaten Orpheus with sanity proceedings unless he changes his will or we can actually seek to have him committed and be put in charge of his affairs as, I think it is called, a committee of the body. In either case, we get control of the money. In either case, either by threat or action, we can make sure that he does not, before we can get our hands on it, give all his money to the Institute. None of this is true, of course. You—"

"Right," Bill said. "I understand your position, Mr. Preson. Go on."

"Very well," Preson said. "Why do we kill him? We invite an investigation which is likely to disclose our plan. If you are right, investigation *has* disclosed the plan—not ours, I assure you. We are forced to contest a will, with no assurance of success. We run the risk of being caught, which means we risk our lives. We—"

He was very logical, Bill thought—very precise. He was also very assured.

Bill Weigand nodded to show he heard.

"You say 'we,'" he said. "You regard the family—I assume you mean you and your sister, and your son and daughter as well—as a unit? Does your son live here?"

He had a room there, yes. He also had his own apartment downtown.

"So actually," Bill pointed out, "you can't speak for him, can you, Mr. Preson? Be certain he thinks as you do?"

There was a moment of hesitation before Preson, with a slight shrug, admitted he could not. But the shrug dismissed the point as academic. "I am in my son's confidence, I am certain," Preson added. "His position in all this is obviously identical with mine. With my sister's."

"Is he planning to get married?" Bill asked. Preson hesitated for a moment.

"I do not see what bearing that has," he said. "However, I believe there is a young woman—a Miss Albrenza. A very charming young woman, I believe. From a very old California family. I do not, however, know what she and my son plan." He smiled faintly. "I am not in Wayne's confidence to that extent," he said. "If you feel that such matters are germane, you will have to talk to my son himself."

Probably they were not germane, Bill admitted. He would, of course, want to talk to Wayne Preson. He was sorry that Wayne was not there; that Emily Preson was not there. He appreciated the co-operation of Mr. Preson, of his sister.

"I assure you," Preson told him, "that we have nothing to hide."

"This is all nonsense," Laura Preson said. "You're wasting time, young man. All this fiddle-faddle about plots!"

"Please, Laura," Homer Preson said.

"Fiddle-faddle," Laura repeated. "Will you please be careful?" This last was to Sergeant Mullins who had, absently, picked up another dog. "Sorry," Mullins said, and put the dog down.

"Mr. Preson," Bill said. "I take it you have tried your brother's glasses at some time?"

"Tried his glasses?" Preson repeated.

"You spoke of not being able to see through them. Of a distorted blur."

Behind Preson's own glasses, the eyes flickered for an instant.

"Oh yes," Preson said. "I did say that. I remember now. However, I merely made an assumption. An obvious assumption, I should think."

"You never tried his glasses?"

"Certainly not," Preson said. "Why should I?"

"Curiosity," Bill told him. "However—"

"At least," Preson said, "I cannot recall that I ever put on Orpheus's glasses, for any purpose."

"Right," Bill said. "It's of no importance. One more question. Isn't it true you felt that your brother was spending too much on Institute projects?"

"Certainly not," Preson said. "At least, we felt that it was his own business. It was no concern of ours."

"Right," Bill said again. "Well—thanks. You've been patient. Will you ask your son, and your daughter, to get in touch with me? Say, some time tomorrow?"

"Certainly," Preson said. "I'm sorry we don't—that they both had engagements this evening."

He moved toward the door and Bill and Mullins moved with him. He let them out, and Laura Preson stood in the living-room door. She was, Bill thought, very pleased that they were going. She was, he thought, impatient for them to finish going. Preson closed the door after them.

Mullins started across the porch, but Bill Weigand touched his arm and Mullins stopped, turned, listened too.

"Why on earth you—" they heard Preson say, and his voice was not modulated as it had been; his voice rasped. He did not finish the sentence. "You know they're not—" he said. But he moved away as he spoke; moved, the eavesdroppers assumed, back into the living room. Then Laura Preson spoke, and her voice carried.

"I thought you'd had sense enough to see to that," she said. Then Preson's heavier voice made a sound without words and, although his sister answered him, what she said was inaudible. Bill Weigand's fingers, resting on Mullins's arm, gave directions. They went, as quietly as they could, to the waiting car. Bill drove it around the nearest corner, turned to face the way they had come, and parked. He spoke briefly, and got out.

Bill Weigand walked back toward the house, stopped in shadows before he quite reached it; seemed to vanish in the shadows. He waited there, but he did not have to wait long. Lights went out in the Preson house, and then the door opened. Brother and sister were much of a height as they came down the porch steps, as they turned up the street. Whatever they had failed to see to, they were going to see to together. At least, Bill Weigand thought, giving them a start and sauntering after them, I hope so. It would be a nuisance if they were merely going to a late movie.

He followed them to the bus terminal and stopped half a block away while they waited for the bus. He watched them get into it when it arrived, waited, with the cold wind biting, until the bus moved off. Mullins, when it was a block away, rolled the Buick to the curb, and Bill joined him in pleasant warmth. The Buick rolled after the bus, unhurrying.

"I don't get it, Loot," Mullins said.

"I'm not sure I do," Bill said. "A policeman's lot is a chilly one, sergeant. He must also, as regulations instruct, be curious at all times. Didn't you ever hear of a Miss Albrenza?"

"Nope," Sergeant Mullins said. "This is another screwy one, Loot."

"You should read gossip columns, Mullins," Bill told him. "Improve your mind. Of course, this may be another Miss Albrenza. If it isn't, I'd think she'd be a bit rich for Wayne's blood."

"Big league, huh?" Mullins said.

If the same Miss Albrenza, Miss Marie Albrenza, big league enough. The competition would be strenuous. To stick it, Wayne would need to be quite a man.

"Then?" Mullins said.

But Bill Weigand shrugged. It was early days or, if the day was not early, they had wasted a good deal of it. There was the audit of the Institute accounts, which might prove interesting—which already had turned up a point or two of interest. There was also Steck.

"Too big," Mullins objected. "Preson saw that."

That Steck was too big was obvious. Possibly, it was too obvious. Possibly, Mrs. Gerald North had something there, if they could work it out.

"She often has had," Bill pointed out.

"All the same, when she gets in things they get screwy," Mullins said. "You know that, Loot." He let the car creep while the bus stopped ahead of them, let it pick up as the bus went on. "You don't think them?" He indicated the bus with a movement of his head. "What he said makes sense, don't it?"

"Oh yes," Bill said, "very good sense, Mullins. But I think they have something to see to, don't you? There they go."

The bus had reached its stop at a subway station. The Presons were with several leaving it.

"On your way, Mullins," Bill said, and Mullins went on his way. Bill watched him, thought that for a large man Detective Sergeant Mullins could be conveniently unnoticeable, and waited until the Presons and Mullins too had gone down the subway stairs. Bill started the Buick then. Almost at once he slowed it and looked at an imported sports car parked near the corner. It was, Bill thought, an interesting place for Wayne Preson's car to be standing. Bill started up again, heading downtown. A properly ambitious motor car agency ought to be open late on Saturday night.

· 11 ·

SATURDAY, 7:15 P.M. TO 9:05 P.M.

They had said they were in no hurry, which was true, and Raul had taken them at their words, which was to be expected. Jerry North tapped the bell on the table in front of them and Pam helped herself to peanuts. The Algonquin's lobby appeared to be the scene of a largish, but relaxed, cocktail party—a party at which there were chairs and tables enough so that even men could sit; a party without pressure, yet with a comfortable mood of unity. Actually, the Norths had met only two or three people they knew.

"The point is," Pam said, through peanuts, "that almost everybody's somebody you might know, if you happened to. You really feel you do."

There was that, Jerry agreed, and tapped the bell again, gently. Sometimes it took a little time. This was particularly true, of course, just before dinner on Saturday evening.

"I wonder if Mullins got Dr. Preson's bones?" Pam said. "Or whether Dr. Steck threw them away, too."

She was too certain about Steck, Jerry told her. "Two more, please," he told a waiter who visited them. She was riding to a fall, unless she could think of some fashion in which a broad man, well over six feet tall, could impersonate a man who weighed, at a guess, a hundred and twenty and stood five feet six or seven in his shoes. Furthermore, he pointed out, Steck lacked the beard for the part.

"As for the beard," Pam said, "who doesn't? But it wasn't a very big beard. It was just around the edges. The muffler took care of that."

"Size," Jerry told her. "Big man. Little man. There's your problem."

"Dr. Preson found out that Dr. Steck was putting the ads in," Pam said. "He put the last one in himself, to confuse Steck. So that—" She stopped.

"Exactly," Jerry said.

"Steck hired somebody," Pam said. "An actor. Then—"

"Then the actor finds he's tied up in a murder," Jerry said. "Then he goes to the police. Then—"

"Steck disposes of him before that," Pam said. "Probably in concrete."

The waiter brought drinks.

"I'm not really sure you need another," Jerry told Pamela. "Your imagination's reeling already."

"Don't think people don't," Pam said. "Concrete, I mean. I've always liked mad scientists."

The preference did not become her, Jerry said. He would, himself, as soon like a heroine bound to railroad tracks. Sooner, if one were forced to so painful a choice.

"Seriously," Pam said. "He stands to profit. He has profited."

"Seriously," Jerry said. "He's too big."

Pamela North sipped. She did not appear happy.

"You can't just buy phenobarbital," she said. "But wouldn't they use it at a museum?"

Jerry thought that few of the specimens handled in an institute of paleontology would require sedation. He said that there were probably hundreds of places in New York where anyone could buy phenobarbital, against the law or not. But if she wanted someone at the Institute, why not Agee? He was more of a size; he would make as good a mad scientist as Steck. He—

"Why?" Pam said.

"I don't know," Jerry told her. "Why not the Presons—any Preson? Eeny, meeny, miney. Right size; family resemblance. Stand to profit, if they win the will contest."

That, Pam said, was one of the troubles—*if* they won the will contest. Why should they have arranged it so that they took the chance?

"Even if Mr. Preson had wanted the money that badly," Pam said, "he wouldn't have killed for it. He's much too—too neat for that. Driving Dr. Preson crazy, or making him look crazy, would have been different. But Mr. Preson would have stopped there. So would his sister. I don't think the girl would have gone that far."

"Wayne?"

"What papa tells him, I think," Pam said. "Also, he's too young to be so devious. He'd never have thought it up."

She paused and drank.

"I want Dr. Steck," she said.

Jerry started to wish her luck. He stopped, abruptly, his gaze fixed on the door to the Rose Room.

"Well," Jerry said, "in a way you've got him, Pam." He nodded toward Dr. Albert James Steck, who was following Emily Preson out of the room. He was very close behind her. He had one hand on her arm.

"Oh!" Pam North said. "Oh—Jerry! *She's* the right size! Jerry— *cement!*"

Emily Preson and Dr. Steck walked toward the door, walked past the desk and the entrance to the small bar which is just beside the entrance. They went out into Forty-fourth Street.

"Jerry," Pam said. "Just coming out of the bar. That's her brother, isn't it?"

"Yes," Jerry said. "I think so."

"Then," Pam said, "come on. We've got to help Bill. We've got to hurry, too." She stood up. "Concrete, I mean," she said.

*   *   *

Wayne Preson, who had been sitting near the end of the bar, where he could see out into the lobby, left money for the drink over which he had been rather outrageously lingering and went, not hurrying, after his sister and Dr. Albert James Steck. He went wondering what in the devil Emily was up to now. None of it made any particular sense, which was disturbing. Emily could, certainly, mess things up. She could get herself into trouble. She had always been able to do that. She could never leave things alone. This did not explain where Steck came into it, or where she thought he did.

It had been evident that she was up to something when she made that curious small movement in the bus. He would not have noticed her except for that—that lifted hand of concealment. It had been a flicker in the corner of his eyes; he had driven on for almost a block before he realized that he had seen Emily in the bus and that, recognizing him and the car, she had tried to avoid being seen, which had meant that she was indeed up to something. Other things, he had then decided, would have to wait, and he had U-turned the little car and loitered in it behind the bus to the subway station. He had parked quickly, had been in luck there, and been lucky that, on the subway platform, Emily had had to wait for a train. It had been easy enough to follow her out of the subway, but very difficult once she was in the crowd. It was, again, pure luck that he had not lost her—luck and the tall visibility of Dr. Steck.

Until just as she met Steck—and it was odd, Wayne thought, to arrange a meeting in the Forty-second Street crowd,—he had, in fact, almost lost her. He had known, or at least been sure, that she was somewhere in front of him in the crowd, but she was not tall enough to be visible. (Neither was he, when it came to that.) But Steck had solved the problem, being visible and unexpected. He had almost lost them when, suddenly, they veered toward the curb and a cab, but fortunately he was close enough by then to hear Steck's rumbling voice. They would have lost him otherwise, since there was no other cab immediately available. They would have lost him if they had, once in the cab, changed their minds as to their destination.

He had, finally, walked to the Algonquin, hoping his luck still held. At first he had thought it did not; it had been several minutes before he located them in a far corner of the lobby. They were, apparently, just ordering drinks. He hesitated, not wanting to go into the lounge itself, and finally went along the wall to the telephone booth near the newsstand. He telephoned his father from there. When he came out of the booth, Steck and Emily were just being served drinks.

If they had been out in the room, he might have taken a chance—he was beginning to believe in his luck's holding. He might have found a seat behind them, but close enough to listen. Steck's voice carried and so, when she was excited—as God knew she usually seemed to be— did Emily's. One cannot, however, get behind people who are sitting in a corner. Where he stood now, he was himself exposed.

He had had an idea which seemed as good as any. He had gone to the newsstand, which included the counter of a theater ticket agency, and begun to enquire about tickets for that evening. He asked for plays impossible of achievement and when, as he expected, they were quickly termed impossible, he went down the line to the merely improbable, realizing he took some risk of having actually to buy a ticket. The improbable plays required telephone calls and the telephone calls took time, which was the idea. During them he could, and did, turn quickly from time to time to see that Steck and Emily were where they had been.

They had finished their first drink, and were talking with intentness—what about? what was the whole thing about?—when there were still two of the probables to go. They had ordered a second drink when the last two probables turned out to be impossibles.

"I seem to be out of luck," Wayne said pleasantly. The friendly woman behind the counter, who had supposed all along that he would be, but who thought of him as a nice-looking young man, lonely in New York, had said that it was, after all, Saturday night. She suggested he should have tried earlier, and he said he knew he should. She suggested a movie and he, ruefully, agreed he apparently would have to settle for a movie. He turned away, hesitated like one undecided as to how the evening was to be spent, and turned back to buy a package of cigarettes. At the cigarette counter he was partly hidden from view of people in a distant corner of the lounge. He lighted a cigarette and stood looking down—having in a sense bought the right—at the displayed afternoon newspapers. The headlines gave him an odd feeling; it was strange to see so much attention paid, in such black ink—except that on the *Journal-American* the ink was red—to events of which one was a part.

He turned away from the newspapers and was just in time to see Steck and his sister leave the table. He moved so that a pillar was between himself and them, since now they might, as they moved through it, look around the lobby. He watched them go to the entrance to the Rose Room, and watched them led in. He should have expected that; food was in season, his own stomach told him that. Wayne realized that his stomach probably would go on telling him that for some time longer. He could not risk the Rose Room, where, since he could not choose his own path into or through it, he might very possibly be seated in plain sight of the two he followed. The Oak Room was even more unavailable; supposing he could get into it, which was unlikely, he would there, for his purpose, be no better off than he would be in, say, Riverdale.

The bar offered an alternative. Its door did command the exit. His stomach would merely have to continue unheeded prayers, be now and then granted a peanut for answer.

He went into the bar and dawdled over drinks. It seemed longer, but it was only about forty-five minutes until Steck and Emily Preson came in sight. Wayne paid and slid from the bar stool.

Wayne waited just inside the hotel's doors until, in response to the doorman's whistle, a cab slowed in front. Then he had to take a chance. He turned up the collar of his topcoat and pulled his hat to an angle not usual with him. He hoped Steck would again give directions before he got into the cab, instead of afterward. Steck did, and Wayne Preson was close enough to hear them. Where they were going didn't make any sense either; none of it made any sense. He watched Steck's cab move east. He gestured to the doorman, who went out into the street and began to blow his whistle.

"Why," Pam North said from beside him, "it's Mr. Preson!"

For a moment, Wayne did not recognize the Norths. Then he did.

"Just stopped in there for a drink," he said, and instantly wished he had not. In his ears, the explanation sounded self-conscious, an explanation not asked for or required.

"Such a pleasant place," Pam said. "Unlike most places. We go there often."

Wayne sought a suitably commonplace remark. He said, "Oh yes," vaguely. Then a cab slowed.

"Here," he said, "you take this one. It's cold out here."

"Oh no," Pam said. "You take it. We're walking."

The cab came to the curb.

"You're sure you won't?" Wayne said.

"Really," Pam said. "We're just going around the corner."

Wayne got in. The cab driver turned toward him.

"Well," Wayne said, "nice seeing you."

The Norths were standing very near the cab door. Wayne pulled it toward him. A cab behind, waiting to discharge at the Algonquin, hooted. The driver of Wayne's cab started up.

"Well?" he said.

Now Wayne Preson could tell him.

"The Broadly Institute," he said. "Up on Fifth Avenue."

"Oh yeah," the driver said. "Up there. Where this guy got killed."

The couple emerging from the taxicab behind had, although nobody touched them, the feeling that they were pulled from the cab. ("New York people are certainly in a hurry," the woman remarked as they found themselves on the sidewalk. "I don't see how they keep it up.")

"Follow that cab ahead," Jerry North said to their driver.

"Why?" the driver asked, with polite interest.

"Because of five dollars," Jerry told him.

"I tell you, mister," the driver said. "You twisted my arm."

"So," Pam said when they were moving, "that's the way you do it. The only time I tried it, the man just said 'Why, lady?' and I couldn't think."

Homer and Laura Preson left the downtown subway train at Ninety-sixth Street. Sergeant Mullins, who had taken the elementary precaution of riding in the car behind and stepping to the platform at each stop, to step back in again just as the doors were closing, saw them leave the car. It was possible they were merely planning a change to a local, and Mullins waited, partly behind a pillar, as unobtrusive as a large man can be. They started off toward an exit to the street, and Mullins went after them. Emerging on the street, they took the first of two taxicabs lined at a hack stand.

Mullins had the door of the second open before he realized it had no driver. Mullins swore, backed out, and looked for the nearest lunch room. He spotted it, two doors up the street, and ran for it. He ran back, more or less dragging a smaller and protesting man. Mullins pushed the man, who was saying, "Hey, looka here! Suppose you are a cop! Suppose—"

"Get going, pal," Mullins told him. "They're getting a start of us."

The taxi driver, plucked by the law from a bowl of bean soup, with spaghetti and franks to come, got going. "This ain't Russia, is it?" he enquired, unexpectedly betraying himself as a listener to Kaltenborn. "Or is it?" he added.

"Not that I've heard," Mullins said. "If you miss the light, jump it."

They just did not miss the light, going east in Ninety-sixth. At the next avenue, the cab ahead just did not make it. They coasted up behind the leading cab.

"I suppose the city pays for my soup?" the hacker remarked, in a tone which indicated his dark conviction that the city would do nothing of the sort.

"I'll tell you what it is," Mullins said. "You're breaking my heart, fella."

The light changed and the two cabs went. They went across Central Park West and dived into the cut through the park. At Fifth they turned north.

The showroom of Sport Cars, Inc., on Broadway in the Sixties, was not large, but it was very bright. Its window displayed a small, gleaming object which, Bill Weigand reflected on his way to the door, needed only passenger space to make it a nice little car. A tall young man, who seemed to be alone in the showroom, greeted Bill at the door with enthusiasm. Shortly, his enthusiasm lessened.

"Wayne isn't here," the tall young man said. "And why should I talk about him behind his back? Tell you our business?"

"Because two men've got themselves killed," Bill explained.

The tall young man laughed heartily. He would, he said then, like to see anyone convince him Wayne Preson went around killing people. He said that all you needed to do was to look at Wayne Preson.

Bill wondered, briefly and as he often did, what people supposed murderers looked like. Did they expect daggers between teeth? The outlines of automatics under suit jackets?

"All I want to know," Bill said, "is—did Preson need money? Was he hard up?"

The tall young man laughed with even greater amusement.

"Wayne?" he asked, as if an entirely new person had been brought, incomprehensibly, into the discussion. "You're talking about Wayne Preson?"

"Right," Bill said, his voice patient.

"Hard up?" the tall young man repeated.

"Right," Bill said. "You've heard the expression, Mr.—uh?"

"Smith," the tall young man said. "John Smith." He laughed again. "Think I'm kidding?" he asked.

"No," Bill said. "I don't think you're kidding. Is Wayne Preson hard up?"

"He's planning to buy a half interest in this show," John Smith said. "That's how hard up he is. It's a good show, too. His family's got it. How'd you think he kept up with this crowd without money?"

"Crowd?" Bill repeated. "What crowd?"

"Marie Albrenza; that bunch," John Smith said. "The people we sell cars to. You didn't think we sold cars like that"—he indicated the shiny object on display—"to people—people named Smith?"

That idea, it appeared from the subsequent laughter, was funnier than any which had gone before.

"Look," Bill said. "I'm a policeman. I'm investigating a murder. Two murders. Two people got killed. Quit being so damned funny, Mr. Smith."

"Listen," Smith said. "You can't—"

He stopped, rather suddenly.

"Right," Bill said. "I can. Don't be funny at all, Mr. Smith. Just talk."

John Smith, whose trouble perhaps, Bill thought, was only youth—high pressure youth—did talk.

Wayne Preson was, he said, part of a group of young and youngish people with money and leisure and with, it was to be hoped, an inclination toward imported sports cars. He supposed they used them to drive between Twenty-One and the Stork, with perhaps side trips to Long Island. A few years before, Smith had met Preson somewhere—he didn't recall, now, precisely where. At that time, Smith had just got the agency for two British manufacturers of light, fast—and for the most part topless—cars. He got to talking about them with Preson; it was Preson who suggested he might make a useful salesman. He had started as a salesman on commission. He had sold cars.

"He makes plenty here," Smith said. "I guess he doesn't need it. Like I said, his family seems to have it. Anyway, he's going to buy in. He's got enough money for that."

"How far in?" Bill asked.

Smith hesitated.

"Twenty-five thousand in," he said. "How far in that takes him is none of your business." He nodded approval of his own point. "Cop or no cop," he added.

"So far as I know," Bill Weigand said, "his family hasn't money in a big way. Did he say it had?"

Smith paused. Finally he shook his head.

"I don't remember that he did," Smith said. "Maybe I just guessed that. But anyway, he's made a lot out of selling cars in the last three-four years."

"You think he saved the twenty-five thousand?"

"I don't know," Smith said. "He could have, if he wanted to."

"Right," Bill said. "Well—thanks, Mr. Smith."

"You're barking up the wrong tree," John Smith assured Weigand as he went with him toward the door.

"I'm barking up several," Bill told him. He stopped to look at the car. "Can you get in that yourself?" he asked Smith.

"Well—" Smith said. "Sure I can. There's plenty of room in there. If you're—"

"I'm not," Bill said. He went.

He drove to his office and looked over reports. There were plenty of fingerprints on the bones. There were prints of almost everybody, including Mrs. Gerald North. Deputy Chief Inspector Artemus O'Malley had been over the routine reports. He had put an exclamation point, harshly, after the name of Mrs. North. He had written: "W. W. See me!" and underlined it three times. That could be left, Bill decided, until the next day. He looked at his watch. It was a few minutes after nine. Inspector O'Malley closed for the day not later than five; he had been known to close at three, particularly on Saturdays. A good many things did. Including, Bill Weigand thought, Columbia University. He wondered if Homer Preson was lying, or had been lied to.

Things were out of hand at the Broadly Institute even before the doors reopened Saturday afternoon. Saturday was normally a busy day at the Institute, as busy days normally went there. From Monday through Friday, a majority of the visitors were fossil fanciers, prone to look long and with sagacity at rearticulated skeletons, to study with purpose the books of the library on the second floor. But on Saturdays, and again on Sundays, most visitors were people who found those days heavy on the hands and who looked at Tyrannosaurus with well-what-do-you-know-about-that? expressions. "No, baby, of course it isn't real," Dr. Paul Agee, passing through the Great Hall, had once heard a young man tell his girl as, arms locked and the future in their faces, they had looked unbelievingly at the past. "I know," the girl had answered. "It's too absurd, isn't it?"

But this Saturday, the eighth of December, was not like other Saturdays. It was blustery and rather cold, but by the time the doors of the Institute reopened a hundred or more people were waiting, impatient to experience paleontology. Several of them went so far as to knock abruptly on the doors of the big building, meanwhile peering in somewhat balefully. When the doors did open, the leaders burst in as if in pursuit of something but, once inside, seemed to have forgotten what they sought. They clustered in front of Teddy the Tyrannosaurus, who bared his ancient teeth. From him, they fanned out.

It can hardly be supposed they, or the hundreds who came after them, expected to find the body of Dr. Jesse Landcraft, the skull in fragments, still lying in front of a Neanderthal cave, a prehistoric axe blood-stained beside it. That would, of course, have been fine and rewarding, but it was not really to be anticipated. There were some expressions of disappointment, and a few of anger, when the scene of the crime was found to be curtained off, but this concealment most of the visitors seemed to have expected. When anything really good happened, the cops tried to keep people away. You couldn't get within blocks of a good fire; when police cars converged on buildings, excitingly, other policemen converged to hold back taxpayers. But you could *be* there. You could stand behind firelines; you could cluster across the street from buildings in which crimes of lurid violence had been committed.

That Saturday afternoon, people could be at the Broadly Institute, where murder had been—where, in some hour of darkness, an axe fashioned in the unimaginable past had been brought down on a man's head, and the head had broken. People could pass the now curtained exhibit, and linger in front of it, knowing that just beyond fabric and glass, only feet away, the cave-man murder had occurred—the one the papers were full of, the one people were talking about. They could discover, and later tell, that this cave-man place, see, is to the left as you go into this big hall, just a ways back of this dragon, or whatever it is, they say is a thousand years old maybe. "Sure," they could say, "I went up there and looked at it. Sure is a funny place to pick to kill a guy."

The Great Hall was uncomfortably crowded by four o'clock and the pressure began to force visitors upward. They reached the second floor easily and invaded the library, to the consternation of several students who were, in a fashion, boning up, and had thought to be left alone to it. They wandered out of the library and scrutinized fossil remains in cases along corridors; finding these of little interest, they climbed higher and began to wander the upper corridors, peering in at empty offices through doors innocently left open. Dr. Paul Agee, who was uncharacteristically in his office that afternoon, was among the objects peered at. He did, then, with some difficulty get the floors above the second established as out of bounds. The police helped him.

None of this was unexpected to the police, and Dr. Agee had been warned. That he had nevertheless decided to keep the Institute open struck the police as foolhardy, but out of their province. They did provide guards. They did try to keep people from carrying off, as souvenirs, parts of Teddy the Tyrannosaurus. (In this, it was subsequently discovered, they were only partially successful.) They tried to keep people from breaking the glass on exhibit alcoves and falling into them. But by late afternoon, things had grown even worse than the police had anticipated.

"Tell him he'd better close this damn place up if he expects to have the place," the precinct captain told a lieutenant, who, in other words, passed the suggestion on to Dr. Agee. Dr. Agee went down to see for himself, was both astonished and alarmed, and gave the word. By a little after six o'clock, there were only a few policemen left in the building; an hour later, they were out. A patrol of two remained on the Fifth Avenue side to suggest that people move along there. Since it was too cold by that hour for out-of-door loitering, people did move along.

Dr. Paul Agee remained in his office, and so far as he knew he was alone in the building. The watchman was not due until ten, the normal Saturday closing hour. He remained there to think things over, and to look things over. The whole thing had turned out unexpectedly, and distressingly. It had even, Dr. Agee thought, turned out dangerously. He had not, he realized, entirely appreciated how one thing leads to another, how one action makes another obligatory and how this continues through a series of actions.

In this affair, Dr. Agee unhappily told himself, the chain of actions had begun quite simply, and, when one came to that, harmlessly. But the extraneous, the not to be anticipated, had become involved, so that now auditors in the employ of the police were going over the Institute's books. This, certainly, was not anything which he could have anticipated. He had not even expected it the day before when the official request came in a telephone call from the office of some inspector or other. He had acquiesced, of course; he had realized that he had no alternative. He had expressed surprise that the financial records of the Broadly Institute could be thought, by anyone, to be informative in relation to the death of Dr. Orpheus Preson, and had been informed—still very politely—that it was desired to investigate thoroughly the financial transactions of Dr. Preson, with which those of the Institute might be involved. "You've got me," Dr. Agee had said, humorously, and then, "Of course." So two men had arrived to go over the books.

Sitting at his desk in the big, deserted building, Dr. Agee wished, in passing, that he had not used the locution, "You've got me." He sincerely hoped he had not been prophetic when he had meant only to say, in humorous idiom, that the workings of the official mind were, in this connection, beyond him.

He did not, for a long time, think of anything which he now could do. The series of actions appeared to have come to an end, and an uncomfortable one. Finally he went out of his office, and down in the staff elevator to the ground floor. He went briefly into the Great Hall, in which two widely separated lights burned dimly—which was a cavern of shadows, with the monstrous one of Teddy dominating the rest—and saw that nothing was amiss. (He was, he realized, like a fussy householder locking up for the night.) He went back through the entry to the staff door and opened it and went out, but just before it closed he checked the keys in his pocket, instinctively. The keys were not there, and he remembered that he had left them dangling from the keyhole of a desk drawer.

He caught the door, which was ponderously closing itself, and held it. He would have, before he left permanently, to retrieve his keys. But he might as well, first, go down to Madison and get the food he had started for. He pushed the button in the door which would render the snap lock inoperative, tried the outer knob to see whether it had, and let the door close. He walked, the wind behind him, down to Madison and to the restaurant he had in mind. He discovered that, once out in the biting wind, he was rather hungry.

to the restaurant he had in mind. He discovered that, once out in the biting wind, he was rather hungry.

Steck put his key in the lock of the staff door, turned it, pushed the door open. He stood aside, then, to let Emily Preson go in ahead of him.

"I didn't know they planned to close up," Steck said. "However—" His hand directed the girl toward the automatic elevator, waiting for them. "I can't say I know what you expect to find," Steck said.

"Something," Emily said. "Anything. Don't you see yet?"

Steck shrugged heavily. He followed Emily into the elevator and closed the door after them.

The telephone rang in Bill Weigand's office.

"Yes?" Bill said into it.

"Oh," the duty sergeant said, "didn't see you come in, captain. Got a couple of messages here. A Mrs.—wait a minute now—North? That sound right?"

"Right," Bill said.

"O.K.," the sergeant said. "This is what the first call says: 'Steck's got Emily.'" The sergeant spoke doubtfully. "That's what it says," the sergeant said. "I didn't take it personally."

"That's all right," Bill said. "It's unusually clear, as a matter of fact."

"O.K.," the sergeant said. "The second just says: 'Gone to Broadly.'"

"Thanks," Bill Weigand said. He hung up. He got up. It was unusually clear for Pamela North, certainly. In spite of that, it failed to add. Apparently, somebody had run up another barking tree.

He was at the door when the telephone rang again. This time it was a message from the auditors who had been comparing canceled checks drawn by Orpheus Preson in favor of the Broadly Institute of Paleontology with receipts noted on the Institute's books. The report was interim; the bookkeeping methods of the Institute were unorthodox. (The auditors were a little plaintive about this.) It did, however, appear that there was a discrepancy. It appeared that the discrepancy was of an even ten thousand dollars—ten thousand dollars which had departed Dr. Preson's bank but not reached the account of the Institute.

Acting Captain William Weigand expressed his appreciation and went again to the door of his office. Just before he opened the door, Bill barked softly.

• 12 •

The Norths' taxi driver progressed with supreme confidence. As a result, he was whistled down by a traffic policeman at Fifty-seventh Street and Fifth Avenue. He was directed to the curb; he was spoken to. Enquiry was made as to his destination; it was pointed out to him that traffic lights are, when red, to be stopped at, not halfway through. Pam North said, "Please, officer," and the traffic man said, "Take it easy, lady. Don't want to get killed, do you?"

"Now, cowboy," the traffic man said, returning to his prey. "Want a ticket, do you? That what you want?"

"It was that bus," the driver said. "Between me and the light."

"Yeah," the traffic man said, "you're in the city now, cowboy. Buses and everything."

The driver bowed his head to the storm, which continued to blow. When it ended, the end was abrupt.

"Get going, buster," the traffic man said. "Watch it."

146

The taxi driver got going. When he had gone a block, he turned to the Norths and said, "Give some of them a badge!" He turned into the right-hand lane and continued uptown, slowly. He said, "What'll it be, mister?"

It was difficult to say. The cab which was taking Wayne Preson wherever he was going had had ten minutes to take him there, and "there" might be any place. Wayne's cab had made the light at Fifty-seventh Street. That had been the trouble.

"He kept on going uptown as long as I could see," said Pam, who had watched. "So I suppose—" She paused, not knowing quite what she did suppose. They continued north, Central Park on their left. They ought, Pam said, to let Bill know what they knew.

"Which is?" Jerry asked.

"About Steck and Emily," Pam said. "And Wayne's following them, if he is. About her being the right size."

"Turn over to Madison," Jerry told the driver. "Find some place with a telephone. I suppose you mean the right size to impersonate her uncle?"

"In men's clothes," Pam said. "She's built for it. She and Steck together. Only—"

"Precisely," Jerry said. "You will have it Steck. Why should she?"

"He must have some hold," Pam said. "Perhaps she's in love with him. I don't know."

"You certainly don't," Jerry agreed.

"This all right?" the taxi driver said, in Madison Avenue. It was. It was her theory, Jerry told Pam. She could pass it on. He waited in the cab while Pamela North, trim, quick, went across the sidewalk into a drug store.

"Sometimes they ain't there," the taxi driver said. "I took a chance."

"It's all right," Jerry said. "Forget it. You still get the extra five."

"That ain't what I mean," the driver said. "I trust you, fella. I mean sometimes in the evening they ain't at Fifty-seventh." He was earnest.

"I know what you meant," Jerry said. Pam came across the side walk and he opened the door for her. She shook her head. She said, "Not there. I left a message. Just that Steck has Emily. I thought the rest would be confusing, except to Bill."

Even that much might be, Jerry thought, and said. The cab remained motionless.

"The museum, of course!" Pam said. "Where else would Dr. Steck go?"

Jerry could think of a hundred places—of a thousand. However, Wayne Preson's cab had last been seen going up Fifth. If he was following Steck and Emily Preson, or knew where they were going, it could be presumed that their cab had gone up Fifth. The Broadly Institute was up Fifth.

"Wait, I'll leave Bill another message," Pam said. She went; she returned.

"The Broadly Institute," Jerry said to the taxi driver. "It's up Fifth about—"

"I know," the driver said. "Where this guy gets killed with this stone axe. You read about that?"

They admitted they had read about that. The cab went on, as confidently as before. But this time nobody stopped it, until the driver stopped it in front of a large, square building which was forbiddingly dark.

"Here you are," the driver said. "Looks like they all went home, don't it?"

It did. Nevertheless, Jerry paid the fare, plus a routine tip, plus five dollars for intentions, if not performance, over and above the call of duty.

"Well," the hacker said, "hope you make out." He departed, leaving the Norths on a cold sidewalk in front of a dark building. The west wind got a running start at them across the park. They went up the steps of the Broadly Institute and pushed without confidence against the big doors. They peered through them. The building was not entirely dark; there was a faint glimmer of light in the Great Hall.

"Somebody's there," Pam said, and was told that that did not follow; that lights were undoubtedly left on every night.

"There'll be a back door," Pam said. "Everything has a back door."

They went down the steps again, the wind jostling them, and around the corner of the building. Halfway down the building's length, they found a door. It was a solid wooden door, firmly closed. They stopped and looked at it.

"No go," Jerry said. "Anyway, we don't—"

But Pam had gone up the three steps to the door. She took the knob, turned, and pulled. She might have been pulling against the solid weight of the building. She considered. She pushed. The door began to open, heavy and reluctant. But by then Jerry was beside her, and then it was easy.

They were, after going up two more steps, in a small foyer. There was a door directly in front of them and there was a door on either side. The doors seemed, in the dim light from a small, high-hung bulb, identical; the call-button of the elevator, which was behind the door on their left, was easy to overlook. Pam and Jerry North overlooked it and, with nothing to guide them, went forward. They came out into shadowed immensity; into a cavern of shadows; into the Great Hall of the Broadly Institute of Paleontology.

Teddy the Tyrannosaurus was at his most formidable in the semi-darkness. He seemed much larger and, at the same time, more porous. One light was beyond him and visible through the great rib cage, where his no doubt tremendous heart once had beaten. The head, which had housed a minute brain, reared high in the gloom, the teeth baleful in the little light, grinning horribly out of the past. The remainder of Teddy seemed to continue indefinitely in the darkness.

"My," Pam said, her voice low and without much confidence. "My!" She considered. "It must have taken him a long time to wag his tail," she said.

Although Pam had spoken softly, her voice seemed to echo in the great room, among the shadows. From some place far away it came back to them. "Wag his tail," the echo said. "—his tail."

"I'm afraid," Pam said, even more softly, "that it doesn't gain by repetition. It was only whistling in the dark."

"As a matter of fact," Jerry said, "it probably did. Took a second or two for the impulse to travel the nerves. He was a little sluggish, they think. What next?"

It was her party, his tone implied. He was along for the ride.

"I don't know," Pam said. "It feels terribly empty, doesn't it?"

It did feel empty; the whole building felt empty. Only the past lived there—the incredibly distant past; only Teddy and creatures like Teddy; only bones dead for times beyond imagination, years beyond counting. Things long dead.

"It was over there," Pam said. "Remember? We looked at it. I said you used to be more shaggy."

It drew them. The light seemed less dim than it had, as their eyes grew accustomed to dimness. As hundreds had done earlier in the day, Pam and Jerry North went to stand in front of the exhibit of Neanderthal man. But now, for some reason, the curtains had been parted and they could look into the cubicle in which Jesse Landcraft had died; in which now the shaggy man of half a million years ago stood by the cave entrance, towering above the crouched figure of his almost equally shaggy wife. But he was defenseless now; the weapon he had seemed to hold, axe head on ground, shaft in hand, was gone. The thing which was almost man looked out at them, looked through them. The past stared at them, through eyes simulated from plastic.

"I don't," Pam said, "think I like it here much. Anyway, nobody's here but us and—and things. They'll be upstairs."

If anywhere, they would be upstairs. Jerry agreed to that. They went toward the front of the Great Hall, from which staircases arose on either side, with public elevators under them. The staircases were broad, the treads of marble. Pam's heels clicked as they went up.

"We're not," she said in a whisper, "exactly slipping up on anybody, are we?"

"I don't know what we're doing," Jerry said. "I don't know why we're here."

Pamela North was not at all sure that she knew either. The only thing was, there had been no one else to follow Steck and Emily Preson, and Wayne Preson who had followed them. And somebody had to. If I'm right, Pam North thought, she's served her purpose. He doesn't need her any more.

The second floor was bisected longitudinally by a reasonably broad corridor. The corridor, lighted by a single overhead light, ran half the length of the building, with doors on either side. It ended in double swinging doors, now closed. At the top of the stair flight the Norths stopped and stood very still, and listened. They could hear nothing. They went down the central corridor, which was lined, between the doors of the rooms opening off of it, with shallow cases in which were objects of antiquity—crudely made tools of stone and of some metals; tiny figures; a slab of stone on which, when it had been part of a cave's wall, some ancient man had tried to picture what he saw. There were also, of course, bones.

They reached the swinging doors and pushed them open. They looked into the library, with a desk near the front, and a railing, and walls book-lined. The room was empty, and as dim as the corridor, as the Great Hall below. They went back up the corridor, past the open doors of dark exhibit rooms. They were back by the stairs, from which they had started.

"Well," Pam said, "they aren't here."

She looked at the stairs, now a single flight, which led up to the third floor. The Norths went up the stairs, side by side. The third floor was different.

There they came first into a transverse corridor, crossing most of the front of the building but ending in a door at either end. Here, again, a central corridor ran toward the rear of the building, but at its end another corridor ran at right angles to it. At first, the lighting here was as dim as it had been on the lower floors. At first, this floor, too, seemed deserted.

But then, midway down the narrow central corridor, a light went on. It came through the glass half of a door. Somebody had turned on a light in one of the offices on either side of the corridor.

"There they are," Pam said, in Jerry's ear. "Some of them, anyway. Come on."

They went down the corridor, not surreptitiously—they might be trespassers but Pam's heart was pure; Jerry was of two minds about his own—and came to the door. It had Steck's name on it. They looked through the glass into the room they had visited the afternoon before.

Wayne Preson was standing at the far end of the room, by a table. He had been looking down at the table; it seemed to Pam and Jerry that he was just reaching out his hand to take something off the table or to put something on it. But as they looked in he turned and faced them and then stood looking at them. Jerry North opened the door, then.

"How did you two get here?" Wayne said. His voice, so far as they could tell, held only curiosity.

"We—" Pam began.

"Followed me," Wayne said. "I wondered if you would." He paused. "I'm damned glad you did," he said. "I can't find them. But—I'm sure they came in." He left the table, which they could now see still held Dr. Preson's bones, and came toward them. "I'm worried as hell about her," Wayne Preson said. "My sister, I mean."

"Worried about her?" Pam repeated.

"I don't know what she's—what she's trying to do," Wayne said. Now his voice sounded strained, betrayed worry. "She—she's likely to rush into things without working them out."

"She's with Steck," Jerry said. "I don't imagine he rushes into things."

"That's it," Wayne said. "Why? Why should she be with Steck? Why would she meet him? Come here with him? They—so far as I know, they've only met a few times. Why does she run to him?"

"Why does she run?" Pam asked.

Wayne shook his head; he moved his shoulders.

"I don't know," he said. "Half the time we—I mean dad and Aunt Laura too—don't know what's in her mind. She can't have had anything to do with this." He spread his hands. "Any of this," he said. "Whatever it is—whatever's going on. Uncle Orpheus kills himself. But then Uncle Jesse is murdered. And—now Emily. She's got herself mixed up in something. I'm afraid she'll—get hurt."

"She'll be all right," Pam North said, because it was the thing to say. She hesitated for a moment. "Dr. Preson was murdered too," she said. "Didn't you know?"

"That's just the newspapers," Wayne said. "Naturally they—" But he stopped because Pam was shaking her head.

"It's true," she said. "He was killed too. Cleverly killed. Somebody poisoned the labels."

"The labels?" Wayne repeated. "It was in the milk. What do you mean, the labels?"

Pam told him. He told her it was guesswork.

"The police found traces on the bones," Pam said. "Where the labels had been."

He shook his head, but he appeared to accept it. He did not raise the objections his aunt had raised, his father had raised. He seemed to think a moment.

"Steck," he said. He gestured toward the table where the bones still were. Nothing much had been done with them since the afternoon before, Pam decided, looking. The bones were still without labels. No—something had been done. The picture was not right. Pam managed to re-create a picture of the table the afternoon before. It was a little shadowy around the edges but— Oh yes, then some of the bones still had had labels on them. Now none had. That could explain the divergence of the pictures.

"Steck threw the old labels away," Wayne Preson said. "He was in a hurry about it. And—he gets Uncle Orpheus's job."

Pam North nodded.

"You're jumping to conclusions," Jerry said. "First Pam. Now you, Mr. Preson. It was perfectly natural to throw the labels away. They weren't of any use—so much wastepaper."

Wayne Preson listened. He said, "Who then?" He said, "Emily must think—" and stopped.

Then he brushed past the Norths to the door.

"I've got to find her," Wayne said. "She's here somewhere."

They could hear him walking, almost running, up the hall toward the front of the building.

"He's right," Pam said. "Whether she helped him or not. Wayne's right."

She started toward the door. But Jerry's hand on her arm stopped her. At the same moment, Jerry flicked off the lights in the office. Then Pam, also, heard the sound. Someone had started to open the door of the office across the corridor which had been Dr. Orpheus Preson's. The door opened slowly; standing in the darkness of Steck's office, just inside the opened door, Pam and Jerry could hear the sound but for a second or two could detect no movement. Then the door was open and two people came out into the dim light of the corridor. They were Homer Preson and his sister.

They stood for a moment and looked up and down the corridor. Then, two slight, swiftly moving figures, they went down it toward the transverse corridor in the rear.

Pam started to speak, but again pressure on her arm stopped her. The Norths watched until the Presons, who seemed to be hurrying, yet who were making very little noise, reached the end of the corridor and turned left into the transverse corridor at its end. Then, softly, Pam said, "Why, Jerry? They're trying to find her, too. Somehow they found out Steck had her here and—"

"Then," said Jerry North, "why were they looking in the dark? They didn't have any light on in there."

"Well—" Pam said, her voice doubtful.

"*I'd* think," Jerry told her, "that they didn't want to be found. I wonder—"

"Jerry!" Pam said. "Come *on!*"

They went quickly across the corridor and into the other office.

It was an honest to God screwy one, Sergeant Mullins thought. It got more so by the minute. He stood inside the door of the office next to Steck's, from where he had been watching the door of Preson's former office; keeping an eye, but only in a manner of speaking, on Homer Preson and Laura. That had been simple, if not greatly rewarding—he knew where they were, if not what they were doing. But then Wayne Preson had come down the corridor and gone into Steck's office. Mullins debated what, if anything, he ought to do about that, and the Norths came down the corridor and joined Wayne. Sergeant Mullins thought speculatively of the door between Steck's office and the one he himself waited in. An ear pressed against the door—

But if he eavesdropped he would have to abandon his post of observation. He had decided to leave Wayne to the Norths, and keep an eye on his own pigeons. But then Wayne popped out of Steck's office, and, evidently, away from the Norths, who did not follow. Mullins swore softly, wishing he could split himself, send part of himself in pursuit of Wayne, keep part on hand to watch Homer and Laura Preson. He vibrated slightly, in indecision and annoyance. Then, from the office across the hall, Homer and Laura had emerged and had taken off. Mullins had started to move, then, but the Norths moved first—across and into Preson's office.

Mullins decided to let the Presons go for the moment, and join forces. He started to come out. But then he heard new footsteps in the corridor, almost closed the door he had partly opened and looked through the crack he left.

The Norths heard footsteps. Side by side, within Preson's office, they peered through the glass of the door. Dr. Paul Agee came down the corridor, walking hurriedly, making little sound. When he reached the door of Steck's office, he stopped and looked quickly up and down the corridor. Then he went in. But he did not turn on the light. The office remained dark.

"Hide and go seek," Pam North whispered, her whisper tense. "What's everybody doing whatever they're doing for?"

Jerry could not answer that one. He was still watching the door of Steck's office. Now there was a faint light behind the glass of the door—a dim and moving light.

"Stay here," he told Pam, and slipped out into the corridor. He went cautiously across to the door of Steck's office and looked in. Dr. Agee, director of the Broadly Institute, apparently was engaged in burglary. He had a small flashlight and by its inadequate illumination he was examining something he evidently had taken from Dr. Steck's desk. Jerry could not see what it was Dr. Agee held in his hand; he thought it was a paper of some sort, perhaps a card. Dr. Agee examined it only briefly, put it down on the desk, and picked up something else from the desk. This time Jerry was almost certain it was a small file card.

Gerald North, who preferred order, sought to convince himself that there was nothing peculiar in this surreptitious ransacking of the desk of a curator of fossil mammals by the director of an institute of paleontology. Jerry failed. It was very peculiar. Gerald North wished for the police, but police did not appear at his elbow. If Dr. Paul Agee was to be caught red-handed—assuming he was doing anything to redden his hands—capture devolved on Gerald North.

Ten years ago, I wouldn't have done this, Jerry thought, reaching for the doorknob. Shows what associations will— He opened the door and joined Dr. Agee in Steck's office.

"Looking for something?" Jerry asked, with politeness; with what he hoped was an air of authority.

What Dr. Agee now held in his hand was unmistakably a file card. Jerry could see, but could not decipher, notations on it.

When Jerry did not come out of Steck's office, Pam started to open the door of the late Dr. Preson's. She was so intent to join Jerry that she did not, for a second, realize that what was delaying her was the touch of fingers on her right arm. She was not actually being held; the touch of the fingers was light. But there were, Pam North thought, no fingers to be there. "Oh!" Pam said, in a breath. She turned.

There was not much light. There was enough to enable her to see Dr. Albert James Steck looming beside her. "Oh!" Pam said again. She allowed herself to be drawn back into the office.

"What are you doing here?" Steck asked her, his heavy voice low, rumbling—so low it was hardly more than a ripple in silence.

"You were here all the time?" Pam asked, and for no reason—except that Steck's fingers were still on her arm, except that they seemed to warn—her own voice was low. "When the Presons were?"

"The Presons?" Steck said. "Here? Emily's looking for—" He stopped. "The offices have connecting doors," Steck said. "I came that way. There was no one here but you, Mrs. North. Hiding."

"Jerry's—" Pam began.

"I saw him," Steck said. "What does he want in my office?"

"I don't—" Pam began. The fingers tightened on her arm.

"What does he want?" Steck said.

"—know," Pam finished. "Dr. Agee went in there and then Jerry—" She felt the fingers on her arm relax. She thought it was very dark—

almost completely dark—in the office. She thought—if there are doors between the offices, perhaps I—

"There's nothing there for Agee," Steck said, and now he had released her arm altogether. Now he was moving back toward the door to the corridor. "Unless—*by God! Arrhythmia!*"

He was, Pam decided, swearing in Greek. She was alone in a dark office with a mad scientist who swore in Greek!

But now the mad scientist, merely looking like a large man, was silhouetted against the glass of the door, his back to her. Pam North moved then, seeking the communicating door—either communicating door, since there might be two, one in either wall. In Steck's office— and now she remembered all of it in curiously vivid detail—there had been a door on either side wall, about halfway down the office. She moved lightly, cautiously; she receded into the gloom of the office and Steck, who seemed to have forgotten her, remained at the corridor door, looking out through it.

He heard the door open, and then he turned.

"Ar—" he began and then he said, "Wait! What's the matter with you?"

There was nothing the matter with her for so long as she could keep going, get a door closed between herself and Steck.

"These damn—" she heard Steck say, as she was closing the door. She heard him move. "Women," she heard Steck finish, as the door finally closed.

She ran across the gloom of an office much like the one she had fled and, midway, bumped hard into a table, fell half on the table. Something seemed to splinter under her outstretched hands. "I've broken somebody's something," Pam North thought. She backed away and went around, having set back, by perhaps a generation, mankind's knowledge of a certain small amphibian which had wandered, but not beautified, the earth some millions of years before. The Broadly Institute had almost pieced him together when Pam North fell on him.

She heard—she was sure she heard—the opening behind her of the door she had just closed. She could just make out the door in the opposite wall, prayed briefly that it prove unlocked—it was fortunate that the institute scientists seemed very trusting about locks—and pulled it open. She went through and was in another office. She was more cautious this time; she avoided the skeleton of something—a gigantic bird, for heaven's sake?—which occupied the center of the room. Pam North fled on, through the remote past and the interconnecting offices of the Broadly Institute, away from the no doubt pursuing Dr. Steck, who swore in Greek—but away, also, from Jerry and whatever was happening to him in the office he had, much to her surprise, entered with the air of a policeman on patrol.

What you needed to be was three cops, maybe four, Mullins thought. When you got one of these screwy ones (with the Norths in it) it was no good to be just one sergeant of detectives. You kept an eye on two people and followed them to this god-awful barn and then the place got full up with people, all acting as if they had gone nuts. This Agee, now, sneaking into somebody else's office; the Norths, now, going into the office across the hall and not turning on the lights. Wayne Preson, up to something. Where the hell, Sergeant Mullins asked himself, is the Loot?

He had an ear to the door which connected his office with that of Dr. Steck, in which Dr. Agee now was doing something—looking for something, probably—which asked for investigation. He had withdrawn to the connecting door as soon as he had seen Agee enter the office. If he had missed something else that way, it couldn't be helped. He was, after all, only one cop, inconvenient as it was. He thought he heard a voice on the other side of the door, but he could not distinguish words. He began, very quietly, very deftly, to ease the door open.

Dr. Agee had been intent when Jerry spoke; he jumped at the sound of the voice. He said, "What the—" and then evidently thought better of finishing the sentence. Keeping the faint beam of the torch on Jerry's face, Dr. Agee began to back further into the room.

"Wait a minute," Jerry said. "It's no good to try—"

But then the torch went out and, for a moment, Jerry was blind in the darkness. He heard movement; he heard what sounded like a door being opened. He went toward the sound. He said, "Hold it!" and then, seeing more clearly now, saw a door in the side wall on his left. The door stood just perceptibly ajar. Agee had gone that way!

It was exasperating; it was in the highest degree annoying. Jerry was annoyed with himself. He had undertaken—against his judgment, uncharacteristically—to catch Dr. Agee with red hands. he was not catching him at all; he was bungling it. He was annoyed at Dr. Agee for making him bungle.

Jerry North jumped for the door, grabbed the knob, and jerked the door toward him. There was momentary resistance; then a man came in with the door. He came off balance, and Jerry grabbed him.

"I told you—" Jerry began. "What're you looking—"

The man he held seemed much larger than Dr. Agee; the man he held was no longer off balance. Something large, something heavy, hit Jerry North in the jaw. Blackness began to close in around Jerry, but now the man who was too large to be Agee—who very clearly wasn't Agee—was holding him up.

"Jeeze, Mr. North," Sergeant Aloysius Mullins said, supporting Jerry, who sagged ominously, "How ud I know? You jumped me, Mr. North! How ud I know?"

The voice of Sergeant Mullins came dimly to Jerry North, through darkness, from a great distance. But then it came again, and now it was closer. Jerry found he could shake his head to clear it; found he was no longer, as he momentarily had seemed to be, in the process of disintegration.

"What did you hit me with, Mullins?" Mr. North enquired.

Mullins continued to support him.

"You all right?" Mullins enquired, anxiety in his voice. "You O.K.?"

"Wonderful," Jerry said. "A blackjack?"

"Jeeze," Mullins said, "I just sort of nudged you, Mr. North. With my shoulder, sorta. You come in wide open, Mr. North. You jumped me."

"Not—" Jerry began, and stopped and shook himself free from Mullins's supporting arms. "Agee. He was in here. Snooping around. I thought you were Agee. He's still here! *You! Agee!*"

But nobody answered. When Jerry turned the lights on, it was evident why. He and Mullins, having captured one another, were alone in the office. A door in the right-hand wall of the office showed, clearly enough, why they were alone.

"All these offices are strung together like that," Mullins said. "You can come in from the hall. You can go from one office into the next. I guess he must of." Mullins listened. He heard the voice of the absent, the sadly absent, Loot. "Must have," Mullins said.

Jerry was looking at the cards Agee had left on Dr. Steck's desk. Mullins joined him.

The cards were, quite evidently, medical records. It appeared they were the records of various—of perhaps half a dozen—members of the staff of the Institute.

"Yeah," Mullins said, "he's a regular doctor, Steck. Along with being a Ph.D. He treats some of the people here. When they don't feel good. It's convenient, I guess."

Jerry nodded, looking at the cards, uneasy that he was invading privacy; relieved that, except for the names of the patients, he was invading it imperceptibly, since nothing he read on the cards had meaning for him. It was medical shorthand. None of the names on the cards was of anyone so far connected with the case. He showed them to Mullins, who agreed.

"The way I'd figure it," Mullins said, "if it was one of the cards he was after, it was his. Wouldn't you, Mr. North? And that he got it?"

Jerry would.

"I guess," Mullins said, "maybe we'd better talk to this Dr. Agee. You wanta come, Mr. North?"

Jerry did. They would get Pam from the office across the hall. They would find Dr. Agee.

But it did not work that way. Pam was not in the office across the hall. Nobody was in the office across the hall—not even, so far as they could determine, the ghost of Dr. Preson.

• 13 •

SATURDAY, 9:15 P.M. TO 9:40 P.M.

Pamela North entered, at what amounted to a brisk trot, the third office beyond the one with the prehistoric bird in it. She had traversed one with a large rock on a table in the center—she had avoided that—and another which, in the dim light, seemed to be occupied by someone with a penchant for snakes, prehistoric, of course. Going through that office, Pam's trot had become indistinguishable from a lope. The third office was largely filled with glass cases, contents better not guessed at, and Pam—who now could see almost clearly where she was going— made her brisk way between them. It had been some little time, now, since she had actually heard the pursuing Dr. Steck. It appeared that she was distancing him. Perhaps he had become entangled with the prehistoric bird.

Pam's mood was, therefore, one of increasing confidence when she reached the far wall of the third office beyond the bird. Another door, another office. Dr. Steck, who swore in Greek, farther and farther

161

behind. Another door— There was no other door. There was only bare
wall. Even the longest series of interconnecting offices must wind
somewhere to a blank wall, a fact which Pam North had not until that
moment considered.

"Oh," Pam said. She considered. "Oh—*damn!*" said Pamela North.

And now she was sure she heard someone in the office she had quit-
ted a moment before. Someone was in there making a kind of scuffling
sound.

She could not go back, into the arms of the scuffler. She could not
go forward. It remained only to go sideways, which Pam did, toward
the entrance door of the office—the door leading to the central corridor; to the harsh exposure of the central corridor, which now, through
the glass of the door, looked intolerably bright and without hiding
place. Pam went toward the door, no longer trotting.

She started to open it and checked the movement. She had come
toward the front of the building; now she was near the point at which
the central corridor joined the foyer at the head of the main staircase.
Dr. Paul Agee was standing there, looking down the stairs. Emily Preson was coming up the stairs.

"I've been trying to find you," Emily Preson said, her tone intense
with the necessity of finding Dr. Agee, with the violence of her need to
find him. "We've been trying to find you."

It was remarkable, Pam North thought, her own fears diminishing a
little (after all, she could hardly be assailed with help so near)—it was
remarkable what intensity Emily could put into the simplest sentence.
If she said, "Here's a cat," you'd expect at least a tiger, Pam North
thought. Hearing her now, one thought of somebody's search for somebody—Stanley for Livingstone, perhaps—in trackless wilderness.

"I," said Dr. Agee, in an equable tone, "have been out to dinner. In
any case, the Institute is closed, Miss Preson."

"*Don't!* " the girl said. "Don't *pretend!* You won't get away with it.
Not now."

"Away with it?" Dr. Agee enquired. Emily had reached the top of
the staircase now. She stood facing Dr. Agee. They were, Pam thought,
almost of a height.

"I haven't any idea what you're talking about, Miss Preson," Agee said. "No idea at all. I have no idea why you are here at all—or, for that matter, how you got in."

"She came with me," a heavy, rumbling voice said, and then Dr. Albert James Steck walked past the door at which Pam North stood. He walked unhurriedly along the corridor, from the direction of his office and Dr. Preson's, from—

Why, Pam thought, then he wasn't chasing me at all! But then—

"I let her in, Agee," Dr. Steck said, and joined the two at the head of the stairs, towered over them. "She wanted to ask you some questions. She's disturbed about several things."

Agee merely looked at him.

"It seems," Steck said, his heavy voice conversational, unexcited, "that poor Preson didn't kill himself after all. It seems that somebody killed him—and then had to kill old Landcraft. Things like that worry people, you know. Miss Preson's quite worried." He looked down at her. It seemed to Pam, listening with the door barely open, that his voice changed with the next sentence. "Very understandable that she should be," Steck said. "Entirely understandable."

"Even so," Agee said, "I'm afraid I don't understand this—er—violent desire to talk to me, Steck. I'd like to help, of course, but—" He let the sentence hang.

"Of course," Steck agreed. "Well, I think she wants to talk about money, for one thing. I think perhaps the police will too, doctor. As a matter of fact, they seem already to have collected Preson's check book. In his desk drawer the other day, you know. It isn't now. Unless?" He regarded Agee. "Unless you picked it up for—safe keeping?"

"Certainly not," Agee said. "What are you getting at?"

"Money," Steck said. "Contributions to the Institute. Oh yes—arrhythmia too, doctor."

The word did not, this time, sound like profanity. It sounded like the name of something.

The word had meaning for Agee; that was clear from his face. He looked up at Dr. Steck, and seemed intently to consider him.

"You're a physician, aren't you?" he said, then. "Things you can't talk about, aren't there?"

"Well," Steck said, "that's a nice point, isn't it? Quite a nice point. We might go somewhere and take it up, don't you think? Medical ethics? And medical records, of course?"

It seemed to Pam, listening, making little of it, that Steck's voice was now anything but soft, but gentle. It seemed to her now that the heavy, rumbling voice had a threat in it.

Perhaps it seemed so to Dr. Paul Agee. At any rate, he hesitated a moment, seemed for a moment at a loss. Then, without speaking, he turned and went toward the corridor leading to his office. Emily and Dr. Steck followed him. Dr. Steck had a hand, gently, on Emily's arm. He was, Pam thought, a great one for putting a hand on people's arms.

What in the world is arrhythmia? Pam wondered, and tried to decide from the sound how it would be spelled. She came, in her thoughts, not too far from it. It might, she decided, have something to do with rhythm. But that did not help much. That—

But then all speculation vanished before the realization, now sharp in her mind, not a mere flicker to be superseded by something else, that Steck had not been following her. Nobody had been following her; she had hurried, panicked, through strange offices. She had broken things, possibly of great importance. And—she had fled without pursuit. It was embarrassing. She—

And then, in the office where she had heard the scuffling, she heard another sound. It was unmistakable, this time—in the other office, someone was opening a door! It was not the door which led into the office in which Pam stood. It was the door which, from the office still beyond it, gave access to the office in which there had been a scuffling sound. But then—but then, she *was* being followed! Slowly, with stealth, but relentlessly, she was being—

Stalked! Pam North thought. That's what it is. The way these—all these awful things in the past used to stalk whatever—whatever they wanted to destroy! And it was not Steck who stalked her.

There was only one thing for it. Pam North opened, with something like violence, the door at which she stood. Pam crossed the corridor, bounding—as some small and succulent creature might once have bounded from the pursuit of Teddy the Tyrannosaurus, who was not, like some of his kind, a vegetarian. Pam made the door directly across the corridor. She went through it, like a flicker of light.

Now what? Wayne Preson wondered. He had just turned into the corridor at the far end, already worried. He was in time to see Pam dart across the hall from one office into another, certainly as if something were after her. But that, to Wayne, did not fit in with anything. Who would be pursuing Mrs. North? He had himself come back from the Great Hall, where he had been unable to find any of those he wanted to find, because he had wanted to talk to the Norths—to Mrs. North, particularly. But he was not, certainly, chasing her.

It occurred to him then that she might be the pursuer, not the pursued. Perhaps, having found something out, or thought something out, she was hurrying, intently, to tell it to someone. Women were like that—at any rate, Emily was like that, and in a sense Marie was too. They got hold of something they thought important, and nothing could stop them until they had got to the bottom of—well, often, things which were apt to get them into trouble.

Wayne Preson walked briskly up the long corridor. He had better talk to Mrs. North. Perhaps he could reassure her. Quieten her down.

Pam, Mullins had assured Jerry North, had merely gone off on an expedition of her own. They both knew she did that. She always came out all right.

"You mean," Jerry said, "she has so far." His voice was worried. "I told her to stay here," he said.

Mullins had not commented on this. It was, he decided, no time to point out that that, also, had happened before. What had not happened before, in his experience, was that he had in so short a time lost track of so many of the people he was delegated to keep track of. He had lost the Presons, brother and sister, who were his special charge. He had lost Wayne Preson, who wasn't. He had lost Dr. Agee, when just on the point of finding him. Now he and Jerry had lost Pam. It was true,

Mullins thought, that he had found Jerry North, but that did not seem to be getting him anywhere.

"The Presons were in here," Jerry said. "Did you know that?"

"Yeah," Mullins said. "Followed them here."

"They could have come back," Jerry said. "Found Pam here and—" He stopped. "Damn it to hell," he said.

"Now, Mrs. North'll be all right," Mullins said. "Take more than those two to stop her. You know that, Mr. North."

"Well," Jerry said, "they're up to something, aren't they? Or why were you following them?"

"To see," Mullins told him. "They came straight here. To this office. Didn't seem to be anybody else around then. Went in the office, stayed—oh, a coupla minutes, maybe. Then they went and I was about to go after them. But Wayne shows up and then you and Mrs. North show up. Then this guy Agee." He considered. "You know," he said, "this place is getting filled up. Why?"

Jerry didn't know. He listened with half his mind; worried about Pam with the rest of it.

"She must have gone somewhere," he told Mullins.

They had had the lights on in the office, by then. It was obvious that Pam must have gone somewhere, since she obviously was not there.

"Yeah," Mullins said. "That's right, Mr. North."

"Emily Preson's here too," Jerry said, reverting momentarily to the filling up of the Institute. "And Steck. Wayne said so, anyway. Said he followed them."

"Jeeze," said Mullins, simply. "I wish the Loot'd get here."

He was looking around the office. He could not see that Homer Preson and his sister had left any evidence of their visit. The trouble was, of course, he did not know what evidence to look for. Abstractedly, he opened the central drawer of the desk. There were oddments there— expected oddments. There were pencils, a scratch pad, a ruler and a slide rule, two erasers, a collection of loose paper clips, a pen with a rusted nib, a spectacle case with glasses in it. It did not appear to be a place in which anyone would have kept valuables which the Presons would have come down from Riverdale to abstract. Mullins closed the drawer and began to open others. Jerry was prowling the office. He found the doors, one in either wall.

Jerry tried the one on his left and it opened. He started through it.

"Hey," Mullins said, "wait a—"

"You go the other way," Jerry said. "Damn it, sergeant, Pam's lost!"

"Now—" Mullins began, but talked to nobody. He sighed and tried the other door. It was unlocked and he went through it.

Jerry hurried into a dim room, avoiding a table on which something appeared to have happened to the skeleton of some small and ugly creature; went in and through another room and just managed not to knock over the skeleton of what appeared to be a prehistoric bird; in a third room avoided a large and uninteresting boulder (which contained fossil imprints of potentially staggering importance) and in a fourth did not, by moving with slow care, destroy any prehistoric reptiles. He opened the door of the next office and stopped because he heard a sound beyond.

"Pam?" he said, hopefully, yet in a low tone. "Pam—that you?"

The sound he heard then was unmistakable. It was of a door opened; then of a door closed.

"Pam!" Jerry North said, more loudly, and hurried into the next office.

It was filled with glass cases. Pam was not in it. Jerry wasted several seconds discovering that the wall ahead of him was doorless. He did not waste much time, then, in emerging into the central corridor. It was empty.

Then it was not empty. Sergeant Mullins emerged from an office at the far end of the corridor. Sergeant Mullins shook his head.

Jerry North moved down the corridor toward him and they rejoined forces. Jerry was, by then, really worried. He was almost certain that Pam had been in the last office; that she had fled it—or been dragged from it? forced from it?—at his approach.

"We've *got* to find her!" he told Mullins, and told Mullins that he almost had. This time Mullins agreed.

Bill Weigand waited in his car near the side entrance of the Broadly Institute. When the prowl car he had called for slid up behind him, arriving without fanfare, without red lights, as per instructions, he told the sergeant and the patrolman what he wanted. Then he went to the staff door, expecting it to be unlocked. He found it unlocked and stepped inside.

He was just in time to see, momentarily, the closing of the door in front. He crossed the small foyer in two strides and yanked the door open. In the dim vastness of the Great Hall he at first saw nothing; then, hurrying among the shadows, he saw two figures—two short and wiry figures. He could, he decided, guess who the two were. He could guess that they had been about to leave the building and that his arrival had stopped them. He hoped they would try to leave again. He wished he knew what had brought them there—wished he knew specifically; he could, in general, guess. Plots have a tendency to come unraveled; often it seems necessary to ravel them up again. This was, Bill reflected, usually very helpful to the police.

He got into the elevator and started it up. He hoped, as the small car climbed slowly, that enough people would do enough things to give him the proof of what was, he had decided on the trip uptown, sufficiently evident—sufficiently evident, in any case, with the underbrush cleared away. There were still, of course, a good many wrong trees which had, dutifully, to be barked up.

"You watch the hall," Jerry said, and Mullins said, "O.K., Mr. North."

Jerry went into the first of the offices on the opposite side of the corridor. He turned on the lights. Someone had been making, out of clay, what looked like a section of layer cake. Pamela North was not in the office. Jerry turned out the lights and went through the connecting door into the next office in this series. Pam apparently had, of her own will or under compulsion, gone from one to another of the offices across the hall. If she had gone up one side, she might be going down the other. With Mullins to watch the hall, he ought, in time, to flush her out. Unless he found—

Jerry resolutely refused to think of what he might find. So far as he knew, Pam knew nothing it was dangerous to know. So far as he knew.

The second office was empty too—empty, at any rate, of Pamela North. There was an interesting display of fossilized starfish, if one were interested in fossilized starfish. The third office did no better. Jerry hurried. But at each new door he stopped to listen.

Pam hurried, too. Although now she heard no sounds of pursuit, she still fled. She would reach the office into which Jerry had followed Dr. Agee; she would find Jerry there. Together they could turn on the pursuer, find out—

Pam could not think, as she trotted across office after office, opened door after door, what it was they would find out. Before, when there had been trouble toward the end, she had known why there was trouble, if not always how it was to be avoided. But now, Pam North thought, I don't really know anything. Not anything at all. If somebody thinks I know something, it's just too bad for—Pam's thoughts jerked suddenly. For me, she thought. It would be terrible to be—be *hurt*—for something you didn't know. Because if it isn't Dr. Steck who's after me, then it can be anybody. Then she thought, perhaps it isn't anybody any more.

She paused on the far side of the last door she had passed through and listened for a moment. At first she heard nothing. Then she was certain that, back somewhere along the course she fled, she did hear someone in pursuit—someone not running, making no more noise than was needful, coming resolutely on. If only I could lock this door, thought Pam, without hope, since she had long before discovered that the doors, although supplied with locks, were keyless. But in a moment more, Pam thought, I'll find Jerry. She crossed this other office, opened the next door. Then, with a sudden coldness, she realized that she had reached Dr. Steck's office, into which Jerry had gone, and that the office was empty.

It was empty, familiar; because of its emptiness, frightening. The desk was there, the book-lined walls, the long table under the windows with the bone collection on it—the collection of bones still unlabeled, with the box of Dennison's labels waiting neatly to be used, with—

But then she remembered. She did not need to look, although, as she passed—and now more quickly than ever—she did look briefly. There was no box of Dennison's labels; there had not been when she and Jerry had stood there, looking at Wayne Preson, who was looking down at the bones. That, rather than the absence of used labels—or together with the absence of used labels—had caused her earlier to feel something wrong with the way the table looked.

But that could not mean anything, Pam thought, as she fled on. Because if the labels had been the poisoned ones—poisoned labels Dr. Preson had not reached—the police would have found them. And if they were not, then what good would they be to anyone? You could buy unpoisoned labels for a few cents anywhere; it would turn out that Dr. Steck had bought these to go on with Preson's interrupted job; it would turn out—

Pam felt suddenly that she was on the verge of something. It was as if the pull cord of a light dangled in the darkness, as if her fingers touched it and it swayed away before it could be grasped. If she could only stop a moment and think!

Involuntarily, with her fingers on the next doorknob, she did stop. The labels wouldn't have been left—the poisoned ones wouldn't. But there would have had to be some labels left. Because everyone was supposed to think the phenobarbital had been in the milk and that the labels had nothing to do with it. So—

She heard a sound at the door behind her—the sound of a knob turning, a catch releasing. She sought the knob of her own door, but for an instant could not find it. Then she did; then she tugged. But she could hear the other door opening.

She did not look around. She did not stop. A low, heavy voice said, "Wait. I want to talk to you," but she did not wait. She ran, now. And now, diagonally across the next office, she ran for the corridor door.

Sergeant Mullins waited until Dr. Steck came out again. Mullins, hearing footsteps, had had a few seconds to get behind an office door, and he had used them. Now, as Steck returned up the corridor from the office of the late curator of Fossil Mammals, Mullins stepped out behind him.

"Well," Mullins said, "what are you doing here, Dr. Steck?"

Steck turned suddenly; Mullins was a tall enough man, but Steck was appreciably taller. Steck frowned.

"Police," Mullins said.

"Prove it," Steck said.

Mullins proved it.

"Then come on," Steck said. "You may as well be in on this."

He started off abruptly and Mullins went with him. It was, Mullins felt, high time he was in on something, preferably something that made sense. They went up the corridor, turned left, and Steck opened a door which had lettered on the glass, "Paul Agee, Director."

"Now we'll—" Steck began, starting in. But then he stopped. There was nobody in the office. Steck turned, abruptly, and made as if to come out again. Mullins blocked his way.

"What goes on?" Mullins asked him.

"Agee and Miss Preson," Steck said, and spoke quickly, biting the words. "They were here. I went to—"

"Went to what, doctor?" Bill Weigand asked, from behind Mullins.

"To get Preson's spare glasses," Steck said, as if it were the most reasonable of statements. "What did you think?"

"I didn't think anything," Bill said. "Just got here. Let's go on in, shall we? You can explain it to me. Go ahead, Mullins."

"O.K., Loot," Mullins said. "O.K.!"

Mullins advanced; of necessity, although he hesitated for a moment, Steck retreated.

"Right," Bill said. "Go ahead, doctor. What about the glasses?"

"I looked earlier in the week," Steck said. "In Preson's desk. No glasses. I looked this evening. Glasses were there." He paused. "So was Mrs. North, incidentally," Steck said. "Not in the desk, of course. In the office."

"Yeah," Mullins said. "And where is she now?"

"She left," Steck said. "I was in the middle of talking to her. Was just going to explain what Agee probably was up to and she left. Excitable young woman." He sighed. "My evening for excitable young women," he said. His own words seemed to recall him. "We've got to find Emily Preson," he said. "I left her here with Agee."

"Right," Bill said. "We will. You went to get the glasses. Why?"

"Listen," Steck said. "Preson was impersonated, wasn't he? Anyway, that's what you think."

"Right," Bill said. "Probably he was."

"You've thought of Agee?"

"I," said Bill Weigand, "have thought of several people."

"To make him appear insane? Preson I mean?"

"Probably," Bill said. "About the glasses?"

"Preson kept a pair here," Steck said. "I knew it. Probably Agee knew it, although now he says he didn't. Trifocals, you know?"

"Right," Bill said.

"Agee could have borrowed them," Steck said. "Used them. Forgotten to put them back. Then remembered to. I was going to test them, with Agee there. Put it up to him."

"Test them?" Bill said.

"Fingerprints," Steck said. "What did you think?"

"I didn't," Bill said. "You've got them now?"

Steck had. He produced them. They were wrapped, carefully, in a clean handkerchief. They were so carefully wrapped that any prints which might have been on them would, almost certainly, have been blurred. Well, Bill thought, he's a professional at mammalogy, no doubt. Bill took the glasses and put them in his pocket. It was true, of course, that laymen did not know too much about prints. Sometimes it was useful.

"Why do you suspect Agee?" Bill asked, mildly.

"Preson was killed, wasn't he?" Steck said. "With an overdose of phenobarbital? On the labels he was licking?"

"Right," Bill said.

"Damned fool not to use a sponge," Steck said.

"Right," Bill said again. "How did you know the stuff was on the labels, Dr. Steck?"

"My God," Steck said. "I'm not an idiot. Men come around and take off bones and test them. Men want to know where the used labels are. Who wouldn't guess?" He waited. Bill merely nodded. "Ingenious method," Steck said. "Long way around, but ingenious. Stuff wouldn't taste, you know. Not with all the flavoring in the mucilage."

"I know," Bill said. It was a point everybody brought up. Apparently it was the first objection of which everyone thought.

"Not much taste to phenobarbital," Steck said. "Mild bitterness. Agee would know that. He took enough." He waited for reaction; got it in raised eyebrows, new interest. "Anyway," Steck said, "I suppose he did. I prescribed enough for him." He paused again. "Of course," Steck said, in his rumbling voice, "I don't really know he took it. Maybe he gave it away."

"Go on," was all Bill Weigand said.

"Cardiac arrhythmia," Steck said. "Know what that is?"

"No," Bill said.

"Irregularity of heartbeat," Steck told him. "Common enough as people get along. Several causes, some of them bad. But some of them don't mean anything, like Agee's. Nerves go a little haywire; functional thing. Disturbing, of course—heart stops and you wonder, 'Going to start up again?' Phenobarbital will calm the nerves down, just enough. Restore the rhythm." He paused. "So will taking a brisk walk," he said. "Agee preferred barbital. Perfectly all right. Wouldn't do him any harm, in the prescribed dosage. If he took it, of course. It was on his record in my desk. He's got the record."

"Hm-m," Bill said. It didn't fit. It was interesting, all the same.

"You people thought of checking the Institute accounts?" Steck asked. "Poor old Preson contributed quite a bit, you know. Meant to, anyway."

"We've thought of quite a few things, doctor," Bill said. "Now—"

"No," Steck said. "You do what you like. I'm going to find the girl." He started for the door. He encountered Jerry North in it.

"Bill!" Jerry said. "Something's happened to Pam. She—" Jerry looked at Mullins. "Where the hell did you go?" he demanded. "You were supposed to watch the hall."

"Jeeze," said Sergeant Mullins, "how many places can a guy be at once?"

"We'll find—" Bill Weigand began, and then he said, "Hey!"

But he spoke too late. Jerry North's arrival had been sufficiently distracting. During it, Dr. Albert James Steck had gone about his business, which presumably was the recovery of Emily Preson. At least, Bill thought, it's that if I'm right. I hope I'm right.

He sent Mullins to retrieve Steck, all the same. Unfortunately, after the habit of people in the big building, so labyrinthine in arrangement, Dr. Steck had disappeared.

"For at least the third time," Dr. Paul Agee said, "I did not ask you to come, Miss Preson. Where is that damned elevator?"

The question was directed to the elevator itself, or its inventor, not to Emily Preson.

"Some fool's left one of the doors open," Agee said, answering the question. "Why don't you go back and see if Steck really found the glasses he thinks are so important?"

He turned away, then, and walked briskly along the rear corridor. He did not appear to care whether Emily went with him or went back to Steck. She went with him.

"I don't believe they're here," Emily said. "Why would they be?"

"Bringing the glasses back," Agee said.

"Why do you keep saying that?" Emily said. "Why should they?"

"He kept them here," Agee said. "How many times do you want me to say it? Suppose the police found them at the house? Need explanation, wouldn't it? Bring them back here, put them back in the desk, then it looks like somebody here. Like me, specifically. Don't be a fool, Miss Preson."

They reached the end of the corridor. Agee opened a door and started down a flight of iron stairs. "Wait!" the girl said. He did not wait. She went after him.

"Why not just throw them away?" she asked. "Anyway, I don't believe they came here."

"Saw them," Agee said. "Headed for the elevator. Don't you know opticians keep records, Miss Preson?" He widened the distance between them. "Too damn many people keep records," he said, and went through a door. For all he had said before, he waited to make sure Emily Preson got through behind him.

· 14 ·

SATURDAY, 9:35 P.M., TO SUNDAY, 6:15 P.M.

Pam burst out into the corridor and thought, Jerry'll be there. But the corridor was empty. She looked up and down it, and was nearer the transverse corridor at the rear. She made for it. She reached it and had two ways to go, and went to the right—went to the right and, almost at once, wished she had not, since she seemed to be hurrying toward a dead end. She thought, "dead end," and the words were discomforting. But then she saw a door in the wall on her left. It must, since it was—surely it was!—an opening through the rear of the building, lead to a fire escape.

Pam opened it. There were iron-bound stairs leading down; beyond there was an area of darkness. The building was deeper than she had thought; behind the part available to the public, the part used for display rooms and offices, there was a space for—for crates and boxes, Pam thought, seeing them vaguely in the darkness. She hesitated, and then went down the stairs. She went down a short flight to a landing, back-tracked across the landing, and went down another short flight. Then she came to another landing, this time with a door on her left. That would lead to the second floor, Pam decided. Probably it would lead into the library, or into some area near the library. She hesitated there, listening. Perhaps she had lost her pursuer.

For a moment of waiting there was no sound at all. She might have been alone in the building. Jerry—all of them—had vanished somewhere.

She reached for the door. She would go through the library, along the length of the second floor and then, if it seemed safe, back up again to the third, where there had last been people—where Jerry had been last, and Dr. Agee, and Wayne Preson. She had her fingers on the knob when she heard the door above her open. She heard a voice say, "Wait!" and Pam North did not wait. There was no time to bother with a door; the door might be locked. Pam fled down the stairs. But as she fled she thought, *that wasn't the right voice!* She thought, *they're both in it!*

She tried to make as little sound as she could, holding to the rail, stepping softly on her toes so that heels would not clatter on concrete and on iron. But her progress was not silent.

She went down a short flight to another landing; down another flight and another and came to a door. She did not hesitate, this time. She pushed anxiously at the door. It opened without protest.

"Thought I heard somebody," Paul Agee said. "Guess I didn't. You want to find them, don't you?"

"I came," Emily said. "Of course. But you're wrong."

"Find them first," Agee said.

He switched on lights in the library. It took only moments to discover the library was empty.

They went out of the library and Agee turned off the lights behind them. At the same time, he turned on lights which illuminated the broad central corridor on the second floor.

"Take that side," Agee said, and gestured to the right. He himself took the other side. They went up, each on his own side, through the exhibit rooms, which were connected by arches.

                                *   *   *

Pam was at the end of the Great Hall. She could look up it through the gloom, see Teddy the Tyrannosaurus in skeletal majesty far up the room. Beyond the monstrosity that was Teddy were the main stairs leading up. Perhaps that way was the best way. She started up the room, threading a quick, not certain way among denizens of the unthinkable past.

She had gone only a few steps when she heard a sound at her right. It was the sound of a door opening. She heard a voice.

"Wait," the voice said. "I won't hurt you."

This time it was the voice she expected. It was a voice that lied. Pam North ran and, after a second, she heard behind her the sound of hurrying feet. Pam tried to run on her toes, but she heard, agonizingly, the clatter of her heels on the marble floor. The great room was filled with the clatter of her heels.

But I don't know *why*, Pam thought, as she fled—fled past unlighted display alcoves on her right, past the one in which (she did not look, but remembered) a man of half a million years ago stood in front of such a cave as he had lived in; finally past the grinning monster who had ceased to live before man was born. She could feel the dinosaur grinning behind her as she fled.

Stairs were no good, now. She hadn't the breath left for stairs; she would be caught on stairs. When she reached the divided staircase she ran past it, toward the double front doors. But they were locked; there would not be time there. She turned to her right again, down a passage and found a door which seemed to lead under the stairs. She prayed it would open; it did open. She went through it. Now, for a moment out of sight, she paused to yank off her high-heeled shoes.

She was in a very narrow passage, windowless on her left; lighted only, far down, by a dangling light bulb. On her right there were doors, one after another. Pam North ran—ran quietly now, except for her quick-drawn breath (but that was loud; she might, she thought, as well be screaming her presence) and knew, was certain, that this time she had trapped herself.

She was halfway down the narrow hall, and had realized that she was running, once more, the length of the building, when the door behind her opened, and closed again. She heard the sound of feet on what was here, in this tunnel, a wooden floor. There was no invitation to wait, this time; no promise of safety.

Pam was almost at the end of the passage; she was at the end, and at another door. It would be unlocked. She would— It was not unlocked! She tugged at it, and it did not move.

She turned and started back, facing the pursuer. She discovered, then, that she could still hear, but could not see—the light hung low enough so that, dim as it was, it still dazzled the eyes, still left the area beyond it almost dark.

If I can't see, I can't be seen, Pam thought, and reached for the knob of the nearest of the doors in the side wall. It opened and Pam was through it, closing it softly behind her.

She was in a meadow. Something that was almost grass came nearly to her knees; she was almost touching a strange beast with too many horns—with a horn growing out of the middle of the back of its head. But it's too dark to see, Pam thought, before she realized it was not completely dark. Light came from beyond the horned animal—the horned animals, because at the side there was another, but this one with a horn on its nose. Beyond her was openness and—and the Great Hall!

But before she reached it, moving slowly in what was almost grass, avoiding the animals which had grazed in Nebraska before last the ice came down, Pam knew that there was a sheet of glass between her and the Great Hall. Before she reached the glass, Pam North knew where she was. In such a glassed alcove as this, old Landcraft must have stood as she stood now, back to glass too thick for breaking, watching a heavy club, with a stone lashed to it, rise slowly in strong hands.

In the Great Hall, nothing moved among the shadows. The Tyrannosaurus grinned, but its back was to her; the light picked up the great curved tusks of a mammoth centuries dead, and it seemed that the mammoth, also, laughed out of the past. Join us in the past, the laughter said; there are no gradations in the past. In a moment, you will be as old as we.

I'll be damned if I will, Pam North thought. I won't have it!

She listened, moving back from the glass, putting an ear close to the door which led to the passage behind the exhibit alcoves. At first she heard nothing; then she heard a door close, apparently some distance up the passage. Almost at once, she heard another door open.

Her pursuer had discovered that she could not have left the passage except to go into one of the exhibit alcoves. Perhaps he had locked the door at the passage's end so that she could not go out that way—he had come from that direction when she heard him first. Now, methodically, unhurriedly, he was searching the little glass-fronted rooms—searching them one by one. He had, he must think, plenty of time. So far as Pam North could tell, her ear to the door, only determination between her and extinction as final as that which had overtaken the dinosaurs, he had.

She could not get out through the doors. She would run into the hands of her pursuer. She could not get out through the heavy plate of glass unless—

If only there were a club in this one, Pam thought, and began to search in the substance which was so like grass. With a club, I could break the glass. Then somebody would come. Then Jerry would come. Then— But there was no club. There wasn't anything. It was only then that Pamela North realized she had, one in each hand, each convulsively clutched, a shoe with a long, hard heel. Then, as she heard another door close, another open—but this time much closer—Pam North stumbled through the tangle which dragged at her legs and reached the wall of glass.

But then she hesitated. The sound would bring him running. It would bring him long before, with only flimsy shoes as tools, she had broken through the glass.

Perhaps something would happen to stop him before he found her. Perhaps Jerry, who was surely searching, had found now where she had fled; perhaps he, with Mullins, with Bill Weigand, was already in the passage, reaching out for the man who had murdered twice and sought to kill again. Perhaps—

There was no use in that, Pam thought. She began to beat on the glass with the little shoes. She beat with desperate violence, and with the first blows the glass cracked. But it only cracked. And the sound of the beating was hideously loud in the little room; must spread out from it through the building. When the door behind her opened, she would not be able to hear it now. If the voice spoke, she would not hear it; if a hand—with what weapon this time?—was raised behind her back, she would not see it. She would not turn. She beat on the glass, and it began to shatter.

She was beating on the glass still, and it was falling onto the marble floor outside, she had cut a hand and blood was on her skirt, when light swept through the Great Hall. She continued to beat on the glass, oblivious of everything else—but still she saw him running in the Great Hall— until Jerry stood in front of her and shouted at her. "Pam!" Jerry shouted. "Stop that. Stop *it*. You'll hurt yourself." For a moment longer she beat the breaking glass. She stopped, then. She looked at the cut on her hand.

"Why," Pam North said, "look. I've cut myself."

Jerry wrenched a great shard of glass out, and then another. Pam, her arms at her sides, a shoe in each hand, could only wait.

Then she knew that Jerry was looking at something, at someone, behind her. It was as if his face were a mirror, reflecting danger which was behind her. But she could not turn—could not look. The door would be opening. Death would be coming through the door, through the tangle of the grass. She—

Jerry North wrenched out another jagged shard. Now he could reach through to her. Now— Now he had his hands on her, was lifting her down from the raised floor of the alcove. Now she was against him, hiding her face against him.

"Somebody almost—" Pam North said, her words muffled.

"It's all right," Jerry said. "The door started to open. Yes. But Bill's—"

Then the Great Hall seemed suddenly full of people. Dr. Steck was coming down from the front of the hall, and he seemed to be supporting two people. At least, he had his left arm around Emily Preson's shoulders and was half carrying a strangely limp director of the Broadly Institute under his right arm. Pam lifted her head from Jerry's chest.

"He's certainly a big man," Pam North said. "He wasn't the one at all because—"

"Got him," Steck said, as he approached. "Just as he was about to—"

"Father!" Emily said, at almost the same moment. "Aunt Laura! You *were* here. You did—"

Homer Preson and his sister were emerging from behind a mammoth. Both were blinking in the sudden light.

"Will somebody," Dr. Agee said, in a weak voice, from Steck's ungentle embrace, "get this—this aborigine—to let me go? Miss Preson will tell you—"

"Shut up, Agee!" Steck said. "You tried to push her down the stairs." He shook the smaller man briskly. "You've done enough," he told Agee. "Save it for—"

But then Bill Weigand was in the alcove with the horned things. Wayne Preson was with him. Bill looked out over the heads of those below, and then the alcove in which he stood was absurdly like a stage, from which an announcement was about to be made.

"Let him go, Dr. Steck," Bill Weigand said. Steck looked at Bill for a moment. Bill nodded. Quite casually, then, Dr. Steck let Agee go. Dr. Steck dropped him. Agee went down on his hands and knees.

"You—you *Cromagnon!*" Agee said. "You—"

"I tell you," Wayne Preson said, and it was as if there were nobody present but Bill Weigand. "I tell you, I merely wanted—"

"Don't," Bill said. "Don't tell me anything, Preson. Not now. You'll have a chance. You can tell it all, then."

"You don't—" Wayne Preson began, but Bill shook his head.

"I understand enough," he said. "That you killed two men and tried to kill Mrs. North." But then Bill paused. "I'll admit," he said, "I don't know what Mrs. North had—"

"Oh," Pam said. "I didn't either, for a long time. You see, he just stole a box of labels. That was all. Jerry and I saw him. And who would steal a box of labels, except a murderer?"

Then Mullins emerged, behind Homer and Laura Preson, and also from behind a mammoth.

"Loot," Mullins said, "you want I should?"

"Right," Bill said. "I think you'd better."

Mullins reached forth two large hands. In each, he took an arm of a Preson.

"The Loot thinks you'd both better come along too," Mullins said. His voice was entirely mild.

Emily Preson said, "O-oh" then, and the sound was a cry. She started toward her father and her aunt, but Dr. Steck drew her back. For a moment she seemed to resist; then she did not. Then she turned so that her face was against the not very well-fitting coat of the large mammalogist, and Dr. Steck glared out over her head.

Good heavens, Pam North thought, he *is* a big man. All he needs is a stone-headed club.

They had talked, Bill Weigand agreed; they certainly had talked. Miss Laura Preson had talked with particular fluency. Bill sighed; he looked tired. He sat in a deep chair in the Norths' living room, and reached out from time to time toward a glass on a low table. The Norths listened; Dorian Weigand, curled in a chair with a blue-eyed cat curled on her lap, listened too.

"She appears to feel we should give her a medal," Bill said. "Her and her brother."

"Not Wayne?" Pam asked.

She did not, Bill agreed, go that far. She appeared to feel that Wayne had been a bad boy. She seemed to feel that largely, however, because Wayne had upset excellent plans—her excellent plans. Because he had rushed in, impatiently, with youthful impetuosity. It seemed to be her idea that Wayne would outgrow all this.

"He won't," Bill said, with some grimness.

Wayne was keeping his mouth shut, which was his best plan. He would make them dig, which was to be expected. Meanwhile, he denied everything. He didn't know what his aunt was talking about. It was preposterous to suggest he had meant harm to Pam North. He had merely wanted to talk to her.

"About what?" Pam asked. "The weather?"

"He says his sister," Bill said. "He was worried about her state of mind."

"Please," Dorian said, "I just came in. Remember? Are you saying all the Presons were in it together? All in a conspiracy?"

To a point, that was quite true, Bill said. Then he hesitated.

"Not Emily, apparently," he said. "At least, she denies it. Laura says she must have known; Emily's father, who doesn't talk much—and doesn't deny much either—does deny Emily was in it. I doubt if she was, actually. She's too—too violent to conspire; too violent to be trusted. She merely suspected, was afraid of what she half knew. Toward the end she was just trying to find out. I think she hoped against hope her uncle *was* insane—that everything was the way her father and her brother and her aunt wanted to make it appear."

"Please," Dorian said. "Shall I leave the room? Is it something I can't hear?"

Bill grinned at her.

Three of the Presons, he told them all, had become disturbed that a fourth, Dr. Orpheus Preson, was dissipating his money—"on those bones of his," Laura Preson said—instead, as would have been seemly, of allowing it to accumulate for the eventual use of his younger brother and sister and deserving niece and nephew. "If that didn't prove he was crazy, I'm sure I don't know what would," Laura had said. This course of action Homer and his sister, and Wayne, found disturbing. They found it far more disturbing when Dr. Preson informed them that he was leaving whatever he would have to leave to the Broadly Institute, and not to them. It was most disturbing for all of them to discover that he had already made a will in favor of the Institute. It was, Laura said—said and said again and still again—final proof that the little mammalogist had become mentally irresponsible.

But—and this was the problem of the other Presons—he had done nothing publicly which would establish him as mentally incompetent. They—and this, also, Laura Preson said repeatedly—had seen him do, and heard him say, a hundred things which would convince anyone that his mind had gone. Anyone in their place would have had no doubts at all. The difficulty, of course, was that no one else was in the place of the Presons.

"Did they really believe it?" Pam asked. "Or just want to? Or not believe it at all?"

Bill shrugged to that. He said he thought Laura Preson believed it;

that Homer had convinced himself; that to Wayne it made no difference. But that was guesswork.

"Probably he did seem eccentric," Bill said. "Many people do—
especially people of limited and intense interests. Probably it was easy
for them to convince themselves, if they needed to."

They had, at any rate, set out to convince other people. There had
not been, in the advertisements they inserted, any intention to drive
Orpheus mad, although perhaps they nearly had. The plan was to make
him appear mad or, as Homer insisted, to make his madness apparent.
Orpheus would complain to the police. The police would start an
investigation. When they were sure the investigation was well under
way, Homer would impersonate his brother at the want-ad counter,
leaving the police to discover that Orpheus had been persecuting himself.

There had been a momentary hitch; the police were not so assiduous
as the Presons had assumed. "Can't be," Bill said. "We get too many.
The town is full of crackpots. Practically every family has one."

"Now," Pam said, "really, Bill."

She would, Bill assured her, be surprised. But then he got back to
the Presons, to the momentary hitch. There was no point to be gained
by impersonating Orpheus unless they could make it reasonably certain the police were paying attention. So the day after Homer had
impersonated his brother, Laura Preson had called the matter to their
notice. She had gone to Orpheus's apartment, carrying phenobarbital
with her. She had taken some, the dose carefully measured. She had
put more in the milk. She had then contentedly gone to sleep and let
nature take its course. Nature—and the police—had obliged.

"A subterfuge to bring out the truth," Miss Laura Preson explained.
"Now we could prove what we all knew."

And then, according to the original plan, they could use their evidence as a club over Orpheus. They could give him an alternative—
either he would quit wasting his money, and change his will, or they
would have him certified. They planned, Laura said—and Homer said—
and Laura said again, nothing more than that. Properly viewed, they
were merely conservationists, preventing the dissipation of Orpheus's

resources. They had had no plan for the immediate enrichment of themselves. Even if they had gone to the point of having Orpheus certified, they would not immediately have enriched themselves. They would have been under the observation of the courts.

"You believe that?" Jerry North asked.

Bill thought for a moment. Then he nodded his head slowly. He was, he said, inclined to. He was inclined to think they had figured without Wayne—without what Wayne's aunt considered the impatience of youth. Wayne didn't want to wait. Bill told them why. And to Wayne, the situation seemed made to hand. Orpheus Preson already was established in the minds of the police as irresponsible—as a man who had not only annoyed himself, but had gone to the point of planting phenobarbital in his own milk supply. It would seem only natural if one of Orpheus's plans overcarried; if, again trying to prove himself a victim of a mythical enemy, he actually became the victim of himself. That the will left Orpheus Preson's money to the Institute would not matter; it would be easy to prove that the will had been made while Orpheus was of unsound mind.

So Wayne proceeded, and all went well. He was first on the scene. For the poisoned labels, he substituted an almost full package of labels not poisoned.

"I thought of that," Pam said. "There would have to be some unused labels. But he wouldn't leave the poisoned ones."

"Right," Bill said. "And, at first, it worked. The Presons took away Dr. Preson's personal effects. The Institute collected the bones and with them, naturally enough, the unused labels. Everything was neat and tidy. But then, Uncle Jesse came in."

As Dr. Jesse Landcraft came in, a little guesswork also came in. Bill admitted that. Neither Laura nor her brother professed to believe that Dr. Landcraft had become privy to their plot. It was nevertheless almost certain that he had. He was much in and out of the Preson house; probably the Presons sometimes forgot that he was there—probably he was hardly more than another chair, or an old man asleep in another chair. It appeared he had not been.

How much he had found out—that was entirely guesswork. He

might not, Bill thought, have realized that the plan had overcarried into murder because of Wayne Preson's impatience to get his share—to get it for a business, through a business for a girl. Landcraft may have thought that his friend Preson had actually been driven mad enough for suicide. But this he evidently had known: enough of the plot to stop the Presons' contest of the will. He had started to take what he knew to Paul Agee, in the interest of the Institute, of science—of mankind's slow accumulation of knowledge. He had not got that far.

How Wayne had learned of Landcraft's journey they had again to guess. Landcraft had telephoned first; probably he had used a telephone in the lower, dark hall of the rooming house in which he lived. At that time—and this they could prove—Wayne had been in the neighborhood but not in the Preson house. (Both Homer and Laura Preson had admitted that, before they realized the implications.) It could be assumed that Wayne had been in the hall, perhaps on his way to see Dr. Landcraft, and had overheard. But perhaps he had merely seen the old man going off, resolutely, at an odd hour, and had followed. Murderers have to keep their eyes open.

"And," Bill said, "murderers have to keep on worrying, which is a good thing for us. One thing leads to another, which is a bad thing for them. You are sure Wayne picked up the package of labels, Pam? Sure you and Jerry saw him?"

"Well," Pam North said, "I am now. I wasn't then. I couldn't swear to anything. Jerry?"

Jerry North shook his head. He had merely seen Wayne standing by the table.

"But he had to worry," Bill said. "He had to assume you had seen him, were sure you had seen him. So—he had to take steps."

"He almost did," Pam said. She shivered.

Bill admitted that. It was lucky that his search for her had taken him to the corridor behind the exhibit alcoves. It was true, of course, that by that time he and Jerry had been in most of the other likely places.

"The odd thing is," Bill said, "that he had no reason for picking up the labels. I suppose he got to worrying about fingerprints. Naturally he had handled them, naturally without gloves. He needn't have worried—we hadn't tested the box for prints, and hadn't planned to. We had, of course, taken samples enough to prove there was no phenobarbital on them; we hadn't thought there would be. But we knew that a dozen people might have handled them, and almost certainly had. Anybody's prints could be on the box innocently, including Wayne's. But Wayne got to worrying, all the same."

"Like not having turned the gas off when you know perfectly well you have," Pam said. "And going back and doing it again." She paused. "Of course," she said, "sometimes you haven't. There's always that."

It had been that way with Wayne Preson, Bill agreed. He had too much wanted to make sure of everything; been too anxious to tidy all behind him. Amateur murderers often were. But it had only informed Pamela North; by then it was only corroboration. The whole pattern was there to be seen, once there were facts enough.

"What were the Presons doing there?" Jerry asked.

"Putting Orpheus's spare glasses back where he kept them," Bill said. "Putting things back in the laps of those at the Institute."

"They knew Wayne was the one?" Pam asked.

Bill shrugged. They denied it. He assumed that, by then at any rate, they did. Bill emptied his glass and Jerry refilled it.

"Bits and pieces," Bill said then. "Wrong trees to bark up. Agee had been fooling around with the Institute's funds. He says, merely to prove they could be better invested than the bank was investing them. That's up to the trustees of the Institute, and the Fraud Bureau. He got afraid that we would stumble on the record of prescriptions Dr. Steck had given him for phenobarbital, and think maybe he hadn't taken the stuff himself. He says he had. There's no reason not to believe him."

"Where did Wayne get the stuff?" Dorian asked. "Where did Laura, for that matter?"

Bill shrugged to that. Probably they would find out; perhaps they wouldn't. Unfortunately, phenobarbital was not too hard to come by.

"And Dr. Steck wasn't in it at all," Pam said, her tone a little wistful. "For a while I was so sure."

"No," Bill said. "He wasn't at all." He sipped. "Sorry, Pam," he said. "He got the idea toward the end Agee was the man. Partly because by then he wanted it not to be someone Emily cared about. He just stumbled into things. Agee hadn't tried to push Emily down the stairs; she doesn't say he had. But Steck was—was looking for things. Feeling protective."

"Knight errant," Pam said. "His armour doesn't fit very well but—I don't know. Perhaps it does." She looked at Jerry thoughtfully. "He's certainly very big," she remarked.

"Listen," Jerry said.

"Oh—too big, of course," Pam said. "Who wants a man who can carry somebody around like a parcel? I mean, the occasion doesn't arise much. Still—"

"About Emily," Dorian said. "What about Emily?"

It would, Bill said, be up to the district attorney, as would the status of Homer and Laura. As for Emily—his guess would be that nothing would happen.

"I think," he said, "she's just a scared kid. Although, of course, she's not really a kid."

"Oh yes," Pam said. "She is, of course. Because she wants so much not to be."

They listened to this. It echoed faintly and was gone. Jerry mixed more drinks.

"The district attorney'd better not do anything to Emily," Pam said, abstractedly, sipping a martini. "Dr. Steck wouldn't like it, I don't think." She sipped again. "He's very big," Pam said. "And I still think he swears in Greek."